ALSO BY NICK HARKAWAY

FICTION

Gnomon

Tigerman

Angelmaker

The Gone-Away World

NONFICTION

The Blind Giant: Being Human in a Digital World

TITANIUM NOIR

NICK HARKAWAY

TITANIUM NOIR

A NOVEL

Alfred A. Knopf · New York 2023

THIS IS A BORZOI BOOK
PUBLISHED BY ALFRED A. KNOPF

www.aaknopf.com

Library of Congress Cataloging-in-Publication Data
Names: Harkaway, Nick, [date]- author.
Title: Titanium noir : a novel / Nick Harkaway.
Description: First Edition. | New York : Alfred A. Knopf, [2023]
Identifiers: LCCN 2022035735 | ISBN 9780593535363 (hardcover) | ISBN 9780593535370 (ebook)
Classification: LCC PR6108.A737 T58 2023 | DDC 823/.92—dc23
LC record available at https://lccn.loc.gov/2022035735

This is a work of fiction. Names, characters, places, and incidents either are the product of the author's imagination or are used fictitiously. Any resemblance to actual persons, living or dead, events, or locales is entirely coincidental.

Jacket illustration and design by Jack Smyth

Manufactured in the United States of America
First Edition

For Clare,
Clemency
and Tom
—my everything.

You can keep the things of bronze and stone and give me one man to remember me just once a year.

—Damon Runyon

TITANIUM NOIR

1

Giles Gratton, sick as a dog from nineteen years spent sleeping in the off hours between bloody murder rooms and the aldermen's bullshit, doesn't knock.

"Get your coat," he says.

"Hi, Captain."

"Yeah, all that."

I get my coat and hold the door for him.

"Hi, Cal," Gratton says.

We go down the stairs together. No need to waste a perfectly good bit of bad news with conversation.

We're in the wrong part of town for something in my line. Not that it's nasty, it's just not perfect. The people I deal with are up there, not down here. Gratton drops me at the building but doesn't come in.

"I've already seen it."

"You got any idea?"

He shakes his head. "Just that it's your thing."

"Confirmed?"

"No, but if you get in there and you think I'm wrong, you can keep the money and go back to bed."

I walk through the lobby and take the stairs up to the third floor. Every single step is shiny clean and smells of off-brand Limonene.

Inside the apartment, the dead nerd lies on the floor. There's a hole in his head, small and smudged with grey ash and a light burn. A close-range shooting: an execution or a suicide. There's some blood, blowback from the moment of impact, but the round must still be inside him. Small calibre, low power. Just enough to do the job.

Down by his feet, Musgrave the city doctor is fussing with a tablet: the police network is achingly slow. Other than that there's not a lot going on. Murder rooms are like train stations at midnight, not much left to do before the last departure.

The nerd looks about forty-five with no habits. He's got dark hair cut nerd style, he's wearing a nerd shirt, button-down, with little hooks for a clip-tie stitched under the collar. Nerd slacks too high at the waist and too short at the ankle, and nerd shoes from an artisan place in the market, with orthotic inserts. The thick soles complete the anti-chic vibe. This was how he lived, wardrobe like an old guy and no mind to be anything else.

There's a lounge chair in front of the big window. I figure he sat there and looked out, so I go and do that too. I can feel the ghost of him in the cushions, pressed down and permanently shaped by his weight. Forensics have come and gone ages ago, but still the other three twitch slightly as I sit because they're not allowed to, not allowed so deep they can't imagine that anyone would.

"You want to get a snack while you're at it?" Detective Felton, standing by the door, doesn't love my way of being in the world. We got nothing to discuss, so I don't.

Outside, the city spreads east and west along the lake. The Chersenesos district juts out into the deep water from midtown, a dog's muzzle lapping from a massive bowl. Behind the skyscrapers the mountains rise up from the farthest shore. Othrys is topographically an alpine lake: the line from the peak to the trench is smooth, and the water is as deep as the mountains are high. Anything you throw in falls for a clear four thousand metres to a cold darkness that keeps its secrets well and never lets them go. Anything, or anyone.

"Oh bloody fucking fuck," Musgrave growls at her tablet. It's not true what they say: good workmen do indeed blame their tools, at least when they have to use what the department can afford. Felton and his uniform buddy can't even be bothered to laugh. Just two of them: there's a serious incident in the Heights. There always is when you need one. Gratton giving me space—or maybe rope.

I go back to the desk and run my hand along the flat surface. It's clean and cold. There's a university terminal, a block of cartridge paper by the printer. The drawers have bamboo dividers to keep everything in its proper place: one cubby for staples, one for rubber bands, one for pens. There is nothing, but nothing, out of place in this room, in this entire apartment, except for the nerd who owns it, dead between the display case and the fish tank.

Koi carp, two, one orange, and one orange and white.

I shuffle all the way back on the dead man's office chair until my feet come off the floor and then I push off with my right hand so that I'm spinning slowly around. The chair is a science chair, translucent and nasty. They take a seed from your ear cartilage and grow it and then you sit in it because something something immune response something biota. Supposedly it's good for you, but who knows? High-ticket item. Round and round I go in the dead nerd's chair, which I guess is technically part of the corpse.

"Hey, Musgrave, you gonna autopsy this chair?"

"Nope."

"Because you know—"

"Yes I do. Technically it's still alive so it would be a vivisection, but let me say again: no, I do not at this time propose to vivisect the chair, because I have an annual budget and it's fucking ridiculous."

"Just figure it's made of his body. If he was maybe poisoned—"

"He was shot in the head," Musgrave says, like she doesn't really want to talk about it any more.

There are no family pictures around the terminal, or on the mantel, or in the display case. There are none in the living room with its view of the harbour, thirty-six storeys down. There are none in the bathrooms. There is a box in the lumber room full of bric-a-brac, and no doubt he intended, one day, to go through it and set some of those things out. Or perhaps he just didn't give a damn. Sometimes you keep things because you don't have time to throw them away.

Alastair Rodney Tebbit, went by Roddy. This address plus a teaching room on campus. Not married, at least for the present. Manicure his only obvious vanity, and a bullet somewhere in his skull: one shot between the ear and the temple, right through the stem and bounced off the concave bone on the far side. The gun is the one he bought yesterday morning, smaller than my palm. The credit card slip is still on the side table where he dropped his keys. Swiss made, with no digital parts. It comes with a spring holster: you twitch your wrist in a particular way and the gun pops into your hand. Another high-ticket item, and fine, he had the cash and not a lot to spend it on, but most of the stuff here is ordinary. Only the chair, the shoes, and the gun are expensive. Roddy Tebbit did not impulse buy, and he did not bother with needless things. He spent money on stuff that mattered, and the gun mattered.

Still spinning in the chair. Look up, look down, look around. There is no part of the crime scene that is not interesting. Cobwebs on the ceiling, but they're new. I can see the spider working. No dirt anywhere else except the tiny blush of ejecta on the carpet where he died, and the diffuse grime that settles wherever humans live, the little tracks of a thousand daily journeys from kitchen to lounge chair to bathroom to bedroom that Roddy Tebbit will not be making ever again.

I roll the chair back and open the drawers. There are two on top of each other, one shallow and one deep. The first one is full of things to write with. Pencils, hard. Pencils, soft. One box of a half dozen in solid graphite. Then pens. Pens, blue. Pens, black. Pens, red. Trifecta. Sharpies, indigo, and only indigo. Personal quirk. The notes on the cartridge paper are in indigo. Nice colour.

Paperclips, one size only. Staples, for stapler, adjoining cubby.

Next drawer. Tape, various colours and sizes. Solder kit. Protective goggles, protective gloves. Lightweight gear for making new charging cables. Solder, different metals. Cable offcuts, cable clips. Latex glue, in date. One empty cubby, no indication of what it held. Maybe it was open: a place for the unexpected. I close the drawer.

And there, on the floor at the spot where the rug folds by the foot of the desk: a tiny piece of shaped metal, yellow and warm. Two loops like a roller coaster track, not more than a couple of millimetres across, a hole through the middle. The butterfly piece from an earring.

"Hey, Musgrave."

"Yes?"

"Got a bag?"

She doesn't say "of course." Musgrave's self-image is anchored deep in the flesh of forensic pathology, and she doesn't need to remind anyone how good she is. You don't work with her even once and not notice. She comes over, curious. There shouldn't be anything. Scene of crime should have seen this, but they missed it, probably because they were eyeballing the corpse. Even here, that's not something you see every day. "Where?" she asks.

I point and she takes a picture almost reflexively. Then I go into my pocket, where I keep a folding corkscrew someone gave me a long time ago. It's a little silver item with a slide-out pin that you're supposed to use to pierce the wax seals you get on some bottles. Great for picnics, and for evidence. I reach down and lift up the butterfly, let it rest on the tip of the pin. Musgrave makes a noise like "hht" then leans over and drops it into an evidence bag, passes it off to the uniform.

"His ears aren't pierced."

You wouldn't expect them to be, or any other part of him, but she'll check, anyway.

I straighten up and look around.

Roddy was a quiet, boring guy who lived for his work. He fed his fish regularly, he shopped local, and he rode a bicycle to campus. He did not, at least in so far as anyone knows at this early stage, run off with other people's wives, gamble in dens of vice or haul drugs over the border in the secret compartment of a Maserati. He had no debts, no known enemies and no obvious worries. Yesterday morning he bought a gun and yesterday night that gun was fired into his head. An accident, a suicide or a murder. And none of these things would be my problem, except for the other bit.

Roddy Tebbit, if he was standing straight without a .22 derringer shell spiralled through what I have to assume was top grade brain matter, would have been seven feet, eight and some inches tall. Two hundred and thirty-six centimetres.

And according to his driving license, he was ninety-one years old.

Roddy Tebbit was a Titan.

Gratton was right. This is my thing.

You maybe could get a seventy-year-old former Olympic basketball player who looks like forty-five. I mean theoretically. In reality your serious sports people pick up injuries, and the longer they stay in, the worse those tend to be. They get cardio problems, craquelure fractures, crumbling joints, hamstring, anterior cruciate ligament, rotator cuff. They might end up with a foot problem, wear orthotic shoes.

What you do not get is a man in his tenth decade looking like his fifth. That is not within the bounds of the normal human healthspan. The only way you get from there to here is T7 therapy, so even if Roddy is in the wrong part of town, in the wrong kind of apartment and wearing the wrong clothes—even if he's so very much not gossip magazines and sturgeon sushi and private planes—he is what he is. Going by age and size it's just one dose, but in policing terms it doesn't make much difference. This is an entire rain of shit for the department. Titan cases by definition involve frightened rich people calling the politicians they socialise with, who call the police chief, who then wants to know everything before the cops themselves do until it's like two guys running in clown shoes, except that when they fall over one of them gets to fire the other.

Meanwhile the Titans think the cops don't really give a shit if they die, which is somewhat true. They think every tabloid hack in the world wants a photograph of a naked Titan with a knife between her ribs, which is entirely true.

I don't hate Titans, cops or journalists. I also don't love Titans, cops or journalists.

I do what I do and I try to do it right.

I poke around some more, open the box of bric-a-brac and find ... stuff. Old train tickets; a branded baseball cap from a diner somewhere in flyover country; work gloves and a tool belt, but no tools. Receipts from everywhere, a pair of hiking boots and a bag of moss. I give the moss to Musgrave, who says thank you, she has always wanted some. I tell her I thought maybe it was important.

But I didn't, really. Roddy didn't think any of this was important enough to do anything with, and for that matter nor did his killer, assuming there was one, who had plenty of time if they wanted his box of things he couldn't bring himself to throw away.

Figure maybe that was all it was: stuff in a holding pattern between being useless and being refuse. Old people get like that, and Titans are old even if they look young. They also get fragmentary amnesia sometimes, if the dosing process was particularly traumatic, if there was a lot of pain. The brain puts itself back together, but not always completely, and it's not unknown for Titans to have little files of the details they can't quite remember, or a desk drawer filled with things that ought to matter, but they don't know why. The cost of immortality is losing part of who you were, and perhaps that's not a bad bargain anyway.

After twenty minutes it's clear the gold butterfly fixture is all I'm getting from the apartment unless I want to question the fish. I do not, so I tell Musgrave I'll see her later at the morgue, and she looks like that is an offer she can take or leave.

I go out between Felton and the uniform into the hall. There's a bag of takeout from last night dumped by the apartment door. The label says it was ordered at seven fifty, but Roddy Tebbit never took it inside. Receipt printout is eight fifteen.

When you stand in the hallway and smell the cold food, you realise you've been breathing death in the apartment. It's not a stink of blood or bowel, but any dying leaves a trace in the air. I feel it as a kind of thinness, like the flavour of a bone broth taken off the cooker before it's time, or the empty pages of a new colouring book.

Apartment 363 where Roddy Tebbit lived is the corner, with big picture windows. 362 is a mid-floor and 364 is pretty much the whole of the other side of the hall, although the building on that side is stepped like a pyramid, so in terms of your square meters it isn't any bigger than the other two, but it probably has a hell of a terrace. I go along to 362. There's a bucket outside. I knock. When no one answers, I ring the bell, and then knock again. Finally the door opens and a guy in a janitor coat looks out. He has greasy hair and muttonchop sideburns and no beard, and he wears a badge which says his name is Rufus. I say hi to Rufus.

"Hi," Rufus says. "You part of—" He waves at the cops.

"External contractor." Meaning I don't care about whatever his hustle is. You got to know a guy like Rufus has a hustle. "These nice people?" Gesturing to the apartment behind him.

He shrugs. "Moved out last week. Going to the west coast."

"I hear it's cold as hell."

"Well, they sure didn't leave anything behind." He sighs. Figure some people leave stuff he can sell on.

"You ever see the nerd next door?"

"The doctor guy?" He raises his hand up way over his head. Not everyone that big is a Titan. In fact right around one in every one million people is naturally over seven feet tall, for a global total of maybe eight thousand; the number of Titans in the world is a quarter of that, even if a lot of them are here, in Chersenesos. But it's not really about the numbers: Titans are red carpet, VIP lounge and champagne. They wear perfect clothes and shoes without orthotics. They're hard money walking. So, sure, maybe Roddy Tebbit was not "that Titan guy" to Rufus. He was tall, and he was a doctor.

"Yeah," I say.

Rufus shrugs. "Sure. You can't miss him."

To be honest I have been wondering if anyone will.

"He okay?" I ask. "Decent fella?"

Rufus nods. "Sure. Just some guy. Shy maybe."

"He date?"

Rufus shrugs. "There was a girl sometimes. A lady, I guess."

"He social with anyone?"

"No." His eyes flick across and down at the floor, but his body twitches a little towards 364. "I mean just neighbourly. Maybe chips and dips. He's a quiet guy."

"Any visitors? Loud music? Like that?"

Rufus laughs. "I think one time some of his students came round and they played him something modern. Three of them. Said they were going to teach him to live a little. It didn't take."

"You recognise them if I showed you a picture?"

"It was a while ago. One of the girls had long brown hair, down to her legs."

"Like brown brown or—" I don't know what the fuck else brown. I was going to use the hair to make him describe the girl, but Rufus gets a look. It's the look people get when they want to ask me how much I'm not a cop. Like am I not a cop so I don't care about jaywalking? Or am I not a cop so yeah, you know, this one time in Vegas—?

I look Rufus in the eye and I offer him cash. Rufus says it happens he is having a particularly bad month owing to some poor financial investments in the field of canine athletics. I help out with this shortfall.

Rufus ambles away to a closet and I watch him go. He has a weird gait, like Chaplin playing a sailor. I ask myself if he has smashed-up hips. I had a cousin who moved that way after a horse walked over him. I wonder whether he might have hated Roddy Tebbit for being a Titan, because Titans don't have injuries like that any more, not after they get dosed, but no one was going to give Rufus a shot at that.

Rufus comes back and he's holding a piece of brown string. When he gives it to me and I realise what it is.

"You took some of her hair?"

"Humans shed hair all the time," Rufus says. "You got long hair like that, more of it. It catches on doors, plants, on a sweater. Then it goes on the floor. This girl, she brushed her hair outside the apartment. To look smart for class, I guess."

"And you just pick it up because it's neater that way."

"I gather it," Rufus says, pious and clean. "I keep it all and I colour-grade it, and at the end of the year I sell it on."

Always something new. I think about how that works and make a mental note not to search Rufus's place unless I absolutely, positively, have no other fucking leads in the world.

"To who?"

"Embalmers. Mostly for touch-up. Sometimes a corpse will lose hair. If they can't use it outside, sometimes stuffing."

"Well," I say, "life is the process of learning shit that you never ever wanted to hear."

Rufus does not like my tone. "Well, that's her hair, anyway," he says, and he's thinking about going.

"He seem different recently? Roddy Tebbit?"

Shaking his head. "Not that I saw."

"And not yesterday, specifically? This week in general?"

"No. Hey—" People always start to get it when you ask that. "Hey, what happened?"

"Fire drill," I tell him. "Excuse me."

Whoever lives in 364 was waiting for the knock but doesn't want me to know it. I hear footsteps, rapid and nervous, and then there's a pause while they stand on the other side of the door and count silently. I count too. People count to ten because that's what they think you do. I get to nine and fix my expression, respectful neutral, and the door opens.

She's long and narrow. She has her hair shaved to the notch at the back of the skull and cut to the line of her mouth at the front, and the jacket dress she wears has a deep collar designed to drag your eye downwards from her face. I fix my eyes on a patch of air a few inches in front of her nose and look as official as I can.

"Good afternoon," I say. "My name's Cal Sounder. I'm working with the police on a serious crime. You mind if I come in?" I badge her, properly, so she has time to read the fine print. She doesn't.

"Of course," she says, "come in."

She sounds sad, but there's something in her eyes like gunpowder and white alcohol.

The apartment is all-over rugs and brass jugs: Mesopotamia chic was in last year. It smells of coffee and vetiver, and in between peacock feathers there's some hardwood modern furniture, as if the Sultan always had a thing for Charlie Eames. The woman's name is Layla Catchpole. She's divorced. It wasn't a good divorce, but it's over now. Her ex-husband lives in Maui with his new wife.

"What can I do for you, Mr. Sounder?"

I play dull on instinct.

"There's been a problem in the building, the official police are investigating, but they've asked me to step in and advise on some technical issues. I need to ask you a few background questions."

"What kind of a problem?"

"I'm a specialist in socio-medical criminal investigations."

Which sounds very white-collar, pushes everyone to think of liability and doctors making side money selling oxy, and they get happy and forthcoming. That is not what happens if you say there is a corpse on the other side of the hall. "You've been here the last four weeks?"

She has.

"Can you recall whether you were here in March last year?"

A sigh as the conversation moves further and further into the abstract. She checks her diary. She was.

"Were you sleeping with Roddy Tebbit?"

She thinks about it.

"When?"

"Whenever."

"Yes. Once."

"When?"

"When he moved in. Just after the divorce. That's quite a personal question."

"It's just routine."

"Is it now? All right. 'Socio-medical crime.' What does that mean, exactly?"

"It's a portfolio."

"That's not much to go on."

"It's the truth."

"I'll trade you answers for answers."

"Why not just tell me?"

"Because I'm bored and you're not flirting. Shall we do that instead?"

Gunpowder and white alcohol.

"Violence, sometimes. Murder."

"That's almost rude, Mr. Sounder. You'd rather talk about death than flirt with me. What happened in my building last night?"

"Someone discharged a firearm."

"And when this someone discharged this firearm, were they aiming it at another someone?"

"My turn, Mrs. Catchpole. You know Roddy Tebbit well?"

"Apart from the sex, no. He's a sweet old man. You know he's old, right?"

"I do. I was wondering whether you did."

"Why did you ask if I was sleeping with him?"

"He's a Titan and you're pretty."

"Why, thank you."

"Just the one time. No follow-up? Never again?" She sighs and doesn't say anything. It dawns on me that she's in the waiting space before crying, the place people go when they're ready, but need something to choke on, to make it begin.

"Just the one time. It was fine. Clumsy. I think he was . . . trying himself out. I think it had been a long time for him."

"Mrs. Catchpole, would you turn your head to the side. Please."

She does, looking to her left. A rounded earlobe peeps out under the line of hair, unpierced.

"Now the other way."

She does.

"You don't wear earrings."

"Who tipped you off about me and Roddy? Rufus, I imagine."

"You think Rufus has a thing for you?"

"I think he has a thing for women in general. I don't think it's a very nice thing. 'Socio-medical crime'—that's what you mean, isn't it? Crime involving Titans and the drug. What's it called?"

"You know what it's called."

"I do. Titanium 7."

"What else do you know?"

"What I read in magazines. It's a rejuvenation treatment given by infusion. It turns the body's clock back to pre-puberty, then runs you through it at speed. It's also used to stimulate regeneration of severely damaged organs and limbs. It really does make you young again, but since it starts with an adult body, it also makes you bigger, hence the name. Oh, and it's so expensive almost no one has it. Strictly for the speciation rich. Did I miss anything out?"

"No, I'd say you're dead-on. The first use leaves you around twenty percent bigger. It's cumulative. I figure Roddy was a first-doser."

"What do you know about Roddy?"

I know he's leaving now, in a bag, because I can hear the gurney in the hallway. "He was a nerd. He liked fish, and work, and now you."

"Well, as you said, Mr. Sounder, he was a Titan and I'm pretty. It was a curiosity to me: a Titan, like you see in the gossip sheets, but also a little, sweet old man reborn in the body of a tennis pro. A nerd, a romantic, and a widower."

"He was married before?"

"Yes, but she died. I wondered if he spent all their money on his dose and not hers. That would be very wicked, wouldn't it?"

It would. I don't like it much, but it could be a motive for someone.

Layla Catchpole shrugs. "It was just once, as I said. For him to see what it was to be with a woman again after all that time, and for me to see if I could make him smile."

I rate her odds as good.

"And last night?"

"What about last night?"

"Did you hear anything from across the hall?"

"No."

"Not even the gunshot."

She turns her head away.

"Maybe. There was a pop. I thought he was opening champagne."

"Alone?"

"He hasn't been entirely alone for a while."

"And you?"

"I wasn't alone either."

I wait, and she leans across to a table and finds a business card in her purse: thick stock, matte finish. A music industry type from out of town.

"He caught a flight this morning. Call him, if you like. It's not going anywhere."

"Thank you."

"Were you alone last night?"

"Yes."

"But I bet you don't date witnesses. Not even after."

"No."

"Then I don't want to be rude, Mr. Sounder, but I'm sure you have other things to do, and I've just found out someone I was fond of is dead. I don't really want to talk right now."

We shake hands, and I make my way to the door. When I get there, I realise I want to ask her straight if she killed him, but when I turn she's gone. I look around and find her outside next to a sun chair, the jacket dress crumpled on the floor, her arms wide and her head all the way back so she can stare up into the sky. There are clouds up there, up above the delivery drones, and a bright winter sun that she seems to be reaching for.

I was right. It really is a hell of a terrace.

In the lobby on the way out I talk to Jerelyn the commissionaire. Jerelyn likes to talk and she's about as tall as my shoulder. Her grandson is studying to be a doctor, she's a Virgo, and behind the desk she keeps a hunk of pool cue. She was born in Nairobi. She grew up there. She knows how to instill respect in the rowdy. There's a gun safe in the back room for emergencies, and her contract requires that she shoot three hundred rounds per month. She does six, and the company pays. She is not a crack shot, but she is a good one. Would I like to see her targets? Well, thank you, she is quite proud. Yes, a few weeks back she had to deal with a situation, two angry drunks trying to follow a resident into the building; never even went for the pool cue, just sent them home with her voice.

I ask Jerelyn if Layla Catchpole was screwing Roddy Tebbit on the regular, but I make it sound respectable.

"Mr. Sounder."

"Call me Cal."

"I'm not calling you anything but Mr. Sounder if you're asking me things like that."

"It's my job."

"I will not be informing anyone as to the social activities of the ladies of this building. Us girls got to stick together. Also the owner's policy is that we do not notice comings and goings. That is my job, Mr. Sounder."

"It's a murder investigation." But she shrugs.

There's no point pretending to Jerelyn that Roddy Tebbit isn't dead. The scene cleanup team needed her key to get the gurney into the freight elevator.

I ask her what he was like. She says Roddy Tebbit was quiet, no trouble ever. From the day he moved in he always got her name right even though he was a white guy. No, there's no other door except the fire doors, and those are alarmed, and if you open them you've got about twenty seconds before the whole floor gets flooded in water from the roof tank. Oh, well, yes, and there's a freight entrance, which she controls from here. Yes, there's a security camera record, but the camera is over there, so it doesn't show faces of guests as they come in. Yes, that's a policy decision of the owner. Privacy matters here. The freight entrance is different, the camera there has a zoom function and night vision, so you can make sure there is no monkey business. Or watch the foxes. No, she doesn't recall Roddy Tebbit having a visitor that night, but the commuter hours are busy and she's not required to check every single entry during that time. So if someone came in at six thirty and left in the morning, she wouldn't know. If they left before nine in the evening, really, she wouldn't know. She is paid to keep an eye on things, but also, as she has already said, to *not*. Yes, Layla

Catchpole did come in with someone, a glossy older fellow Jerelyn took to be up to no good.

I ask her about the takeout delivery. Roddy got meals from a takeout place around the corner sometimes. Yes, he got one last night. Oh, dear, that means he did have a visitor, after all. She meant no one social. Yes, she buzzed the kid in. She uses the same place sometimes, it's not expensive. It's mostly Goan food but the chef is Hungarian. The combination works. Go figure. The kid's sweet, it's good to see a young person working with their parents. Education is a fine aspiration but there's such a thing as a family business. We need both in the world. If I go over there, tell his mother that Jerelyn says hi.

I look around for the security camera. Too high and too far away, and like she says, intended to give everyone a little privacy. Perfect for compliance and liability, not so great for an actual investigation. Gratton's people can do the hard labour, matching entry and exit to residents. That's what uniforms are for.

I give Jerelyn my card and tell her to call me if she thinks of anything she doesn't want to tell the police, and I walk out into the winter. I can smell snow between the mist and lake water, and the heat from the cars.

The Goan-Hungarian place is called Bela's but the chef's name is Atilla, pronounced like oh-tah-loh. His wife, Mâri, runs the business and she's the brains. Oh, Jerelyn from over there? That's a good woman. And yes, Mâri says, she knows Roddy. Occasionally he comes and sits in. He always orders the same things, very particular. He doesn't drink much. Always used to come in by himself. No, never with Mrs. Catchpole—Mâri does not love Mrs. Catchpole—but there was a girl, a pale, pretty girl, she looked tiny next to him but she was about the same height as Mâri. Atilla says she was a singer. How does he know she was a singer? She told him so. And when was he talking to the pretty singer, exactly? When he brought the sorpotel and the paprika feijoada. Well, he should keep his eyes on his cooking, then, and not disturb the female guests. I was going to ask whether the singer wore earrings, but I figure I'm not getting an answer to that now.

Atilla goes back to the kitchen, and when a kid comes through the main door with a skateboard Mâri immediately brings him over and sits him down.

"This is Andor. He made the delivery last night. Tell him, Andor."

The kid says he made the delivery last night. "But the guy never came to the door. No tip."

"Andor!"

"Sorry, Mom."

"You're not supposed to leave food. If they don't come to the door we bring it back. Keep it warm."

"But he called out to leave it."

That's interesting. "You sure about that?"

"Pretty sure. I knocked, he didn't answer. I knocked again and he said to leave the food."

"Him or someone else?"

"I . . . guess it could have been either."

"Andor!"

"No, he's right, Mrs.—" What did she say the name was? "Adami. Through a door, one sentence like that, he can't know whose voice. Not to be sure. That's important. Thank you, Andor."

"S'okay." He gets up to go.

I lay a couple of bills on the table. "Since you didn't get a tip." Leave my finger on the top one. "You think there was someone else in there? Or was he by himself?"

"Someone else. I figured it was his girlfriend. I thought there was, uh," a glance at his mother, "kinda heavy breathing. Like if someone had been, uh, getting a lot of exercise."

She scowls, and he takes flight. "Do your chores!"

"Yes, Mom."

The kitchen door closes.

"Good kid."

She smiles then, like sunrise. I go outside and think about

Roddy Tebbit ordering food before killing himself, and Roddy Tebbit sitting in his chair overlooking the city, and Roddy Tebbit dead on the carpet, and I think about someone breathing heavy enough to be heard outside by a kid who had other things on his mind.

Musgrave's office is on the first floor, with the mortuary right alongside. The entire south wall is made of white smoked glass so the autopsy room can use natural light. The other wall is the cadaver bank, row upon row of square doors with corpses stored behind them one on top of the other like a library of grief.

I put my head round the door and say: "Hi, Musgrave."

"No DNA on your earring," Musgrave says.

"I'm fine, thanks."

"If you wait, I'll give you my first impressions."

"Hey, Tidbo, does she talk to you like you're a real person?"

Tidbo, the chain of evidence sergeant, looks up from his magazine and says: "Oh, shit, no."

"Hi, Felton."

Detective Felton raises his middle finger. It's like he's toMAHto and I'm toMAYto.

"Fuck you doing here?" Felton says.

"Roddy Tebbit."

"The suicide?" Tidbo says.

"Okay, if you like. But he's a Titan, so here I am."

"What makes you think he's not just a big guy?"

"He's ninety years old, Felton, so yeah, he's a big guy because someone jacked him up with T7 sometime."

"Fuck the Titans and fuck you."

"That is the general consensus."

"Take your general and consensually shove it—"

"Oh Jesus, shut up!" Musgrave says. "Felton, he was a Titan. One dose, for services rendered. Contractual perk, for God's sake. I never saw that before. Sounder, stop being an asshole."

"Fuck we need him for?" Felton says.

"So you can blame someone when you fuck it up," I tell him, and apparently that's just too far. Felton raises his fist like he's showing it to me, then turns away like he's done. Then he actually goes for it. It's a good punch and I don't know if I'd slip it, because I really wasn't expecting things to get physical, but it doesn't matter because Musgrave, without looking, reaches back and tases him.

I'm serious. With her off hand she sticks a Taser into his backside and fires it, what they call a shunt tap: the barest contact. Felton jerks once, the strong muscles in his stomach crunching him forwards. He yells and falls over, gets his hands in front of his face so that he doesn't break the nose, but still catches himself a good one.

"You're welcome," Musgrave says. "Now you're not gonna punch a civilian consultant during an autopsy, spoil the trace evidence, and get fired and sued and all that shit."

"Are you out of your mind?" Felton yells at her.

"You're bleeding, detective," Musgrave says, because there's a little red line coming out of his nose now. "That's a big no-no in my space." She tosses him a bottle of aspirin. "Get him out of here, Tidbo. And you," she adds to me, "don't imagine for one second I don't blame you for that shit."

"Fuck did I do?"

"Just don't do it any more."

Tidbo rolls his eyes and helps Felton out to clean up. I don't argue with Musgrave. I just sit there and wait for her to be ready, and eventually she is. She tosses me a mask and starts to cut.

Autopsies aren't as bad as people make out. There's a stink, for sure. In fact there's all kinds of stink from all kinds of different places, and there's wet stuff. But mostly what there is is a wonderful, broken thing. Most times the interior landscape is hidden, and we only get to see it when it goes wrong, but there's an astonishing beauty beneath the skin. We are remarkable.

Musgrave is gentle as she works, and she's not afraid to touch the dead, even to embrace them so she can reach what she needs to tell their story. In her hands, a corpse is like one of those old Bibles chained up in a dusty room, not only the printed text and the rich colours of the pictures, but the records of marriages and births and deaths in the back pages, the history of a town. It's a shame we don't think of ourselves that way more often.

Musgrave sees me watching and puts a thermometer spike directly into Roddy Tebbit's liver.

"Time of death was mid–late evening. Call it eight p.m." She takes the liver and puts it in the scales. She makes a note and transfers it to an icebox.

"He listed himself as a donor," she tells me, before I can ask. "Livers regenerate, don't worry about the hole."

"I wasn't. You mean he's a standard organ donor?"

"Looks like."

"Would that even work?"

"Sure. Cut it in half, even, two for the price of one."

"But with the T7?"

She shrugs. "It's supposed to clear the system. Once it's done, Titan blood and cells are just blood and cells. Whether that's true . . . Search me. Not an expert."

A Titan and a donor. I've never heard of that happening before. But then, I've never heard of a Titan living by himself with a couple of koi carp, teaching and reading books. And for sure I've never heard of anybody getting T7 as a perk.

Add it to the motive list. I can already feel this case ballooning, the sheer number of possibilities getting beyond the headache stage and into migraine by end of day. Unless he really did shoot himself in the head. Then we can all go home.

"He was murdered," Musgrave says.

Of course, he was.

According to Musgrave, Roddy Tebbit was probably conscious when someone held his hand like a lover and put the gun to his head, then pulled the trigger. There's a void on the skin of his fingers where the burn residue was blocked. You can trace the outline of someone else's thumb: a slim hand but large—it would have to be, to go around Roddy Tebbit's. There's some bruising too, mapping the palm and little finger of that other person on his skin.

Musgrave tells me to draw the blind. When I do she flicks the UV lamp on and you can see the lines of pressure on Roddy's flesh, the ghost of an embrace. Someone overpowered Roddy Tebbit. There wasn't much of a fight about it.

Musgrave leans down close to the hand, tracing the shadow on the skin with a marker: cartoon fingers like sausages. A big man or a big woman; a smaller person wearing gloves. Maybe just a magnifying effect, a puff of wind at the crucial moment. Maybe the skin pinched by the grip so the shadow looks bigger than it was.

But probably—and this is where the ceiling falls in—most probably a human hand as big as, or bigger than, Roddy's.

Which would mean another Titan.

Bang.

Musgrave still has plenty of cutting to do, and I leave her to it. I take the waterbus across town and step out at the Reddington jetty, smelling mud and water freight, and something down by the bank that died. From one corpse stink to another, and this one's cleaner.

In my pocket there's an address written down on paper, the organ service Roddy Tebbit was signed up to. The building is a square redbrick, a converted customs barn from fifty years gone, and likely a smuggler's den or a shooting gallery a decade later. Now it's commercial, owned by a company in Nassau, so exactly that much has changed. There's a main door on the front but the one I want is round the side, the loading dock where the drones are lined up with cooler boxes, and the pilots—kids, mostly, and one or two old lags from the Afghan Raptor crews—are vaping bubblegum flavours and telling one another stories about that time when: Once I saw a woman naked on a rooftop, or a man.

Once I crashed a movie star's pool party. Once I flew a MOP bomb right into the mouth of a bunker and you better believe no one got out. Once I was a hero, or a joker. Once I was a pilot. Now I'm here.

I walk through them without stopping. They don't try to stop me. It's not clear who cares less.

I hop up onto the concrete dock and walk in. The stuff on the floor only looks like sawdust. It's a synthetic. They sweep it up at the end of each day and wash it, then lay it out again. When it gets wet, it leaks menthol, so the place smells cold and crisp, not bloody. There's a mixed production line: robot arms packing and despatching, sorting and passing to the drones. The actual harvesting—I'm sure they don't call it that—is done by humans, because however efficient the hardware is, nobody wants to imagine themselves, however deceased, being xystered and guillotined by a thing with a hundred tiny mechanical hands and empty silver eyes like a bead of mercury. I read where they bring cadavers here from all over. One of the many things the city is good at: the upcycling of the dead.

I raise my voice to call out. "Doug Krechmer?"

A man in red scrubs puts down something with a rotating blade and says: "How did you get in here?"

"Yeah, it's a regular fortress."

I point back to the loading dock. He comes out from behind the operating table so I can't see what's on it. Fine by me. I like to keep my dismembered bodies to one per afternoon, and even then, only if they're professionally relevant. "Need to talk to you."

"We don't allow—"

"I can come back later—"

"You can come back with an appointment, sir—"

"—with a dozen cops and a warrant."

Magic words. Everything human gets quiet. The parcelling machine keeps going, wrapping one little spool of nerve tissue after another in cold foil and passing it to flight control. There's a national database now, running a sophisticated placement system. Day-to-day non-specific items like nerves get put into a transit pattern so that wherever your hospital is there's always a package within a couple of hours' travel. The rare stuff goes to the medical spine depots and sits in a pulsatile-perfusion system getting fed nutrient soup and staying viable until needed. Life after death, unevenly distributed.

Krechmer leads the way to a spic-and-span little alcove with pictures of smiling dead people and the smiling living people whose lives they have prolonged. There are smiling relatives too, in all directions. I think it's supposed to be uplifting. It's probably not.

"What's this about? Who are you?"

I tell him my name and what this is about. It doesn't make him any happier.

"Murdered?"

People always say that like it's shocking. Murder? In this postal area? Write to your representative. Demand better service—but the truth is it happens all over.

I'm tired of telling Krechmer things I've told lots of other people today, so now I just sit and wait for him to run out of steam and tell me I can have whatever I need. It doesn't take very long.

"Did you run any assays on Roddy Tebbit before taking him on as a donor?"

"We prefer—"

"I don't care. Did you?"

"The standard tests, yes. No blood-borne infectious disease. No problematic organ damage, no addictions. He was in wonderful shape. Hardly surprising, at his age."

If he knows he's got a Titan on his books, he's remarkably relaxed about it. A murdered Titan. I don't think he does. I have no idea what effect it would have if you implanted organs from a T7 body into a normal human one. Assuming they fitted—not all of them would. I'm pretty sure it's not covered by his insurance.

"Do you have any facility for allowing a donor—" Krechmer twitches again, he really doesn't like that word—"what the fuck do you say instead?"

"Benevolent."

"You say benevolent every time you mean donor?"

"Yes."

"It's honestly amazing you get any work done at all. Do you have a facility for allowing a donor to specify the recipient?"

"Of course. Some have very particular requirements, others broad generalities. Some just want to be useful. It's a little like adoption. Though we absolutely do not accept criteria based on race."

"Did Roddy Tebbit specify?"

"Yes. He left his organs to the storage bank of a private clinic, in fact. The Travis. It's quite well regarded."

Depending who you talk to.

I tell Krechmer he's to treat the information he holds as evidence in a criminal trial. He's to lock it down, and hand over the access rights and any physical detail to Captain Gratton personally, or to me. Anything he would maybe prefer did not trouble the police, directly to me, without delay.

"If anyone asks," I say, as I'm leaving, "I came to see about making my own donation. All that badge stuff was just me jumping the line."

"And . . . what did you decide?"

"You didn't like my tone and you threw me out. You can yell at me while I'm leaving. It'll impress your boys."

I open the door and after a minute, he does. He's terrible at it, but I don't turn around, and him being completely unpersuasive makes it look pretty real.

The lake smells like must and geosmin all the way back to the office, and the air is thick and cold. The sun sets behind the mountains, snatches the day away and puts it to bed.

climb the stairs thinking how much they don't smell like Limonene, the way the ones in Roddy Tebbit's building do. Not that my building is a dump. It's a good building with good people, and on the second landing there's a bunch of flowers in a vase that

Mrs. Khan puts out on her little table, the one the superintendent says is a fire risk but never actually removes because he's a human being too.

It's cold in the stairwell, and the skylight at the very top is letting in a blue steel light: winter nighttime and mountains. I can see my breath curling away towards the roof.

When I go in there's someone sitting in the chair in my office. Sitting behind my desk. Not searching through my things, not holding a gun on me. Just sitting in the dark.

I know it's her. There's just something in the silence. Perhaps, at the edge of my hearing, I'm registering the sound of her heart. Perhaps it's the air moving in and out of her lungs. I used to listen to her sleep. Even changed, I know her in the dark.

Athena.

Although most everyone else in the city calls her "Ms. Tonfa-mecasca" these days, or just "ma'am."

"When were you going to call me?"

"I didn't want to bother you."

I hear a rumble somewhere, and it takes me a moment to realise that she's just growled, deep inside her chest like a hunting cat. "We've been through this."

"Yes, we have."

"And you promised to call."

"You promised I'd call. I didn't say anything."

When we first met, she'd put her hands on her hips like Superman in one of the old comics you see in museums now. Action number 9, World's Finest number 2.

Instead, she leans forward into the light and I see her face. So very nearly her as she was. You could look at her now and see a woman built from birth on a grand scale, the daughter of Finnish giants, a cheerleader the size of a quarterback, but more than that: it isn't just scale she has, it's density, as if the ordinary world has to make space for her, and does. You can see the challenge, the wit behind the smile, the sorrow behind the wit.

"Come on. What can I do to help?"

I sit down in the client chair and look at her.

"There's nothing yet. I don't know anything."

"You know he was murdered."

"That's not public."

She snorts, racehorse deep. "Sure it's not."

Not public, but everyone who matters knows. Of course they do.

I say: "What have you got?"

"Not much. Less than we should have."

"I hear he was dosed as a contractual perk."

"So it seems."

"You ever hear of that before?"

"It's . . . generous."

"A fucking house in Malibu is generous. I don't think there's a word for what this is. What was he doing for Stefan?"

"Something research-based, obviously. He was part of a team, but it was years ago and Stefan doesn't remember."

"Sure, why should he?"

"Yeah, like you remember client details from last week."

"I'm paid to forget those."

"And Stefan has people to remember things for him."

"So you ask Elaine? Or Maurice?"

"I don't talk to Maurice unless I have to."

Which means she talks to him in the office, but not otherwise, and as often as possible through assistants and subordinates. Maurice, Stefan's sister's son, is a human lifetime older than Athena, but roughly the same time out after his first dose. He wears his collateral status heavy and has dreams of the top floor office: years of service, deep working knowledge of the company, blah. When Athena came back into the fold—my fault—she took his job and his promotion ladder. In fairness he was only ever keeping it warm for someone else, and everyone except Maurice knew that. He wants to turn back the clock, and on some level he must know he never will. Athena meanwhile can't stand Maurice, but that's less professional rivalry and more because Maurice has a crush on her mother and Elaine lets him hang around.

Family's never easy, but it gets nastier if everyone's rich and lives basically forever.

Athena carries on. "Stefan doesn't like this thing of my mother being the company historian. He says she should just get on with her life."

"They're divorced. It's not his business."

"Cal, it is literally his business."

"I think he's just squeamish because Maurice is his nephew and is dating his ex."

"They're not dating."

"They're not related like related. And age-appropriate isn't really an issue either."

"You think?"

"I figure anyone over eighty can legitimately date anyone else over eighty. And hey, if they actually got married, that would make him look all kinds of legitimate. Maybe he could even steal his job back."

She shakes her head. "Just none of what you said is happening."

"Sure, it's platonic. There was a great picture of them dancing platonically in the *Post*."

"You read terrible newspapers."

"It's my job."

"That's the other thing. Stefan's pissed you didn't call right off."

"How is he?"

"He doesn't change, Cal."

I don't think that's true. Stefan Tonfamecasca is a four-dose Titan. In some sense, changing is the essence of what he does, even as he remains the same ruthless bastard he's always been. The cumulative increase in height and mass takes him beyond the merely human into some new territory I don't understand. No one understands. Not even Athena, his youngest and best beloved daughter, and probably the last natural child he will ever have.

I say: "Nor do you."

She looks away, leaning back into the dark. The chair creaks. Athena was five feet five and twenty-nine years old when she was crushed under a collapsing wall. She lay in hospital in a coma for two weeks, something like seventy of the bones in her body broken into more than one fragment, most of her organs on the brink of shutting down. She and Stefan weren't talking. He'd cut her off and she'd told him where to shove it. She was living a normal life.

With me.

I sat with her every hour of that coma, and the doctors came every day and told me it was never going to change.

So I called Stefan, and he came.

Now she's just over seven feet tall, and weighs in excess of one hundred and thirty kilos. She is the notional heir to the Tonfamecasca family company—not that Stefan ever proposes to step down.

But what she isn't, any more, is mine. And though I try to take care of her, the truth is she doesn't need it, and I do need her help.

So I swallow my pride and I ask her again what Roddy Tebbit was doing for Tonfamecasca.

"We honestly don't know," Athena says. "Stefan can't find him anywhere. He just appeared out of the air."

"Would he tell you?"

"He tells me everything."

"I hope that isn't true."

Huge eyes look into mine across the desk. She finally has a body big enough for the soul within.

"I'll call you, Cal, if I get anything more. Say you'll do the same."

"I'll do the same."

"Now mean it."

"I'll do the same."

The floor creaks as she leaves, huge hand trailing across my shoulder for just an instant, soft like snow.

I'm calling it, or maybe my bed is calling me. My apartment is tucked away next to the office; most people think the plain little door just alongside the one with my name stencilled on it is a closet, but it's a nice, cosy space: a galley kitchen dining, and a bedroom with a glass roof section like a little greenhouse that looks straight up into the sky. I can lie down and watch the storms as they roll off the mountains and pass overhead. In summer I have to pull the blind across or the sunrise wakes me almost before I've gone to sleep. Tonight I can sit there with my hands around a hot mug and stare into the stars, thinking of the great cloud of possibilities and motivations, things that might have happened or might not, roads and crossroads and snarls and tangles. I can fall asleep with no idea and wake up with less of one.

That's what I'm doing when Bill Styles calls and asks me if I'd like a drink at the university.

"Not really, Bill. It's been a long day."

"Come on, Cal, you need to get out more. Let's chat."

Sure, Bill.

The university is a twenty-minute ride this time of day. The bus goes over the Tappeny Bridge and along the water. The campus looks towards Chersenesos, like a message to the student body: this is your goal. If you do well; if you thrive; if you excel; one of those offices will be yours, and all that goes with it. Everything in the city looks towards Chersenesos, one way or another.

Right now the moon is rising behind the ridgeline and the campus streetlamps are lit, each casting an X of shadows over the central path. I walk through the gates and find a guy standing by himself in the middle of the court. He's short, a little plump, and he wears waistcoats and corduroy so hard you have to think he's making a statement. Oddly flat lenses in round spectacles, so they catch the light and flicker when he turns his head. I guess he has a certain image to maintain. After all, he's the Dean.

"Hi, Cal."

"Hi, Bill."

"Let's walk."

"Sure." But we're not heading for his office, so I guess I'm not getting that drink just yet a while.

A university is a small, fractious mini-state all its own, and it has heroes and villains and victims of circumstance and it is not always easy to tell them apart when you're in the top chair. On the other hand, if you are just some guy, you might be able to go somewhere and ignore certain things that you see, and escort a talented young person home from what might otherwise be a bad place for them and their sparkling future. If you're in the top chair and you're a little devious—which is kind of a basic qualification for the job—you might seek out such a person so as to know who to call if ever the need arose, and if you were that kind of person, you might make it your business to let that be known, so that your name comes up at the right time.

Nine times, actually, in six years.

"It's so good to see you, Cal. And look: the winter honeysuckle is very fine this year. And the quince."

"I'm a sucker for quince, Bill. How did you know?"

Bill Styles used to be a moderate teacher of history, but he has the politics and the administration skills to run a place like this, and so these days he does. Bill is not some sort of holy educator. He's not even a particularly nice person. But he does take care of his own, like a goddamn lioness.

"I have an instinct about my friends. Horticulturally speaking."

"Is that what we are today? Friends?"

"I like to think that's always what we are, Cal."

"I can go with that, unless you shot someone in the head last night."

He laughs, white teeth almost as bright as those flat lenses in the streetlamp light. "If I did, it must have slipped my mind."

"You'd be amazed how often it does."

Bill leads the way down another little avenue of trees: Autumn Higan cherry, but I'm at least a week too late for the blossom. The bark is slick and black on either side of the path.

"You should have seen them in October, Cal."

"I'm sure it was lovely."

And then, at last: "I gather I'm short a professor tomorrow."

"Yes, you are. You know him?"

"Not well."

"Tell me. Off the top of your head."

"Absurdly tall, of course. Young, talented, shy to the point of rude. Marine biologist by training, synthetic biologist by career. Something something freshwater algae something. Very annoying, very fussy, but he publishes occasionally, teaches adequately, and doesn't seduce the seniors. Or the staff. I do like the absence of emotional drama from my common rooms. Should I be concerned?"

"You're already concerned. That's why we're walking around with bats overhead rather than having coffee in your office tomorrow. I don't have anything for you, Bill."

"But it's nothing torrid? It's just him dead, not him and a call girl, say?"

"Was that his thing?"

"Christ, I hope not. Not that I know of. And not that I'd know."

"No call girl. Although there is a woman in the picture. Two, actually, but one says it was over and I buy her denials for now."

"Good god. He hardly seems the type."

"What type did he seem?"

"Brilliant, anti-social asshole. The boring kind."

"How'd he come to work here?"

"Direct from the University of Burfleet. Achingly well credentialed, but to be honest he was foisted on us by the board—family connections, I suspected at the time. No doubt there's a library somewhere that I wouldn't have without him. And as I say, so long as I don't actually have to deal with him, he's a perfectly acceptable addition. A good one, even. And now I'll have a hell of a time replacing him, I suppose."

"I'm going to need to see his office. All his correspondence. I need to know what he was working on and with whom. I'll have to talk to anyone he was close to. There's a student, a group of them, who visited his place. I need them as well."

Bill shakes his head. "I can get you into his room, of course. You'll be discreet about any confidential research?"

"Sure. Figure the black market for synthetic algae patents is a little slow this winter anyway."

"You'd be surprised. Slime sells. As for the students . . . that's a red line, as far as the university is concerned. They are the fragile minds of tomorrow's great possibility blah blah blah. So unless you're looking for something very specific—no, actually, especially if you're looking for something very specific—"

He stops because I've stopped walking, and when he turns around he has to squint because I'm standing between him and one of the lamps. I wait for him to look uncomfortable and lift a hand to shade his eyes.

"Bill, I'm sorry, I'm sure you've got a terrific speech about why you can't help me, and I'd love to hear it, but I'm really tired and you've got this upside down. The regular police are holding off for now. Giles Gratton wants this done quiet and I'm the soft option. If you give me everything, you might get away with a pro forma visit. Otherwise my case won't hold water, and the cops'll come through here like a plague of ants. They'll be in everything. They'll catch all kinds of shit they don't care about, but once it's there in front of them they'll have to run with it. Maybe the football team is juicing, maybe someone's printing MDMA in the chem lab. Maybe the head of the business school lied on her tax return. For sure there's weed growing in a closet somewhere because there is always weed in a closet, and I guaran-fucking-tee some of your students are engaged in blameless but illegal sex work to pay tuition. The cops will find all of it, some of your kids will have to be expelled, the news people will have a field day."

Bill sours behind the hand. "Are you putting the screws into me, Cal?"

"I'm throwing you a lifeline, Bill. I can help, and what I need is what you need me to do, but if you can't go there, then you can't. This is why you got me up here, remember? I was going to bed."

"I figured you'd help me calm it all down, not turn my school inside out."

"That is what I'm doing."

"Sure doesn't feel like it." But he lowers the hand and we go back to walking. "What the hell is going on? Tebbit, for Christ's sake? What's he into? Was he a serial killer? A spy? A drug trafficker?"

"He was a Titan, Bill. It's on his driver's licence, he was ninety years old and change."

Another moment for him to put that together and then he drops his head into his hands. "Fucking private limited personal health disclosure. It's university policy, Cal. I'm not allowed to ask questions about medical status unless they are directly relevant to an acute situation. That covers his birthday, even."

I'd feel sorry for him if I didn't know they made that rule a few years back so that Bill's predecessor didn't have to trace embarrassing infections transmitted through her senior staff.

"Sleep on it. Let me know in the morning. I was going to swing by about nine, so call me any time before then."

"You put a strain on friendship, Cal, you surely do."

I leave him to his general sense of the sky falling and I go home, again. As I open the door the stupid part of me expects Athena to be there, the way she never is any more, asleep on the sofa or curled up in the bed. I lie down where she isn't and listen to the sound of the wind. Up above the city there are high clouds, like a second ceiling, and the sky is orange and purple with deep spaces giving onto the endless black. Every so often a helicopter or a drone flies over. Every so often a smattering of rain comes down. When the traffic stops there's a silence that goes on for miles.

I don't know when I fall asleep, but when I wake it hasn't been enough, or maybe it's too much and I can't tell the difference.

2

I t's officially official," Gratton says, in his officially official office. You can imagine it like the bottom drawer of a filing cabinet with a desk against the side wall, and a guy like a skinny cook behind the desk. The precinct house is tucked hard by the border between the real city and the dreamland of Chersenesos. You can see the towers, but your feet are still firmly in the mud, and Gratton's been in the job so long his eyes are the same colour as the walls. There's a three-bar electric fire at each corner and the room still feels cold from September to May. In summer the lake tugging at the foundations makes it smell like old clothes and old guilt.

"It's a murder investigation," Gratton goes on, "and you're hired in support."

"Who am I supporting?"

"Right now we're very busy. I can't spare a detective for full oversight of your investigation." More room to move, more rope. "On paper, you're working with Tidbo and Felton." I start to object, but Gratton waves his hand. "I spoke to Felton. He won't be an asshole any more so long as you can manage a minimum of collegial respect." Eyebrows up in polite warning: don't fuck with me on this. Message received. "Both Felton and Tidbo have regular duties, so unless you need the input of a senior detective—in which case I'll come in—you can assume neither of them needs to know anything you're doing. You can lean on them to detail a rookie or two if you have scut work. But don't waste time. I want you to bring me answers, not questions. Understood?"

"What about paper?"

"You mean warrants?"

"And such."

"If you need one, you need one. There are sensitivities around this case, that's why you're here. We apply and see what happens."

I make a note not to ask if I don't want to be told "no."

"Cal?"

"Giles?"

"Bring it in. Quiet as you can, but bring it in."

He locks eyes with me until I nod. Then he pushes the buzzer on his desk. "Brief him on the ballistics, please."

Felton's voice says "Yes, sir." He sounds as happy as I am.

"He's really going to be nice?"

"Sure, Cal, he actually won a charm contest in Scotia last year. He's going to make pikelets with conserve."

The shine on his sallow head says I'm dismissed.

Felton, instead, tells me about ballistics and forensics for what feels like the better part of an hour, which he does to his credit with a minimum of bullshit.

There are no prints on the gun except Roddy's. The apartment has the usual load of assorted DNA traces, but all the analysis team can say for sure right now is that it has been visited by several humans and—until Felton explained about the aquarium—apparently also a cuttlefish. There are no crucially revealing follicles, secretions or giveaway boot prints.

Felton's nose looks like it hurts a lot. I ask a few questions. He answers them. I ask more, trying to sound as smart and respectful as possible, as professional. We are polite as hell. Finally:

"Hey, Sounder?"

"Yeah?"

"She ever tase you like that?"

"Oh, Musgrave?"

"Yes fucking Musgrave. You got a list of other people who—Never mind, don't answer that. But she ever—"

"No, but we have history."

"I can work with you. I don't have to like you. But how do I go in her office now?"

"You just go in. She doesn't care."

"I honestly thought she liked me."

"Probably does."

"How can you tell?"

"It's Musgrave. I don't mean to be a pain in your ass, you know."

"Sure, you do."

"Okay, yeah, I kinda do. But it's not personal."

"What you said back there that made me mad? I never realised it before, but Gratton made me think it through. It's true, isn't it? You're the fall guy. You do okay with detective work—actually pretty good—but the reason you're there is so cops don't get fired over Titans."

"You coulda said it a little nicer, but yeah, that's a big part of it."

"What's another part of it?"

"Very occasionally I get to stop something bad happening before it happens, rather than after."

"Well, that's nice."

"Very occasionally."

"But other than that it's a shitty job."

"Yeah."

"Why d'you do it?"

"I don't know. I fell into it, now I'm here." I know just fine, but I don't want to talk about Athena with Felton.

Felton looks at me a while longer. "I don't like it, but I get it now. I can deal with it." He puts his hand out. I shake it. We both look like we'd rather be anywhere but here.

"Okay. Thank you."

"You want any more about the gun?"

"You think it's important?"

"In my cop judgement? Fuck, no. It is not."

"You get anything off the security tape yet?"

"Take out the residents, there's fourteen people come in that evening. So far we got a racketball teacher, four dinner guests and a massage therapist."

"Like massage massage or the other kind?"

"All I can tell you is expensive. That kind of expensive, it's honestly a little hard to tell. Then there's a few more we don't know yet. No faces, no one's owned up to them. You know there's going to be two or three we can't get, right? People doing things they shouldn't do."

"Yeah."

"You gonna share? Did you get anything?"

I'm about to say I'm only supposed to tell Gratton, but I can still feel his handshake.

"Janitor collects hair. Like, he gathers it up and colour-matches it."

He stares at me. "The hell?"

"He says it's commercial. I don't think it's a thing."

"Oh, it's a thing I'm gonna think about when I can't sleep nights. Jesus, Sounder. Anything that isn't freaky as shit and might be relevant?"

"Not yet. You want me to call if I do?"

He nods and we look at each other like we're ten years old and trying to share a pushbike.

I walk out before one of us fucks it up.

Twenty minutes with a cup of bad street coffee in my hand gets me to Mick's Guns on Highdown Road. Mick's is a militia-aspected executive hipster venue catering to nervous senior vice presidents and Doc Holliday wannabes with deep pockets. They carry the Armani Armour range as a cheap option and head north into bespoke Dyneema, Dragonscale and monofilament. There's impact cloth ballgowns in the ladies' section: bulletproof so long as the shooter doesn't aim for the décolletage, but they solve that with a shawl which'll take a direct hit at ten feet and keep the contessa standing to return fire with a range of purse-carry accessories. The same pepperpot gun Roddy bought comes in a thigh holster and ships with a selection of replaceable grips in non-slip pearl or abalone. There are no cash registers, so you'd think these items change hands as a courtesy, but in the middle of the room there's a tall woman—ordinary tall, not Titan tall—in what I'm guessing is about twenty grand's worth of ballistic spidersilk formal wear. She says her name is Celine. The accent is French with a trace of somewhere else, maybe Bangkok but maybe not.

"Hi Celine, I'm Cal."

"And what can I do for you, Cal?"

"Suppose you had to guess?"

She nods and looks me up and down, checking for cost. Feet, wrist, neck. My shoes say I walk; I don't wear a watch because they're unnecessary now and I don't wear a necklace because men who wear necklaces look like mob lawyers in TV shows. Also because they can be used to strangle you in a tussle. No easy markers of wealth, yet here I am. Tech bro, maybe. Musician. Film asshole. Or: Celine's eyes flick to the arms of my jacket, looking for a holster. Then she walks around back, looking at the lines of my clothes.

"Federal," she says at last, "I hope."

"I'm a consultant."

She sighs. "Couldn't decide if the suit was really good or if you just weren't carrying." She hits a bell and a kid comes out of the back room. He's wearing hayseed overalls and a Henley shirt. A stitched tag on the left cuff has a mock fire service badge and the words "no-burn." Celine tells him to mind the store. "But call me, Aaron, if anything comes up." Aaron ducks his head, twice, and I wonder if he's her son. Mick's is a family business, but in keeping with its executive spy vibe it's hard to find out what family. Though probably not hard enough that it's actually interesting.

We head into the back office, plush leather and fitting rooms for the bespoke set, and on through into the warehouse space behind, where the real work gets done and the lacquer gives way to chipboard and bare concrete. Way in the back someone's cutting fabric with hydraulic diamond shears.

Celine pulls two old office chairs up to the same side of a trestle table and we sit. There's a working tablet propped up on two old coffee cans, sleek lines buried in shock-absorbent foam so you can drop it and keep working. The foam looks cheap and homemade, but I figure it's offcuts from something halfway nuke-proof.

"I really look like a Fed?"

She shrugs. "If you were a Fed you might actually be here to buy. What do you want, Mr. . . . ?"

"Cal," I remind her. "Sounder."

"You mind if I call you Cal?"

"If I can call you Celine."

"You'll have to. I haven't told you my other name." Someone brings a jug of cold water and two cups, and she pours one for me. We both drink, and she makes a movement with her free hand. Get on with it.

"You had a nice young man in here day before yesterday. Very tall. He bought the wrist pistol. Did he get anything else?"

She shakes her head: "We don't give out details like that."

"His name was Roddy Tebbit, and if we assume that he also bought a suit, I regret to inform you that Mr. Tebbit will not be attending his fitting."

"Should we expect him soon?"

"Not unless you're really religious."

She nods as if that's just something that happens. "In that case: he bought the shawl from the Resilience line, but not the gown."

"Did he take it with him?"

"No. For delivery." She taps at the touchscreen. "Susan Green. An office, I think. 154 Mapleton Street."

I don't know Susan Green. She's not anywhere in Roddy Tebbit's top layer of contacts. Someone new, or someone old, or someone secret. I do know the address. It isn't an office and hearing it doesn't make me happy.

"Is that all he bought?"

"Yes."

"How did he seem?"

"Big." She glares. "We haven't talked about that at all."

"We both knew he was big when I came in and he hasn't gotten any smaller."

"You called him a nice young man."

"I was being poetic. How did he seem?"

"He was shy and a little bit scared. He made a change to the standard kit. We sell the gun with three boxes of ordinary bullets. He traded for two, one standard and one other."

"He wanted armour-piercing."

She nods. "He did."

I think about what Roddy Tebbit's office would have looked like if he'd been shot with an armour-piercing round. A lot redder. So he bought it, and then hadn't changed the loadout when whatever happened to him happened.

Lot of men would buy armour-piercing because it's cool and they've heard about it in movies, but Roddy Tebbit was a nerd. Armour-piercing rounds are a pain in the ass unless you have a specific need. They go through people, walls and other people, and other walls, and on and on. Roddy Tebbit wouldn't bother with that noise unless he had a reason. The reason wasn't that he was looking to shoot up a car or scare a bully.

He was expecting to have to shoot someone in armour.

Or someone with really thick bones.

I call Felton to tell him about Susan Green and the address Celine gave me.

"Victor's, huh?"

"Yeah." I shake my head. Felton laughs.

———

Figure if I'm going to Victor's I may as well drop in on Ostby since he's in the same part of town. Ostby won't like it much but I don't much like Ostby.

I swing by right about when he takes his morning coffee. He's not going to offer me any but he always has a meeting set for ten forty-five so that he can drink it in peace.

Most people in Ostby's position would have an assistant but Ostby doesn't care for it. He likes to take his own calls and keep his own appointments book.

I walk in and the place is quiet like three a.m. church. Ostby's in the back room drinking his sacred coffee. I take a moment to appreciate the decor. The floor is textured sheet metal with Turkish rugs. The desk is extruded composite that looks like stone. There are no metal leg chairs, no sprung loungers. The cups on the sideboard where customers can help themselves are the same stuff as the desk, so you feel like a caveman picking them up. New addition in back: a rack of gym weights in the top load range, and a bench.

Floyd Ostby is what you call a creep. That's to say he's an ordinary guy who aspires to be a Titan so much that he's already trying to live like one—but because he's not a Titan and doesn't actually deal with any, he has no idea how that goes.

Titans do like stone; they do like stuff that doesn't break all around them. But they're so rich that it either looks like it's made of glass or it's heavy enough that you have to reinforce the floor. No Titan is going to have anything made of resin, even if real granite is brittle. Resin looks like resin, and if you snap a piece off a stone item you buy another one. It'll be with you by close of business, with champagne.

Ostby's just a wannabe to them. Half of them wouldn't even realise what he was trying to be, and the other half would laugh their enormous asses off.

———

walk on through the waiting room and open the door to his workspace. The man behind the desk—resin legs and a slate top the size of a pool table—looks at me and scowls. He's got wide shoulders and a bald head, and moist eyes like a bloodhound.

"Hi, Floyd."

"Get out."

Ostby also hates me because I know a couple of Titans and I don't find that exciting.

"Nope." I sit down. He stands up.

"We gonna do this, Cal? You want to see what happens?"

He comes out from behind the desk to loom over me. Big muscles, big man. Genuinely a big man. In any other period of human history he'd be all kinds of imposing. I look up at him.

"I'm not going to fight you and you're not going to fight me. You want to talk about all the shit that I know?"

Ostby is a financial advisor with a big shiny logo and a whole host of nice family clients: good ordinary folk who put their money to work. A hundred grandmas owe their prosperity to Floyd Ostby and he does not let them down. He puts their money in safe stocks and good apple-pie companies and it grows a little, stays strong when there's a downturn, and a little bit saves the whales too.

Ostby can afford to be cautious for his good family clients because he has five or six other clients whose money comes in a little dusty, maybe grey, even a little shady, and he helps it wash off that grime and make itself presentable in polite society. In amongst the sheep: wolves in casual knitwear.

Murder cops have to talk to financial cops about money when they need to know something and financial crime is frustrating and intangible. Right now Felton is sitting with his eyes closed, wishing he was dead, half listening to Wade Kinsella and Joanie Fontana from Forensic Fiscal Division go through money flows and Roddy Tebbit's legitimate expenditure.

But me, I like to talk to Ostby, because if you want to know money laundering you want to know a money launderer.

Which is why I make it my business to know Ostby's business. Not the money and certainly not the clients. But I know Floyd Ostby has a little issue with pills and I know where he goes to enjoy those pills, and what and who he does when he gets there. The last Mrs. Ostby paid for some really great recording equipment.

Ostby knows I know this but today he's not buying.

"Maybe I don't care any more."

"Maybe you don't."

"Maybe I've got new friends, Cal. The kind of friends can make that kind of problem go away."

"It's been tried occasionally. It didn't stick. You threatening me, Floyd?"

He shakes his head, but it's interesting he'd get that close to it. That's not Floyd Ostby's home ground at all. He's strictly a gym bunny, not a thug.

"What's got into you, man? You find yourself a shiny new client from the cartels? I didn't think you liked that action."

"Someone—" he smirks a little bit. "Bigger."

"I can just call Stefan and ask who it is, Floyd. You know that."

"Damn it, Cal! How long you going to try to hold this shit over me?"

"Pretty much until one of us dies, Floyd. And if it's me pegs out? I'm going to bequeath it all to Gratton."

"Screw you."

But he sits down again. Another way he's not like a Titan. They don't talk about it much but I'm pretty sure Titans get stubborn when they get dosed. I'm not sure if it's a chemical thing or just having your body get tougher than everyone else's and spending time exclusively with the mega-rich. When a Titan says "no" they mean it, and if you push, they push back. There's no meeting you halfway.

I toss him the little drive with Roddy Tebbit's numbers on it.

"I need to know what's happening there."

"I'm sorry, Cal, I'm all kinds of busy this week. Why don't you have your people call me . . ." He sits down, flicks through a calendar, "no, that's not good . . . no . . . yep. Here we go. Call on the sixth of go fuck yourself and we'll set something up."

"First blush I'll take right away. You can come back to me with detail later."

"Did you not hear me?"

"I figured you were just letting off steam." Because if he actually turns me down I will burn him to the ground. That pill habit will draw heat. His grandmas won't hang around and his other clients won't like the feeling of exposure. His business will blow away on the wind and with it whatever tiny chance he has of buying his way onto the Tonfamecasca patient list. I sit there with my face blank and expectant and let him run through it all in his head.

When he's done he puts the drive in the side of his nifty little terminal and I wait while he browses.

It doesn't take long.

"Vanilla."

"Completely vanilla?"

"No."

"What no?"

"Can't tell you yet."

"Tell me something."

"New business is pure as the driven snow. Man has a job, spends within his means. Sizeable salary, not many outgoings. No surprising shifts, no mysterious withdrawals. Proper citizen. Old business is something else. That's a wall. I'll come back to you."

"Am I gonna have to press you?"

He waves me away, still staring at the screen.

"Am I?"

"No."

"I don't want—"

"No, Cal, get lost. This is professional now. I'm going to learn something. It's well done. Shoo. Come back and I'll put it all into little words."

"Thanks."

The wet eyes glance up for a second like he's a different person. Say one thing for Floyd Ostby, say this: he cares about his craft. "Thank you for bringing me this."

He goes back to the numbers, and I head over to 154 Mapleton.

Victor's is where east meets west. It's the bar you go to if you know. It's not a nice place.

When Titans first get dosed, the actual change is absurdly fast. Systemically they go from old to young in a week, which is to say the skin gets flexible and the body changes so quickly they have to be sedated and fed through a tube. They start aging backwards, hypersenescence kicking out dead cells and erasing keloid scars, then crash through a repeat of the transition from child to adult in a matter of weeks. For six months they're hungry all the time, they sleep a lot, and from month three to five they're in constant low-grade pain because their bones are still up-massing so fast you can almost watch it happen. The company keeps them in a healthcare environment for the worst of it. Towards the end of the process they're notionally functional but batshit crazy. They're pissed off, horny and overstimulated but think they're bored. That can last a few years, and it's during that time that they go to Victor's. It's a bar with a speakeasy vibe: a velvet door that you go through from a smart-looking foyer in the business district. The ground level belongs to the bar—they keep the booze fridges, food and paperwork up there, and there's overnight rooms you can book which are basically fuck hutches but double as drunk tanks for new-minted god children who can't hold their liquor. The first floor is a gym, also owned by Victor, which means they can make as much noise as they like and no one gives a shit. If you want to get in, you go to the admin layer and they vet you. If you want to work there, same thing.

Victor's has what you call a rep, and that's fair enough. Some crazy shit goes down here, though Victor keeps it—not legal, by

any means, but law-abiding, in the grand scheme. It's not a murder house, blackmail is frowned upon, and if you don't want to
play the games—games which can get pretty fucked up—you can
just leave at any time. Vic will make sure you do, in good order.
Though you also won't be getting back in; Victor's is strictly a one-
chance venue. That knowledge also keeps the Titans in line when
they come. Which they do more seldom than the cool crowd here
would like to think. There just aren't that many Titans in the world,
though by definition, the number is increasing.

Less so this week, I guess.

The door is 154 Mapleton, where Roddy Tebbit sent a bulletproof shawl for Susan Green, and the doorman is called Sam. Sam
and I go way back.

That's why I walk in with my hands where he can see them.

Sam is stocky, built ordinary scale, but you'd have to be an idiot
not to see him for a hard case. The cooler in a place like this is
by definition one dangerous son of a bitch. Sam did some kind of
private military thing that isn't the kind you talk about and now
he does this instead. Turns out he likes danger and money but
he's not great with air travel. He has tattoos on his arms and scars
all over his body, and a year ago I saw Sam walk up to a raging
two-hundred-kilo billionaire who got handsy with the wait staff,
break his nose in two places and tranq him to the ground before
manually dropping his bodyguards as a courtesy so they wouldn't
get fired.

Nineteen seconds start to finish.

I keep asking him to come work with me. He keeps saying no.
He's probably right.

Sam says "Hi, Cal."

"Hi, Sam."

"Nice quiet night."

"Room at the bar, then."

He glances up for the first time, looks right at me. "No, Cal, it's pretty loud in there. The quiet, that's what I'm asking for from you. You got business to transact, transact it tomorrow. You feel me?"

"Something special about tonight?"

Sam shrugs. "I got wind."

"Okay."

"There's a new chef. She's from Laos and I can't stop eating the tam mak kluay but some part of my intestine is a weak motherfucker and I get wind. Like all the damn time. I keep waiting for it to get better but it doesn't."

"That's hard, man."

"It is."

"Your chef—"

"Not my chef."

"She the only new hire?"

"Naw, there's a bunch for the winter. The summer kids mostly take their tips and go to college. Winter teams are a little older, bit wiser. I don't know them all yet. Victor does."

I look at him. "It possible this chef is a little bit easy on the eye, Sam?"

"I guess, but that isn't the point. She's talented." I swear to god I'm waiting for him to put his hands behind his back and turn his foot on his toe.

"Whatever you say."

"What I say is that if I have to fight tonight it's gonna piss me off. Could be I'll fart. A man's got to have his dignity in this job and if I fart then someone's gonna have to lose an eye. So don't put me in that position, is what I'm saying."

"Okay, Sam, I feel you. I promise."

"Fine, then. Go on in. There's room at the bar." And he opens the door.

Back in the day, Victor's was a vaudeville theatre, all red velvet and gold and a high ceiling with satyrs chasing nymphs around a lake of wine. When Victor bought it she kept the style but retrofitted a series of platforms into the seating, so that the whole place starts in the gods and falls down an endless stair to the dance floor. What used to be the director's box is now a dais with a Last Supper table and a bridge made of actual obsidian called the Stairway, blocked by a single velvet rope, which dancers of particular talent and desirability may be offered the right to ascend. Some of those who go up think they're going to meet a soulmate, a lost heart bewildered by new youth. They watch too many movies and think they'll be the one to teach an ancient innocent in a college kid body all about what it is to be young today. Others are just looking for the wildest time there is.

I don't know who's at the Last Supper table tonight. Not unless it's a woman named Susan Green. I slip through the tables to the bar and pick a seat with a view of the doors. Victor catches sight of me and rolls her eyes.

Victor looks like your auntie if your auntie wore a vintage catsuit in burgundy velvet, accessorised with a domino mask. She has silver hair in a boy cut and a lazy smoker's voice you can't help but listen to. Last of the great local originals.

"Vic."

"Cal Sounder. Sam let you in."

"I promised to be well behaved."

"Why, yes, Cal, I'd love to buy your shiny bridge."

"Susan Green."

"Have a mojito instead. She's not on yet. And don't call her that. It's Diamant when she's working."

"She a singer?"

"Yes, Cal, my star singer is a singer, isn't that amazing?"

"She got any particular admirers? Regulars?"

Victor doesn't think much of that question. "In this place? Honey, she has hundreds. You wait."

"Titan. First-doser. Mama's boy hair, bad shirts."

"Ugh. The boyfriend."

Roddy and a cabaret singer. "You're not serious."

"That's what I said to her. But the two of them, honestly, Cal. Like lovesick fauns. I banned him, of course. All the sass went out of her when he was watching. All that sparkling sex just . . . poof. As soon as he wasn't here, it was better. But still she went from 'none of you can keep up with this vagina' to 'look but don't touch' in the space of a week. I could cry." She helps herself to my mojito instead. "Well, you weren't going to drink it anyway. Sit here and brood, darling, and don't start anything. Diamant will grace us with her nun's cabaret in twenty minutes."

"He's dead, Vic."

"Who's dead?"

"The boyfriend."

She stops, eyes hard on mine. "No shit?"

"No shit."

A long silence. "Damn."

"Yeah."

"And you're on it."

"Yeah."

"You maybe change your profession recently? Become a grief counsellor?"

"Still a detective."

"Damn."

"Maybe you'll get your singer back."

"I suppose I might. Do me a favour?"

"I'll do you two."

"Don't tell her until after the set."

"Sure."

"And be as kind as you can."

"I still owe you two favours."

"Piss off, Sounder," Vic says, but if you listen real close it sounds almost like "thank you."

Hi, Ugly," someone says. I feel a weight on my shoulder. "Why don't you come show a girl a good time."

Vic's away along the bar.

"I'm working," I say. "Sorry. There are some groupies at table seven just waiting to be asked."

"That's why I'm not interested. I want you."

I turn around into a big, beautiful face. There are two of them, a woman and a man, gym fresh and hardbody, but not the real thing. They're Titan wannabes like Ostby, all kinds of invested. These two are taking the creep game to the next level. They're trying to live the Titan life already, take on the attitude, except they have no idea what it really looks like because they're wannabes. Maybe they think if you live Titan hard enough, the real ones will notice you, bring you into the circle.

Not how it goes, but whatever gets you out of bed in the morning.

Physically these two are real imposing but it's not like you can't tell the difference. The muscles are big, but not the bones. They're both ripped, and for the evening they are wearing what looks like armour from a fantasy game. The man's hanging back, but he's the driver. I can see it in his eyes, avid and intent. He must be clear over thirty centimetres taller than me, half again as heavy. She's maybe just a third. They're chiselled, aquiline, glossy. They look like extras from a *Ben-Hur* remake.

"Sorry. Not available right now."

The woman's hand doesn't move, just stays, too heavy, where it is. "Not how it works here, Ugly. This is Victor's. Shit goes down."

"You must not've been here too often," I say, "if you think that's how it is. You meet Sam yet?"

"I did not and I don't care. Come and have a drink with us."

"Yeah, that's not how it is either. Ask Vic. She'll give you the talk."

"I'm really not interested in the talk. Now come along and behave, or you'll upset me. You might hurt my feelings. That's unhealthy."

I look up at her, and past to him, urging her on. "That how it has to be?"

The woman just smirks, playing with the clips on her chest plate. Guy says: "Yeah."

I call along the bar. "Sam said he isn't feeling well. He says to keep things quiet."

Vic nods without looking up. "That's right."

"You want to issue a judgement on what the quiet thing to do is here?"

Finally she looks over. Her eyes travel up and down the hero twins and I realise I should have just called to Sam. I see it spark in her eyes: the spirit of commercial enterprise.

Goddammit, Victor.

She makes her way over, taking her time. "Well, now. Who are these beautiful kids?" One long white-fingered hand like a bird-spider, touching the biceps of the hero. That shade of lipstick, just a little bloodier than cherry, as she smiles. "Truly lovely."

The man looks down at Vic and sees a bartender, maybe a retired hooker.

"No problem here, old lady. Walk on. My girl is asking this boy to join us at our table. Seems she's taken a shine to him. I'm down with it. The gentleman was just about to accept."

Vic looks all kinds of delighted, and I'm getting that sinking feeling in my stomach.

"Is that true, sir?" she says to me. "You about to go and show these pretty children a good time? You don't look like their type, but maybe they like their evenings a little rough sometimes. That about it, honey?" She looks at the woman, who grins.

"Oh, yes. I think so."

"No," I say. "Misunderstanding. I was declining politely, but some offence was taken. I'm not polished like some of your other customers."

"No, I'd say it's pretty clear all the original edges are still on you," Vic murmurs, stroking the oiled arm. "Come on, kids. Let me find you someone a little more suitable."

Kids. Suitable. Grandma voice.

Thanks, Vic.

The guy pushes her away. Vic staggers theatrically into the bar, and a little pyramid of champagne glasses crashes to the floor. The smashing echoes and people stop talking and look. Vic uncoils off the copper top like she's made of plastic, smiling wide enough to swallow an entire cat.

No one in the whole place isn't looking now. The heroes know it. The woman stretches slightly, pushing her shoulder blades together. Her boyfriend turns his hands in so that his deltoids ripple, and leans in my face. He's about to speak but Vic gets there first. She pulls a cord mic down from the ceiling and lets out a rebel yell.

"LAAAADIIIES AND GENTLEMENNNNN! AND OTHERS MORE INTRIGUINGLY COMPLEX! WELCOME! GOOD EVENING AND WELCOME! I'M VICTOR DEVINE AND THIS IS MY PLACE, AND AS YOU KNOW IT IS THE OOOOONLY PLACE TO FIND. WHAT. YOU. NEED!

"With all due respect to Mick—and we all love Mick—I done went and created a place where—whatEVER you like, whatEVER you crave—you can, you can, YOU CAN GET . . . SATISFACTION!"

There's something happening on the stage level that I've never seen before. The tables are sliding apart and an object is rising up out of the floor. An enclosed metal frame four metres by four. Or, no. Not a frame. A cage.

Oh, for fuck's sake.

Vic has one hand flung out over her head like a prophet. "Here at Victor's we like to think we can make anything happen for you, make everyone happy . . . but dis-agree-ments. Do. Arise.

"I love it when something tasty ARISES. Don't you?"

A fat wink, white teeth flashing. She only comes alive in front of the crowd. Vic was never a hooker. She was never a hitman either, whatever you may have heard. She never ran guns out of Lisbon and she never divorced a billionaire.

She was a televangelist.

It's not even a secret, yet somehow no one knows but me.

"AND TONIGHT . . . we have something a little special to whet your appetite. Oh YES WE DO." The cage slides into place, and the door opens with a massive crash. "A DUEL! For the honour of—well now. I wonder. WHICH OF YOU WILL STEP INTO THE CAGE?" The spotlight picks out the heroes and they love it. She jumps on him, wraps her legs around his hips and drives her tongue into his mouth, then bucks off again and raises his hand in hers:

"WE DO EVERYTHING . . . TOGETHER!"

Vic throws back her head and lets out another mad laugh. "OF COURSE YOU DO! Ladies and gentlemen—and others more intriguingly complex! IN THE RED CORNER WE HAVE THE BOLD! THE GORGEOUS! THE MUSCULAR, SALTY AND DELI-CIOUS! THE AFFRONTED . . ." she leans down and listens "MAC AND MINI!"

Laughter.

"Well, that's not their fault, they hardly knew they were coming out to fight this evening. They had something ENTIRELY different in mind . . ." she grabs the man by the ass in passing. Huge laughter from the room as Mac jolts upright, grinning in outrage.

"AAAAND THAT'S THE STAKE! IF THEY WIN . . . THEY GET TO TAKE THEIR PLAYTHING HOME . . . IF THEY LOSE . . ." she stretches it out, staring at the couple, who have just realised there's a downside in this for them and don't like it. Too late to back out now. The room loves their loss of confidence. Vic leers, taking her hand off Mac's ass to flick Mini's armoured skirt up.

"COMMUNITY SERVICE!"

A roar of approval. She walks down towards the cage, the mic trailing its long tail behind her.

"AND HERE HE IS . . . THE APPLE OF DISCORD! THE PRIVATE, THE PRUDISH, THE PRIGGISH OBJECT OF THEIR THWARTED AFFECTIONS . . ."

And now the spotlight's on me. The room's laughing again. Vic nods, palm down.

"I know! I know! He don't look like much. But a girl wants what a girl wants. We all have URGES don't we? Now myself . . . these days . . . cookies and a glass of milk. A good book . . . And two or three of my favourite lovers to warm eiderdown! But for now: what's your name, son?"

"Cal."

"CALLIPYGIAN CAL!" A smattering of laughter. "The rest of you can look it up when you get home! CAL OF THE GORGEOUS ASS—THE GOLDEN ASS OF DISCORD! GET DOWN HERE!" More laughter. "Fighting to defend HIS OWN VIRTUE! A rose so sweet it's never been picked—LADIES, WHAT WERE YOU THINK-ING? . . . Oh, look at that half-busted nose, the lantern jaw . . . and yet you put them all together and there's undeniably something, isn't there? I could bounce myself off that face, couldn't you? And you? . . . Many many takers, Cal. You're going to have a great night."

Jesus Christ, Vic.

"IF CAL WINS . . . HE DOESN'T HAVE TO FUCK ANYBODY HE DOESN'T WANT TO! Honestly, honey, you sure you don't want to ask for a better prize?"

"Sure I do," I say, loud enough that the tables nearby can hear me.

"HE DOES! HE DOES!"

I see the frown on Vic's face. This is her game, and if I fuck it up, I'm in big trouble.

"All right, Cal, darling—CALLIPYGIAN CAL—if it's within our collective grip"—sniggers—"what do you want?" I think she's hon-estly curious. Vic always wants to know everyone's vices.

"Twenty minutes alone with Diamant."

Vic shakes her head, just for me: Cal, Cal, Cal. She folds it into her act.

"A HIIIIIGH PRICE! DIIIIAMMMMANT! The SIREN! THE SONG-BIRD! Very well, Cal sets his prize, and what happens in the room is between him and Diamant. Those whom Victor's has joined, let no one put asunder . . . IF HE CAN WIN which to be honest . . .

it's not looking good, Cal, not good at all . . . BETTING ON UNLI-
CENCED PREMISES IS ILLEGAL please ask your server how to
make your wagers! You have two minutes. Fighters! Take your
places by the cage. There are no rules, no limits! There is no place
for compassion or hesitation! WELCOME TO VICTOR'S! HAVE A
NICE NIGHT!"

I take off my coat and my shirt and put them on a chair by the
cage. The heroes have to take off their armour, which leaves them
standing there in black athleisure underwear and us exactly as
equal as one ordinary-size guy facing off against two steroid muscle bodies can be, which is to say not a whole lot. Mac looks me up
and down and sneers. Mini does the same but looks like she just
bought a high-ticket item cheap.

Vic stands on top of the cage, colour commentary. She's recruit-
ing a party of Hollywood C-listers as ring girls. I can see the faces in
the front rows: scandalised and low-grade aroused. I look around.

"Can I get a lipstick from someone? Something in a dark red?"

In the second ring of tables, an older woman raises her eyebrows, then tosses me one from her clutch. I smear about half a
day's pay of it on the fingers of my left hand, pass it back. Then I go
through the door into the cage. Inside, it's big enough that I can be
a safe distance from the sides and out of arm's reach of them even
when they spread out to make us into a triangle, but that's about
it. Not a huge space to work in.

Mac and Mini file in, the door closes, and Vic says: "AND THE
FIGHT BEGINS!"

It does.

I wait for them, and they come. Mac looks angry, Mini looks all
kinds of fucked up. They move together. I think they've done this
before. I put my hands up in a boxing guard and I see Mac get
just a little bit smug. With no gloves and a small space, I can't hit
hard enough with my knuckles to take him down fast, and I can't
hide. If I'd shown him a grappler stance he'd at least have had

some respect, but now he knows this is going to be over pretty quick. I don't think he's even disappointed. This isn't about violence for him, or sex. It's about control. He likes to control situations and people. Violence and sex are how he does that. I'm guessing he does a power job, too. The people who work for him do as they're told or they get fired. His favourite moment is when someone doesn't meet quota, and he bawls them out, and then they don't meet quota again next time and he fires them, and as they walk through the room he can see the others feeling it: feeling his power.

That's his thing.

Pretty sure Mini's thing is sensation. When she's hopped up, screwing, drunk or fighting, she doesn't have to think about whatever rides her. She lives in the moment, zen by overload. And what rides her? Probably the memories of the last hundred things she did while she was hopped up, screwing, drunk or fighting. What are you gonna do? If either one of them was possessed of a rich and healthy interior life, we wouldn't be meeting at Victor's.

Because to be clear: both of them will love this. Smacking me down. Taking me apart. Then taking me to a booth for victory sex. Sending me out again when it's done so I have to walk between the tables. That's where they live. And by the numbers they can't miss. Two reasonable fighters with serious mass in a cage with one skinny guy? Sure, I got runner's muscle, but that's not enough, and it doesn't matter, honestly, how good I am. There's a ceiling on the skill dividend and it's right here, in an experienced fight team working together, throwing combinations that I don't have enough arms to defend against. Best case, I duck and weave and I have to be able to fight twice as hard as they do for the duration. As soon as I slow down—and I will—pow. Their most serious concern is not to wear me out before the main event.

This will be quick and dirty, over before it begins.

Mac stamps and shouts, then makes a grappler lunge under my guard and I have to dance back, but Mini's thrown a kick right into where I'm going. It's a roundhouse, high and hard, not intended to make contact, just to force me to evade. I slip under but it deforms my core line. I have to twist and bow. Mini follows the kick in with a series of jabs and the last one grazes my cheek, for a value of "graze" that feels like walking into a plate glass door. I take the hit as the price of admission, cross block another jab and flat palm her forehead with my left hand, dragging my fingers down into her eyes. Red lipstick trails four lines to her cheeks. She snarls and launches a knee at my chest, sending me back into Mac's arms. I turn and get my hands up outside the noose, but he closes the bear hug and it's huge, like an actual fucking bear. He puts his face into my stomach and hunches his shoulders, ready for the elbows he thinks I'm going to bring down to make him let go.

Mini hisses "fuck!" and claps her hands to her face. Dark red lipstick is made with eosin: fluorescent acids which inflame the skin to give you plump lips that last all night. Get enough of it in your eyes, though, and you can't see for half an hour. Also it hurts like a sonofabitch. Tears are streaming down her face and out of her nose.

Yeah. I cheat. Go figure.

Mac roars and slams my back against the cage. Ribs flex but don't break, spine feels like I got wired up to a battery, then a second later it's on fire. I keep my head forward and see white, then red, then brown, wish I had the simple intelligence to take a clerical job somewhere in the countryside, get a fucking dog. Take a second to remember what I'm into right now. Mac's about to do it again. He's cursing me, fight-porn smack. "You better get ready for what's coming to you, boy!"

I don't even try to hit him. I just put my hand into his mouth between words.

All the way into his mouth.

Mac tries to bite, but I'm not done. I'm still feeding my hand in so my fingers are touching the soft parts of his throat, and he's still holding me so tight—hasn't realised yet he needs to let go—that I've got plenty to push against. By now it's hurting him. He doesn't work out his jaw muscles at the gym, and his arms are still locked around my waist, so what's he gonna do? I feel his shoulders soften and I lock my legs around him so he can't shove me away. Then I clench my fist and feel it fill up all the space from his windpipe to his teeth.

Looking around, I can see the crowd hasn't tumbled to it yet, but they're starting to. There are whispers. They're making faces at one another: what's going on? Is this a fight or what? Why isn't there blood?

I lift up and push down hard. I feel Mac's jaw dislocate on one side. Now it's easy. He shrieks, but it barely makes a sound. He can't breathe, and something's twitching under my knuckles: his body's trying to vomit but I'm in the way. He lets go and starts whirling his arms, batting at me open hand, an old man in the park waving at flies. I keep him between me and Mini. She's still got her guard up, but her face is streaked with wine-dark tears. Her sclera are about the same colour: the old lady's brand must be waterproof.

I hook my first two fingers in the soft tissue of Mac's throat and pull. Having someone tug at your trachea from inside triggers a horror reaction in most people that pretty much never goes away. Ten to one he has PTSD from this. Fuck knows, I would.

Mac goes down onto his knees. His face is turning purple because there's not enough oxygenated blood in his body. He starts to thrash, so I lean him back a bit. I don't want him falling towards me. I look over at Mini.

"Tap out," I tell her. "It's done."

"Fuck you!"

She swings in the direction of my voice. It's not easy manoeuvring with Mac stuck on the end of my arm, but it's not what you'd call hard, either. And I've done it before, so there's that.

Mini comes in again, a creditable blind combo of kicks and punches. She clips her husband and loses her balance, drops and rolls out. I lean down to talk to him.

"I'm moving my hand now, Mac, because I don't want you to die. If you get up, though, I'm going to take that very seriously. Okay?"

He doesn't answer, but I pull my hand out anyway. He falls over and chokes on the mat. I watch him for a second to make sure his breathing starts properly. It's ragged, but good enough.

Mini has her back to the cage wall and she's weaving her hands in front of her, juking and skipping. Like I say, it's creditable. Every fifth step or so she's rubbing her eyes, pushing more lipstick into them while trying to get it gone.

"Tap out," I tell her again. "Mac's down. You're blind. Come on, let's call it."

She runs at me, arms wide.

If she hits the far side of the cage like that she could be seriously hurt. If she catches me she could actually pull this off.

I let her fingertips tag me as she goes by and she spins, grasping, but I've stepped on around with her, I'm behind her.

I put her in a sleeper hold and drop her next to Mac.

And that's that.

Silence.

Vic says: "CAAAAAAAALLLLLL SOUUUNDEEEERRRRR!"

Thunderous applause.

In the soundproofed back office behind the bar, Sam passes me a cold cloth for my bruised face.

"That's your definition of 'quiet,' is it?"

"I did what Vic asked, I didn't seriously injure anyone, and you didn't have to get out of your chair. Don't be a baby."

"They will still be talking about that in a month," Sam growls.

"In a year," Vic says. "Hell, darling, in ten. That was epic! Brutal. Elegant. Chilling. They thought they were getting blood and grunting before the first course, and instead they got something altogether more frightening: competence. You fight like an accountant, Cal. Passionless. Forensic. Absolute. Which of course triggers all the opposites: passion, dreams and disinhibition. My diners are already ordering the expensive stuff, and if table eleven aren't naked and moaning by dessert I'll eat my hat. Fucking stupendous. You should stop by more often."

"Not really my scene."

"Oh, but it is, darling. You hate it, but that doesn't mean it's not yours. It wants to rub itself all over you. And you never quite have the good sense to tell it no and move on, do you? This world has its hooks in you, Cal. Maybe you should just admit it and have some fun. I'll put you down for a gold membership. No charge."

"I'll take my twenty minutes with Susan Green."

"Diamant, please. And yes, just as soon as she's finished. You warmed up the crowd perfectly. Oh, that reminds me: the Dentons—that's Mac and Mini, to you—sent their business cards and would really love to see you again. They promise, no sex."

"Sure. I'm known for my poetry recitals."

"They want to socialise, Cal. They're tremendously impressed. Maybe just a little bit in love."

I can't even. "Vic, could I possibly have an East European imported beer, and five minutes to hate myself in peace?"

Sam slides one of two bottles across the table. He doesn't pass the second to Vic. She huffs.

"Boys and their beer. Incorrigible. All right, you have your peace and quiet. Susan—oh, bloody damn, Diamant, now you've got me doing it—is onstage."

She leaves the door open as she walks out, and the sound of a woman singing comes through from the main room, high and full-throated, clear like Lake Othrys and almost as beautiful.

Sam smiles, and raises his bottle. "I can't believe you foie gras'd that motherfucker," he says. "You've got some balls, Cal."

"What would you have done?"

Sam shrugs. "Eardrums and joints."

"But then they wouldn't be able to hear the concert."

He takes another pull. "That's your problem, Cal. You're soft at the beginning, so you end up going hard later."

A while after that, Diamant finishes her set, and Vic takes me through to the dressing rooms to give her the bad news.

Susan Green has on the ballistic shawl Roddy bought her over the top of a peach Louis XIV dress with a waist small enough to make you worry. There's some crazy whaleboning around the back so she can breathe deep enough to sing. Under the beehive wig her hair's so pale it's almost silver, and her dark eyes make her seem ghostly in the warm light of the dressing room fireplace.

She wears ear studs, black pearls, but she's hardly the only woman in the city with pierced ears. The shawl is silver brocade, just different enough to match.

"Wait a minute," she says, reaching behind with both hands. I look away, and hear a *whomp* and a thump as the dress hits the ground.

"You can look," she says, amused. "I'm decent."

That might be an overstatement, though it's technically true. Some kind of strapless sports top and shorts. She laughs at me and wraps the shawl around her middle like a beach dress.

"Better?"

Actually now instead of looking like an attractive woman in sweaty workout gear she looks like an attractive woman wrapped in a silk thing that's not really big enough for the job, but never mind.

"Cal Sounder," I say.

She laughs. "Mr. Sounder, there's no one in Victor's tonight who doesn't know that."

"I guess not."

"What can I do for you?"

"You can tell me about the bulletproof scarf."

She touches it gently. "A gift."

"Someone worried about your safety."

"I'm a singer. I get the wrong kinds of fans sometimes. I get letters, flowers, even visits. People see me onstage and they're moved, but they don't have the sophistication to understand the difference between an emotional response and a relationship. A little extra protection never hurts. Besides, I think it's beautiful. Don't you?"

She shifts her shoulders, making the shawl shimmer.

"And the . . . concerned party? They understand that difference?"

"Yes. He does."

"A boyfriend."

"I hope that isn't disappointing to you, Mr. Sounder. This is going to be a conversation, between us. Nothing more."

"No, that's what I came for: to talk."

"So talk. I'm secretly hoping you work for a record label."

"I'm a police consultant. What can you tell me about the man who gave you the scarf?"

"Roddy? Is he in trouble?"

"No." Which is not exactly a lie. "I promise I'll explain, but I'd like to talk first so your answers aren't coloured by the situation now."

"Consultant, you said. Not detective."

"No. Officially retained, but not actually police."

"I don't know whether I want to help you. How do I know you're on my side?"

"Ask Victor."

"Because everyone trusts Victor."

"Everyone who knows her." Which is true. Victor is a whole bucket of crazy in that velvet catsuit, but in the end, she has rules and she follows them all the way down into the mud.

"And what would Victor say about you?"

"That I can help you. That I'll do my best for Roddy. That I play straight as I can. She made me promise to be nice to you."

"Doesn't that mean she thought you might not?"

"Means she thought my promise was worth something."

"And Sam?"

"Sam would say I'm an asshole. But he wouldn't argue the rest, and he did pour me a beer."

She laughs. "That's about as good as it gets with Sam."

"It is. He serious about that new chef?"

She grins. "Are you a gossip, Mr. Sounder?"

"Tell me with your hand on your heart that Sam being romantically entangled doesn't blow your mind."

She puts her hand on her heart and opens her mouth, then shakes her head. "I actually can't."

"What's her name?"

"Iolani. So . . . is he serious?"

"Deadly, I think. Is she?"

"Am I talking to Sam's drinking buddy now?"

"We drink in the same place sometimes. I don't know about buddy."

"Well, okay. She likes him. She doesn't really know what to do with him, and I think she never really saw this world as her target zone. She wanted the kudos from Victor's so she could start her own place. Upscale. She gets involved with Sam, she can still do that, of course, but she'll never get her feet out of the door of his world. She knows that already: he's never changing."

"People can surprise you."

"Do you think so?"

"Sure. Don't you?"

"I'm a believer, Mr. Sounder. I believe love conquers all, in the end."

Yeah, that's not gonna make this any easier. "The shawl, Ms. Green. Roddy Tebbit."

"Roddy . . . is a Titan, of course. But not like the others who come here. I saw him the first night and he was . . . quiet. Alone in his corner. Long out of his first dose, not all hopped up and horny. Just a guy sitting by himself at a table for two. I sang a whole song just for him. I couldn't get anything back at all, not a blink. He just stared into space. But at the end, he clapped, the way people clap when they're crying inside. That's a thing, by the way."

"I guess it is."

She cocks her head. "I thought you'd ask me how I know."

"You're a pro. Of course you know."

"You really aren't a cop."

"I'm really not. So he clapped."

"He clapped. And I—I honestly do not know why, it's not how this works—I sent a drink to his table. I didn't know what to send. I mean . . . if I send champagne that's either intimate or commercial. Classically, men are supposed to like whisky, but not in the middle of a meal."

"So what did you send him?"

"White wine, with a note to say that it was my favourite."

"And he came by to say thank you?"

"He played the piano to me. Right there in the club."

"Vic let this happen."

"Of course. It had dramatic potential."

"So he . . . serenaded you?"

"No vocals, he just played. Not brilliantly. It didn't matter. Damp squib from Vic's point of view, nothing more than a snack between courses for the crowd. Comic relief, even—he was so tall and weird. But after it was done it turned out one of the other guests was an opera singer, and he was far more accommodating. Sang for kisses and belly shots. One serious kiss, one shot, one song. Then someone wanted to duet, and, well, you can imagine where it went from there." She shrugs: another night at Victor's. "But Roddy and I were in here, just talking. Well. Not just talking, after a while. I pretty much told him I was going to jump his bones and to shut up and let it happen. He sat in that chair. Sex was . . . logistically challenging. But lovely. Am I telling you too much?"

You're writing his eulogy. "Please go on."

"We saw each other again, and then again, and it went from there."

"But recently he's been worried about you."

"He was worried about himself first, then me because he thought someone was watching me. I thought so too, but I figured it was just a pervert. Or a photographer. The singer dating a Titan. Always good for copy, especially if the Titan is unusual.

Roddy doesn't want to be in the paper, for sure, but he also doesn't believe that's what's happening, so he bought me the shawl. It's electro-something or other, bunches up on impact, so even though it's very thin you get plenty of cushioning. Punched across the room, he said, rather than shot. But it's lovely. God, he hasn't hurt someone, has he? By mistake?"

"Do you know who he thinks might be following you both?"

"Someone from his work."

"At the university?"

"His research work. He has contracts through them into the private sector."

"You know what he's working on?"

"Something ambient oxygen something perfusion something? I think? He keeps promising to explain it to me, but . . . we get distracted. It's all still so new. We talk about music and what we'll do together. We eat. There's a bunch of things he's never tried, food-wise."

"He propose to you?"

"Not yet. He was married before. A really long time ago, it's so weird. My mother was a kid. You know?"

"I'm sorry, I don't."

"No, I guess most people don't." She looks away.

"Ms. Green, I'm sorry, I have to ask: you're only seeing Mr. Tebbit, right now? Not anyone else? And he didn't, uh, displace anyone?"

"Yes, and no, he didn't. Clean catch."

"Okay."

She doesn't add to that, and nor do I, so we sit together without talking. The sound of the rowdy tables ebbs and flows. Then she looks right at me.

"I worked reception in a hospital once. There was a nurse there who was a complete bitch to everyone. Everyone except the critical patients and their families, and the way you knew someone was getting better was she didn't have time for them any more. The smart ones got that, and when she was rude, they started to cry, because they knew everything was going to be okay. I think you're the same way, and I think you've wasted enough time being kind."

"I don't know what to say to that."

"You can tell me the truth, Mr. Sounder. He's dead, isn't he?"

"What makes you think that?"

"You do. I saw what you did in the cage. It was hideous. But here you are being nice to me. Am I right?"

"Yes."

The affirmation hits her. Her face is so pale anyway that when the blood drains out of it she's almost translucent. I keep my hands in my lap. I don't reach out. It's better that way.

She cries silently for a long minute, maybe a lifetime, and then the tears stop. It's not that there aren't more, she's just not sharing them with me. There's a hollow moment, after you tell someone, when the first grief is exhausted and the long mourning hasn't begun, when they're almost not in pain. They can do the needful things, like pass on the bad news, find a babysitter, or talk to a murder detective.

"You have more questions."

"Just a couple."

"Then I need a cigarette and some air. Come with me."

She picks up her coat and I follow her down the service corridor. There's a metal door into an alley. On the outside there's a mechanical keypad under a smeared steel cap. Vic changes the combination every week. She steps out, a slim figure among the dumpsters and discarded crates, almost magical in that long grey loden with a deep hood. The cigarette is black, scented. She offers me one from the packet.

"Ms. Green, did he say anything at all that I can use? A name, a place? Anything?"

She's looking past me over towards the water, and I turn and follow her gaze. Birds sitting along a ledge. A newspaper floating in the vortex at the corner of the street. The sound of electric engines whirring as they carry people out along the shore to the suburbs.

"Some place he went to had a wood fireplace. Real wood. He

was impressed, because the carbon capture made it expensive. That made me laugh: a Titan, impressed by money. I mean, he was rich, but not rich rich. Nice apartment, nice life, but not crazy. He said that was my job. Become a star and buy him nice clothes."

It happens so fast I don't understand. I hear Susan Green say something that sounds like "Harpo." The way she says it makes me think it's important. I start to say "Like Harpo Marx?" because they still screen those movies on an endless loop at three a.m., like a secret church for insomniacs and gumshoes. Then I feel her body slam against my back, and then pressure and flight. I'm in the air, spinning, and so is she. The car is passing under us. We bounce off the roof and I see her face go blank as she clips her head. Not dead, maybe, but out for the count. We hit the ground together, and I roll her away with me because the car is reversing, coming back for us: black wheels, dark paint, low slung with some kind of hook for a mobile home or a trailer. Maybe the bad guy likes to go antiquing.

The car misses, stops, and a man gets out. Mask and heavy shoes, working man's boots working me over. It hurts, which is bad, but there are two things that are worse. The first is I'm probably going to die here. The second . . . the second is the scuff down the inside heel on the left boot: a thick line like a child's drawing of a moon. I watch it go up, and come down, and every time it hits me I try to see something else, but all I see is that line.

Then the man takes a few steps, pulls a gun, and puts a few into Susan like it doesn't matter, but since he's come all this way he may as well. He turns back to stand over me and I can hear his breathing, slow and even. Little sigh as he checks the gun to make sure nothing goes wrong. I say something like "please" because it's what I have. I don't expect it to work and it doesn't. The guy shuffles his feet around so he doesn't have to worry about the ricochet.

I shut my eyes because as it turns out I don't see why I shouldn't.

The bullet hits me off target and it really fucking hurts. You hear a lot about how when you're shot you have this moment where you don't really understand, you think you're okay. I can only tell you that sometimes when you're shot you have a very clear understanding and that understanding is that it hurts like hell. I open my eyes to tell him not to dick around. Again: you try it and see if you can do better. I can feel the path of the bullet in my side. Guy's not even paying attention to me: he's looking off at something outside my angle of view and that's why I'm still alive. I hear him say, quite clearly: "What?" Like someone is telling him his zipper is open.

He flies away to one side and out of my life. I hear another gun firing, maybe more than one, but by this time I'm feeling cold and tired and I can see Susan Green. I wish to hell I couldn't. She's so pale and white she looks like she's made of snow, and her body is in all sorts of the wrong places. Her tears look like snow too.

Then I realise it is actually snowing. First of the year, burying me in soft white flakes where I lie.

Someone leans over me and says, "He has been shot."

"No shit," I say, but it comes out real quiet like.

"Indeed, Mr. Zoegar," another voice says, cocktail formal, "we are unforgivably late."

I hear a sound like someone dragging a corpse. The cocktail voice is picky and fastidious, but deep. I try to turn and look, but it hurts like hell—bullet, beating, run over. The cocktail man's shadow is crazily distorted by the lights of the cars, so that on the wall next to Zoegar he looks like a child's toy from a Saturday morning cartoon: an egg with long, thin arms and a fat head. One of those jelly monsters with their hands in the air that you stick on the end of a pencil.

It can't really be who I think it is, but I think it is.

Until just now I'd have given you even odds he didn't exist—just another fish story in a city on the shore of a deep, deep lake. I figured there must be something to it, because I've busted a couple of his guys, and I've had a couple of cases fade away that I was sure were good, but suddenly a witness changed their mind or a cop got sloppy in the evidence chain. It's like you go in a room and you think someone's just left. You can smell that familiar smell, that steak, that cigar, that particular half-drunk drink, but maybe it's just three guys with three bad habits and you're imagining one fat one. Or maybe not, as it turns out. No cause for alarm, no bad blood between us. I hope, anyway, and since he just saved my life I guess not.

"Hi," I say. "We haven't met. I'm Cal Sounder." It comes out kinda funky. I try to reach up to shake his hand but my arm still won't move.

"Hello, Mr. Sounder," says cocktail man. His voice is heavy but fussy, like he wants you to know he never orders from the menu.

Cocktail's friend, Mr. Zoegar, looks at his watch and tuts. "We should leave, sir. The ambulance will be here shortly." He looks down at me. "St. Helen's, Mr. Sounder. You will find it the most interesting of the available medical facilities. Do you hear me? St. Helen's. Say it."

"St. Helen's."

"Keep saying it. Whenever anyone speaks to you, what do you say?"

"St. Helen's."

"Very good."

"St. Helen's."

I keep saying "St. Helen's" and that's where they take me, even though it's all the way on the other shore.

When you spend time in the shadows you know shadow people. You meet Doug Krechmer and his harvesting team who won't say "donor" in case it makes someone sad. You meet Victor, who used to grift for God, and Sam the tough guy who's in love with a doubtful chef. You meet the late-shift watchmen and the janitors and the all-night delivery riders on Day-Glo bikes, with their dreams of the Tour de France. You meet tricker kids who can run and jump through the urban sprawl so smoothly it's like watching water on stone, for whom the whole city is a playground and the people who don't run look like statues of grief. You meet drone chauffeurs who always have something for you to buy in back, or know someone, or have a tip, and you meet the dealers and mules and thieves who keep the whole shadow economy running. You meet waifs and strays, and people like Mac and Mini who think they're tough but who don't really understand the difference between dangerous and durable until you make them eat it.

And if you press on through the shadows, and you don't get tangled up in them and devoured, you come to the far edge where I make my living, in sight of another world, where the Titans are. Their world is bright and shiny and full of the best of everything, as if all that's good naturally rolls down a slope to the warm towers of Chersenesos. It's a fairy-tale world where no one thinks about money and there's only a couple of thousand real people on earth. The rest of us are flickering fairy lights: cheap, disposable and fragile. The doorway belongs to the Tonfamecasca Company, and the daylight and the shadow worlds line up on their lawn, hoping to be let in.

They do, very occasionally, let people in. You can buy entry, but the cost is ridiculously high because Stefan Tonfamecasca isn't sure yet just how many Titans the world can sustain, and he has no intention of making too many, ruining that post-scarcity for the few. You can trade your way in if you have something impossibly valuable: legislative power, or science on the same order of magnitude. You can be given a dose if someone inside loves you and is willing to go to bat with the Titan king on your behalf. There's even a piece of emergency legislation for senior government and witnesses in high-profile trials: if you get assassinated, and T7 can save you, they might dose you up. Might, if there's time, and they really care, but don't count on it.

Or sometimes, just sometimes, Stefan will walk out in the street and pick someone who catches his eye. Three times ever, that I know of. One chance in eight billion during the course of a human lifespan.

And because people are superstitious in the face of what they fear—and there's plenty to fear for all of us, even Titans, because once you've seen the heavenly city you have always to fear being kicked out of it—there are myths and ghost stories here in the city.

The same ones from Chersenesos to Tappeny Bridge; the same ones in penthouses and poorhouses; the same ghosts seen over different shoulders in different mirrors.

There's the mad Titan called Mr. Streetlight, grown impossibly tall and thin and trailing silken threads like a spider as he walks through the suburbs, lifting people up and away by the neck and dropping them strangled by the side of the road. There's the Drowners, also called the Fates, the three weird sisters of Lake Othrys, so big and old they can only stay alive underwater, who snack on passing swimmers and pleasure boats that wake them in the reeds. Over on the other shore, there's the Devil Dogs, escaped test subjects from the T1 lab at marker 9, hounds like bears supposedly living in the desert a hundred miles to the north. There are human monsters, too: half awful and half admired, like Flens, whose husband was supposedly killed by a Titan, and who picks them off one by one in their pleasure palaces and leaves them jointed for Stefan Tonfamecasca to find. Last month I heard someone say that Titans can only get high on baseline human adrenaline. A month before that, it was that they can only have sex if they inject freshly harvested hormones. And then there's Doublewide, the Titan victim of some experimental offshoot that didn't work, who grew sideways but not up and escaped euthanasia to live in the sewers until he became the king of beggars, and then the king of thieves. The Humpty Dumpty of crime, more recently known to me as Mr. Cocktail.

All the new ghosts of the city, the things I laugh about. At least one is true.

My dreams, in the hospital, are full of them.

"Welcome to St. Helen's," the nurse says, his hands cold on my forehead as I come back. "Again."

"Again?"

"We had this conversation earlier. You remember?"

"No."

"Then welcome to St. Helen's. That's a nice clean gunshot wound you have there. I'm impressed."

"Thank you."

"Somehow I don't think you can take credit."

"I piss off very clean gunmen."

He chuckles. "Okay, tough guy, you're with us. Well done. Now shut up, get some sleep, and when you wake up I'll bring you some food."

"Hospital food."

"Yeah, sorry about that. You want Le Chat Noir, you need to duck faster."

"All the nurses in the city, I get the funny one."

He smiles, and there's not the slightest hint of compromise in it. Just kindness.

"Go to sleep, Mr. Sounder. When you wake up, you'll feel like hell. That's how you know you're getting better."

On that basis it sounds like a terrible idea, but the sneaky bastard has put something woo in my saline, so off I go.

3

You're a fucking optimist."

"Chew your food."

"It's pudding."

"Chew it anyway. How's your back?"

"Feels fine."

"Because it looks like someone threw you into the side of a metal cage."

"I'm a professional wrestler. Steel chairs, backflips. But it's really kind of wholesome, we pray together too."

"I'm going to ask the doctor to anaesthetise your mouth."

"Is there still a hole in my side? Then I'm allowed to be an asshole."

"About that hole—"

"Wild Bill fired a prop gun and it turned out to be loaded. Mr. Fantastic duplexed him and next week I'm gonna get the girl."

"Suplexed."

"Excuse me?"

"You said duplex. It's suplex."

"See? You sneer, but you still drunk-watch the show."

"Someone called Detective Felton rang and asked after you. Wants to know how you're getting on."

"Did you tell him I died?"

"I did."

"Did he buy it?"

"He said he'd send flowers. Although he also said to tell you you're an asshole."

"He didn't buy it."

"That's what I thought too, and I was super-convincing. Chew your food."

"I literally do not know how. When can I leave?"

"You see this?" Middle finger.

"I do."

"While you were sleeping I filled your bullet hole with flesh putty and lattice. When it's set so that I can't put this"—middle finger—"right up it, you can go."

"How long will that take?"

He pokes the hole. It feels like I have a burning golf ball in my stomach. I hiss at him.

"Looks like you're about done. Maybe an hour. Then we're gonna keep you in overnight so we can be sure you don't haem-orrhage or go into putty shock."

"What the fuck is putty shock?"

"New therapies, new problems. What does it sound like?"

"Just cauterise it and let me go home."

"No, because cauterisation smells like pork and I'm eating at the Lakeside Grill this evening. When we send you home tomor-row, don't go swimming or do heavy manual labour of any kind for a week. The putty will knit you back together by then. Oh, and if it gets dirty, wash it."

"It's not anti-microbial?"

"It is, but if it gets dirty you end up with a dirt-coloured pucker-mark on your baby-soft skin. In this case it'll look like you have a new asshole right there. Is that what you're into?"

"Not really."

"So. Wash. It. My god, everything's adversarial with you."

"Did she make it?"

He doesn't answer.

"The woman who was with me. Did she make it?"

"Your girlfriend?"

"My witness."

"Patient Jane was pretty dinged up by the car. Two broken legs, cracked pelvis, concussion. Then they shot her."

"Where?"

"In the designer bulletproof item—so her brain is still inside her head—but from real close up. Those things are good, but they're not magical. Figure she got hit three times with a sledgehammer. She is all kinds of fucked up inside, my friend. No idea if or when she will wake up."

I stop eating. ". . . shit."

"Marcus," he says.

"What?"

"You never asked me my name, asshole. It's Marcus."

"Hi, Marcus. I'm Cal."

"I know. You talk in your sleep. So listen to me, Cal: if she does live, it's because of you. If she doesn't, it's because of them. I know that look you have. I've seen it on soldier boys and cops and firemen and every other kind of desperate life-saving son-of-a-bitch. I will be honest and tell you I see it in the mirror on those days when God in Her wisdom decides to fuck my scorecard good and hard and I lose every patient on my round. That happens. It is statistically inevitable. We get up, and we do it again, and we save someone else. We can't do that if we're still carrying the ones we couldn't get to. Okay? Guilt is a luxury no one can afford in this life, least of all people like you. Don't buy it."

I look at Marcus the nurse and I see someone who's got an old head in a young body for reasons that have nothing to do with T7, and I nod at him once because after a certain point you can't dick around any more.

"Sleep tight, Cal. I'll see you in the morning."

And he leaves me to sleep.

Which I don't, because this is St. Helen's, and I'm supposed to find it interesting.

open my door and there's a uniform. Her shirt says "Kristoffsen, J."

"Hi there, Kristoffsen J., I'm Cal."

"I know, sir."

"You looking after me today?"

"Sergeant Tidbo says you're not to get any more shot, sir."

"Figure Susan Green has friends here too?"

"Yes, sir."

Thank you, Tidbo, for doing the obvious right thing. Cop life has its rhythms, and Tidbo hasn't missed the beat. Speaking of which:

"You happen to come here by squad car, Kristoffsen J.?"

"Of course, sir."

"You ride shotgun in the squad car?"

"Yes, sir."

"And that squad car have the battery pack for your non-lethal there under the shotgun seat?"

She laughs. It's a cop bugbear, that battery pack. Go over a pothole and you feel it in your ass bone. Get out of the car too quick—and cops have to do that—and the edge will trip you up.

"Yes, sir." She turns the inside of her left boot towards me, and there it is: a short line, curved, like a child's drawing of the moon. The scratch from a half dozen moments in her every day when that damn battery tries to throw her on her face.

"Every uniform gets it," Officer Kristoffsen says. "Pain in the ass."

Yeah. Every uniform, and some of the detectives, and anyone who rides shotgun in a police car. Someone on that list ran me down outside Victor's, and put Susan Green in a coma.

"I'm gonna go for a little walk around, Kristoffsen J. I'm not supposed to, but I'm going crazy in there. Don't rat me out to the night staff. I swear to you I will be back safe and sound before the change of shift. You okay with that?"

She probably isn't but she's too smart to let me know it. She smiles again, freckles and dimples: a perky recruitment poster, but if Tidbo detailed her for this then I'm guessing she can put three in the ten ring faster than I can say her name.

I wander away down the corridor. I'm pretty sure Kristoffsen J. isn't going to shoot me in the back right here. I'm pretty sure she wasn't the guy who shot me in the first place—at best, he's thanking his vest he's still alive—but there could have been two of them. I wasn't at my most observant.

The back of my head tingles, waiting for the instant of a bullet arriving. I walk, and wonder if it'll happen. I don't whistle because my mouth's too dry, and because I'm a professional and we don't whistle when we're lying.

Hospitals never sleep. They don't even drowse. But the lights do go down in the corridors when the recovery patients are resting and there's no consultants or registrars walking their patch. Nurses grab moments of stillness as they can, and in the intersection of those moments, a place like St. Helen's, high ticket, almost gets calm.

I switch my patient's robe for porter scrubs lifted from behind the night desk. The duty nurse is getting some Zs in her chair. You would too if you were awake thirty-one hours. Then I walk back and forth along the corridors, listening to the murmurs of the graveyard shift. I listen to Mr. Polson's respirator and Martha Jane's tachycardia. I hear Marcus's relief nurse complain about how he leaves old contact lenses on the washstand. I sit and nod in the ward room, giving up my bunk to Carlo the midwife when he needs to crash, and always always always listening for something I won't know until I hear it. I walk all the way along to the persistent state ward and check in on Susan Green.

"Hi, Cal," Tanya Garcia says, and she's not asleep at all.

"Hi, Tanya. Tidbo put you on this?"

"Put myself on it. He didn't object."

Sergeant Tanya Garcia, steel hair and long bones, hollow cheeks, has done most of everything in her time. Not least close protection. Not least hostile entry. Been a detective, too, but she went back to uniform last year as part of a retirement track, passing on what they call non-quantifiable skills to the rookies. That means how to tell when your partner's on the take, or screwing a witness or using—the stuff they can't be seen to teach, but every young cop needs to know. Garcia's boots don't have that moon shape on them, because she always drives.

"You mind I look in?"

Garcia doesn't mind. I look in. Susan Green looks very small with all those tubes, like the dog that believed in you.

I say thank you to Garcia and walk away, looking in doorways and on wall maps for whatever it is I'm supposed to see.

And then I see it, the thing that Mr. Cocktail wants me to see, at the very far end of the walkway, past the theatres and the crash rooms, past the critical care unit and the lung machines. At the very end of the line.

A chair with a pump tank in a room with a view, and all the machines they use to monitor, measure, tweak and tidge. It isn't even locked, and there's a scrap of red ribbon on the floor, the ends tied to the chair and the tank. It's what they call an Atlas Suite, but to anyone who doesn't work for Stefan Tonfamecasca's PR department, this is an emergency T7 unit, and it's brand-new.

You're new," the duty nurse says, as I bring her coffee from the machine in the hall. It's a bad machine and it makes bad coffee. She's grey-headed and round-eyed. Pretty sure she's the one who knows everything, the one the admin staff lean on. The one they ought to pay better, and don't have to.

"New this week," I confirm. "Still finding my feet."

"I can tell," she says, raising the coffee. "Everyone else brings a flask."

"You don't."

"I like to be in the place I'm in and not pretend. And this way I get to meet people. Like you."

We drink. The stuff in the cups is mid-warm and recognisably brown, so there's that.

"Big shindig just before I started," I said. "Sorry to miss it."

"Shindig?"

I wave back towards the Atlas Suite.

"Oh, that! Hardly. I'm sure it looks like a shindig in the papers, but it was so short." She looks properly scandalised. "That man was here, the giant."

"Stefan Tonfamecasca, in person?"

"I hear he opens all the new suites himself. I'd never seen one before, a Titan."

And Stefan was her first. No wonder she looks a little stunned. I make a wide-eyed face. *O Gosh!*

"How big is he?"

"Just . . . huge." Hands reaching out to sketch bigness in the air. "He had to use the special elevator, for MRI machines and so on. The ordinary one just wouldn't have been safe. He was bent over in almost all the corridors except the main one, and the ceiling there is five metres high. When he talks, he whispers, but you still hear it because he's just enormous. Is there something wrong with his larynx, I wonder?"

"That must have been amazing. I wish I'd been here."

"Well, it was amazing, I'll say. Definitely one for the diary. If I'd had the chance to have my picture taken . . . But honestly it was just a little bit weird, too. Like he was the Queen of somewhere or something. Everything had to be just right. All his people running around before he got here, prop open that door, make sure there's nothing in the way, like the man's too important to have to move a chair out of a corridor, and this is a working hospital. And after all that, he just left! He was supposed to stay for the whole evening and mingle with the staff. Although I bet he wouldn't have, just talked to the director and the board. He didn't seem like someone who mingles."

No. He doesn't.

"Still, kinda rude to just pack up and go."

"Well, I thought so. But I suppose he has things to do, and it was just a ribbon cutting. Maybe the stock market crashed in Tokyo or something."

"Oh, that kind of left? Like in a hurry?"

She grins.

"Like a man seeing his ex-wife show up with her lawyer. First proper human thing I saw him do. He got a call and: poof. He was out the door and down the line. Didn't even hang around for the thank-you speech."

"Ouch. Girlfriend, you think?"

"I couldn't possibly say," she says, then ruins it with "but the things one hears about that man it could hardly be anything else. Now shoo! I have to figure out this rotation. Go carry someone!"

"Can I bring you another coffee later?"

"If you want to find the way to my heart, bring me one from the place over the street."

"Yes, ma'am."

Stefan Tonfamecasca was here the night Roddy Tebbit was killed.

And he left early.

Sometime after I get back to bed, Marcus the nurse brings a Jell-O shot full of nutrition that tastes of steamed broccoli, and he's pleased to poke me in the bullet hole again and remind me to wash it. He gives me a squirt bottle like the ones boxers have to drink from between rounds and says I can just sluice some soapy water over myself. A passing registrar makes an inappropriate wolf-whistle and later a tired nurse-administrator ticks boxes and signs me out. I'm done.

I walk down the street through the snow. The city is still white, with inclusions of anthracite and brown mountain dust. I can feel the putty in my side, less like a golf ball and more like a hard steel grape. It's itchy but I'm not allowed to touch it—"I don't want you to fucking fiddle with it, Cal, I want you to pretend that it's a little tiny feathery bird nesting there, and if you touch it the other birds will stop loving it because it smells of your fingers, and they will peck it to death and that will be on you"—so I don't touch it. But I really want to.

I stop by my place to change clothes because the ones I was wearing when I was admitted are a mess. The hospital laundry got the blood out but they're still busted at the seams and there's a hole in the jacket and the shirt where the bullet went in. I look like the ghost of Jack Ruby.

I shower and I'm having fantasies about raking my fingers over the skin. I do what Marcus said and splash water over the wound from the bottle and that makes it about a billion times worse. God knows how I'm going to survive doing that every six hours and not touch it. Maybe it's better I don't try and just end up with a skin discolouration that looks like a sphincter.

I breathe in the steam, tasting metal pipes and the deep mineral background of Othrys, ice and iron and shale.

Why did someone want to kill Susan Green?

Was Roddy Tebbit right that she was in danger all along? If he was right, did he die because of her? Or did she get run down because of him?

Or was she run down because she was standing next to me?

In which case, what the hell do I know, or what am I about to find out, that's so very important?

Him.

Or her.

Or me.

pick up the phone to Gratton.

"It's Cal."

"You sound great."

"I was shot."

"Seriously? I had no idea. You should call the cops."

"Thank you for looking after me."

"You're on the clock for us, Cal. You get messed up, you get the guard."

"Yeah, but still."

"You're welcome. Now please go unfuck this situation for me before it gets any worse."

"We should meet."

"You got stuff we need to talk about?"

"Yes. Was there anything on the security camera at Roddy's building?"

"There was not."

"I was hoping the murderer would just walk right in. I like it when they do that."

"When do they ever do that?"

"I like it in prospect."

"Sure, don't we all."

I think about Susan Green and the church of insomniacs.

"If I say 'Harpo' to you, what do you think of?"

"Like Groucho and Zeppo?"

"Like that."

"Are you serious?"

"What do you think of?"

"Ice cream."

"Ice cream?"

"When I was a kid, I used to watch their movies when I was home sick."

"You got ice cream when you were home sick?"

"I had fucking recurrent tonsillitis, as if it matters, so yes, I did. Why?"

"Susan Green said 'Harpo' just before we got hit by the car."

"You sure?"

"No, I got hit by a car. And then shot. Did I mention I got shot?"

"No, that's news to me. I hear when you get shot they give you ice cream."

"I got broccoli Jell-O."

"Maybe Susan Green was just saying the whole world's absurd."

"Shit, maybe she was. Say, it's no big deal but here's a thing: the guy who shot me had a little moon shape cut in his left shoe."

Gratton doesn't respond.

"I said—"

"I heard you."

"So what I was thinking was—"

"I know what you were thinking. Leave it with me."

"Just like that?"

"Leave it. With me. Don't go home." And now I can hear the anger, deep like the lake. "You got somewhere to go?"

I could go to Athena. "No."

"Get somewhere."

"Okay."

"Somewhere quiet."

He's right. The smart move is definitely to make myself scarce.

Oh dang! Sorry," I say, "I got cans of beans up to the hairline," and this is true. I have the biggest brown paper bag of groceries, and I'm carrying it like a momma bear in a hug in front of my chest. There are beans in there, but on the top there's a two-pack of baby feeder bottles and some wipes that I'm trying to push down with the tip of my nose and that dog clearly won't hunt.

The woman I just jostled is small enough that I have to put my chin on the whole bag and lean forward to say sorry. She's pretty and she's wearing an actual gingham country girl shirt. She doesn't know I know her name, but it's Liz Felton. I'm climbing the steps to her building with my shopping just as she's going in. Total coincidence, me with my new-father supplies and just in need of a little helping hand, and gosh I'm so darn clumsy I could die.

Careful not to lay it on thick, but thick enough.

Liz Felton is all kinds of good people so she helps me inside. She's what they call petite, which isn't fair because petite sounds like fancy and schmancy and she's all business, and working muscle under that coat. She's a trainer at the gym halfway down the boulevard: cycle cardio and something else. Good work, plenty of shifts when you want them and time off when you don't. Perfect for a cop's wife.

Turns out my name is Dave. I'm from Neuberlin. Yeah, it's our first child, just moved in upstairs, and oh dang once again! It seems like my wife's taken the baby out and I don't have a key, so of course a good woman like Liz is going to ask me in for tea. It's just neighbourly.

The Felton home is proud but not fancy. I'm pretty sure one of the chairs is handmade out of an old door. There are pictures of the Feltons with other cop couples, hanging out in their backyards.

Cop life is complicated. Three quarters of the problems they get asked to solve they can't, and shouldn't have to, and don't know how. The rest are just fucking terrifying. That makes them hang together, and that causes trouble because they can't belong to one another more than they belong to ordinary people—but they inevitably do. Add in all the ordinary human vices and cops can be a mile away and to the side of the population they're supposed to protect. Bad things will happen. I work near cops, around cops, between cops, but I'm not one of them and that makes a difference.

The difference is much easier to deal with when you don't get to know them personally.

I put my bag down on the counter and sit while she boils water and we chat. I make sure to make no sense, and go on and on about my little girl, nine weeks. I even have pictures. Liz Felton is glad to talk because her husband's running late. She doesn't have kids yet. They're waiting for him to make Sergeant. Yeah, she worries when he's late, but he's a smart guy and he knows he has responsibilities. He'll come home.

I make like I'm embarrassed: I don't want to take up your time, you're so kind, I should go and see if she's back yet, but could I just use your bathroom, and of course I could.

So I get into the private space and look around. Detective Nat Felton—Liz calls him Nathaniel every single time—likes a wet shave, a spearmint toothpaste and dark-coloured towels, and when I get out of the bathroom and I'm thinking I might just have a quick look along the hall, his wife is holding a gun on me, dead steady and not amused at all.

"Don't feel bad," she says, "you did it really well."

She waggles the gun and I sit back down at the dining table.

"What gave me away?"

"Nothing. I'm a cop's wife. I smelled you."

"Cal Sounder."

She acts like she doesn't know the name. Maybe she doesn't. She doesn't talk to me and she also doesn't sit, or stop looking at me, for an hour. She just holds the gun level at my face until Felton gets home and calls me a fucking asshole.

"What the fuck are you doing in my house?"

"I guess I nearly trust you."

"You nearly trust me so you sneak into my house and go through my shave bag?"

"Yeah."

"Well that is a messed-up way of being in the world you have there, Sounder, so why don't you fuck off? And actually when you get there you can just keep on fucking. How would that be?"

"I'm sorry, man."

"The fuck is wrong with you?"

"A guy with a scratch on his left boot drove a car over my witness and put a bullet in me."

Felton's all kinds of pissed off but it doesn't take him even a heartbeat to work that one out.

"What kind of scratch?" I can tell he really wants me to say it looked like a picture of Marilyn Monroe.

"Like a little moon."

Felton huffs a big breath and all the asshole goes out of him on it. He bows his head and says: "Shit."

Then he looks at me and he thinks about it, and I know what he's thinking. He's thinking what he would do if that would happen to him and he's counting the people he really trusts and coming up with a short list, and he's realising that in a very real way he was on my short list and that is a thing between us now. He waves at Liz and she puts the gun down but not away, super-proficient.

Figure the other thing she teaches is pistol.

"You just got to the part where you trust me sorta kinda but you'd turn over my place real quick just in case."

"Gratton told me not to go home, so I came here and it turns out I'm not quite a good enough person that I just took it on faith, which you know about because neither are you and nor is your lady wife which is why she has a pistol in a cereal box."

Felton looks like he wants to argue but I'm right. He says "shit" again. Liz says something about how the gun is taped under the breakfast counter, and adds:

"I could have shot you, dumbass."

Yeah.

"And then," she adds, "I'd have had to clean that shit up again."

I think about it and do not ask about "again."

"You can sleep on the couch," Felton says, like I was expecting top and tail with them in the bedroom.

But he lends me a blanket someone knitted once, and I go to sleep wondering if it was his mother.

————

Wake up, Sounder."

"What is it?"

"It's morning, you asshole, and real working people have real work."

"Hey, I have work."

"Yeah, sure."

Felton slams the carton of milk down on the table and it spills. He snarls at his whatever the fuck those things are in the bowl. I don't ask what's wrong because I feel like that would not help.

Liz says: "There's a missing cop."

Felton growls again.

I ask what sort of missing.

"He's not on a beach in Hawaii, I can tell you that."

I wait. I don't say "that happens to cops sometimes" because although that is true it is not something that Felton wants to hear right now.

"Gratton got on the radio last night," Felton says at last. "I guess a little after he talked to you. Guess he took some time to work out what he wanted to say."

"What did he say?"

"He gave a speech about what it means to be a cop. It was all kinds of moving and total shit. Then what I hear is he got on the private channel to about twenty guys one at a time. Like he was working down a list. Spoke to each one of them for a bit. Sometimes it's a good conversation. Sometimes not so much. We had three guys hand in their papers this morning. And one guy—"

"Is missing."

Felton's head drops again like there's an answer hidden somewhere in the crumbs on the table. Moment like this you can keep looking for a long time before you realise it's not there.

"He's missing because we haven't done notifications. There's no mystery where he is."

"So?"

"Officer Mullen ate his gun, Sounder. I guess it's your fault for not dying like you were supposed to."

"Yeah, not apologising for that."

"Damn right. Fuck it, though. Fuck it actually a lot."

Liz Felton sighs and puts her hand on her husband's shoulder.

"You know Mullen?"

"Of course, I know Mullen." He points his hand at the pictures on the wall. I don't know which one is Mullen and I don't ask.

"Nice guy?"

"What do you want to hear? He was okay. Awful karaoke singer. Good with prints, not bad at talking to people. Would I have figured him for this? No. Do I believe it? Ab-so-fucking-lutely because I'm a terrible person. Except it turns out he's a terrible person and I'm just an asshole. The funeral's gonna be on Friday, I guess, and you're not coming. Before you ask, yes, I will fucking snoop for you and if I hear anything I will tell you, because: like I said I am a terrible person. Jesus."

"I'm sorry, man."

"Stop doing that, Sounder. He took money to kill you and now he's dead. Have some decency and gloat a little so we can hate you for twenty-four hours."

"Thanks for the couch."

"Go away, Sounder."

Liz Felton shows me out and shuts the door.

Figure I've been kicked out of one place I don't belong, I may as well go for the double. It's not even that far away, on the other side of one of those squares of mud and dead trees the mayor's office likes to think of as a park. The bare branches of a hawthorn scratch at me as I cross to the building where Susan Green has a rented room in another woman's apartment. It's not the kind of place anyone watches the front door, so I just go right on up and ring the bell.

Abigail Gaines is tall and slight and looks like she might be a librarian in waiting. In fact she teaches dance, which I can believe because the apartment looks like it belongs to someone who teaches dance. The colours on the walls are bright to the point of irritating, and the furniture is tall and elegant and not very comfortable, but at least it isn't pretending everyone who sits on it is a Titan. It's almost the opposite, like everything here is standing on points. Figure that says something about Abigail Gaines, too.

"It calls itself an academy," she says. She sounds offended.

"Is that not what it is?"

"A dance academy should strive to model standards of excellence within the profession."

"Okay."

"I mostly teach singers how to move their hips. It's a school, Mr. Sounder. What can I do for you?"

"I wanted to talk to you about Susan."

She sighs. "Poor Susie. You were there?"

"Yes." Unconsciously touching my side, where the putty is. It starts to itch on cue. Goddammit.

"Is it—bad?"

I'm trying to think of a way it could be anything else. "I guess it's as good as something like that can be."

"I suppose. Do you think she'll be all right?" She looks at me. People think if you're an investigator you're obviously a connoisseur of unhappy endings. Which I am, and I don't, but I'm not saying that to Abigail Gaines.

"Ms. Gaines—"

"Abby—"

"Ms. Gaines—"

And so we dance the dance of the nearest and dearest, which in this case is a dry dance because I don't think Susan Green and Abby much cared for one another. They didn't dislike one another either. They just shared space and got along as best they could in the city. They had compatible schedules.

I ask her about Roddy Tebbit. She nods and says it was strange.

She wouldn't have seen Susie with a Titan, but she wouldn't have seen Roddy being one if he hadn't been so tall. He was shy and sad. He was just some guy who happened to be old and big. He was tragic, but getting along. Gaines wonders whether, if you lose someone as a Titan, your mourning goes on longer because you have that much more life in you.

In my experience it does not.

"Were you ever a thing?" I ask, and Abigail looks at me.

"Why would you ask that?"

"Because it's the kind of intrusive bullshit question that if you don't ask it you regret the shit out of it later when it turns out to be important. I don't even think it is. You can tell me to fuck off, I don't mind."

She shrugs. "No. Not that I wouldn't have, before she moved in. But no."

"Thanks for your candour."

"Thanks for yours."

Gaines takes me into Susan's room and shows me her things. It feels wrong, as if doing this will bring on the moment of death. Gaines asks me if someone will come for them. I guess someone will: either Susan, or more likely a father or a mother or a sister. Maybe just a city officer, if there's no one else.

I ask if Susan has family. I keep tripping over the tense; so does Gaines. It's making both of us feel like shit.

Gaines doesn't know about family. I'm guessing Susan's people maybe were not okay with her chosen career, or her decision to live in the city, or maybe they're just far away and very busy. You'd think they have to know by now that she's in trouble, but maybe not.

Does Susan have any hobbies?

Yes. She likes life drawing, museums and eating out.

I ask about Harpo and the Marx Brothers, but Abigail doesn't know. She hates old movies and TV shows. A lot of people do, without knowing why. It doesn't occur to them to notice that we're locked to the patterns of life in the moment T7 was developed, as if there can't be new new things because the old ones aren't going away.

I stare at Susan Green's room for a little while longer, wondering if I should go through her drawers. I read her bank statements instead. Money in from Victor, money out to Abigail and the grocery store, some expenses. What looks like a regular girls' night. It speaks to a small life, well-enough lived. Four weeks ago she bought Roddy a tie. I figure it was a dull one, and that he liked it.

There's a sketch book on the night stand: dark blue hard covers, orange elastic holding it closed. Inside, towards the middle, I find a series of sketches of Roddy Tebbit naked as the dawn. Susan Green is working in that mid-brown pencil art students use that makes everything look provisional except dogs. His ribs and shoulders stretch the skin as if he doesn't eat enough. Yoga and running, I figure, looking at the long muscles, and maybe less Goan-Hungarian takeout food and more granola.

Roddy as Rodin's thinker.

Roddy as naked superman.

Roddy as Achilles, with a shield and a hooked sword.

Roddy's hands, close up, and the big knuckles on his fingers. I wonder what it must have been like to be Roddy, to have arthritis one week and then look again and find this.

And to find love again, with a girl like Susan Green.

Maybe he'd have been better company than you'd think.

Go figure.

I go do the next damn thing.

There's two dozen cops at Officer Mullen's place and every one of them is giving me that look. Tania Garcia frowns when she sees me and I can tell she thinks I shouldn't be there. I think that too. I also think Mullen shouldn't have shot me and that nice things should be free to nice people and really expensive for assholes, but this is not the day when any of us gets what we want.

The apartment is a walk-up and I walk up. The cleaning product in the stairwell is strawberry, but it doesn't cover the sharp scent of dried xiyoli and Uzbek tobacco from a hookah. Someone on the floor overlooking the street is having a great day, but that's not where I'm going. I get to Mullen's floor and Musgrave throws her hands in the air and says "shit."

"What's the skinny?"

"There is no skinny, Sounder, it's just shit."

"Yeah, well, you never take me anywhere nice."

She shakes her head. Not playing.

"Cal," Giles Gratton says.

"Sorry."

"Fuck are you sorry for? You need to be here. You care too much what cops think of you."

"Wonder why that is?"

"Not like he shot you because he knew you." Gratton glances at me. "You didn't know him, right?"

"I can honestly say I was shot by a complete stranger."

"At least he missed."

"Check my fucking abdomen, Giles."

"Mullen took two in the vest sometime before he died. You know anything about that?"

"I'm going to speculate it was after he shot me. I wasn't really paying attention." Zoegar's rounds, but given he saved my life I'm leaning hard into not having actually seen him fire.

Gratton sighs. "You're here to poke around?"

"We consulting detectives prefer the term 'investigate.'"

"Sure, Cal, let's have an English lesson." But he waves me in, even though I used his first name.

I investigate on my best behaviour. Not like I'm trying to search like a cop. Trying to search the way I do it, show them something they haven't seen, but make it look less like daydreaming. It's hard to freestyle when there's a little voice in the back of your head telling you every cop in the room is thinking you have no fucking clue what you're doing.

Bad furniture, bad carpet. No girlfriend, no boyfriend, no kids, no dog. Dating profile on the terminal doesn't say he's a cop. Lots of young cops don't advertise that. Fridge full of surprisingly healthy food. Mini-gym under the bed.

"What are you doing here?" Tidbo growls.

"I'm looking for a big black canvas bag full of used notes."

Gratton puts his head round the door. "Fuck you, Cal."

"Sorry."

"That's okay."

"Fuck you too."

"You're welcome."

I keep looking. It's so not like Roddy's apartment. So very not. I won't find a butterfly piece here, or if I do it's not taking me anywhere.

"You talk to the neighbours?"

"No, Sounder," Tidbo says, "because we never did this before."

I'm going through the motions. There's nothing I can do here except be seen and go away. I ask Gratton to pass me anything he thinks I need and he says okay. Then I tell him I'm sorry for his loss.

"That's what's fucking wrong with you, Cal. You actually are."

call Bill Styles at the university and he answers on the first ring.

"Bill, it's Cal."

"Cal! How are you?"

"I have a bullet hole stuffed full of putty that's itching like a sonofabitch and someone kicked the shit out of me before pulling the trigger. Roddy Tebbit's girlfriend is in a coma. So on the whole not great, and if you haven't found those students of his yet, do it now, before one of them ends up on the casualty list."

"Jesus, Cal, you think they're connected?"

I do not, but I'm not telling him that. I want Bill Styles nervous as hell. Bill is not just Bill, much as he would like me to believe that he is. When I speak with him, I'm talking direct to the university financial machine, which is big and stubborn and dangerous like an elk. I want that machine to know it is going to tell me about Roddy Tebbit, and his money, and his research partners, and for that to happen it looks like the elk needs to see some wolves in the trees.

"They could well be, Bill. You figure out who they are?"

"I have a fair idea, yes. I was going to call you."

"Get them in so I can talk to them."

Three kids, as promised, waiting in a tutorial room on the ground level, with a picture window looking over the lake, all the way to Tonfamecasca Tower, and Athena's office, if I knew which one it was.

That one, with the warm light on, high up above the world.

Bill is hovering like a mama duck. He says he can't leave me with the students even though they're legally adults because he's responsible for their welfare. It's a safeguarding issue, which I take to mean that I mustn't shout and if it turns out one of them killed Roddy for kicks and just flat out breaks down in the room Bill's going to get sued for letting me find out. There's no way that's what happened, but Bill doesn't have to know that just yet.

The boys are Miles and Richard, the first a wannabe life sciences magnate with a finance haircut, and the second a quiet kid with big feet I figure is one of those slow-rolling people just now finding his way. The girl, Hester, has that flavour of sorrow about her that some people carry even though they haven't got anything to be sorry about. The long straight hair does indeed fall to her waist, and it's combed flat and mournful like an old flag on a bad island. Rufus the collector must have just about drooled when he saw her. Figure on a good day he might have just made her an offer for the whole crop.

I say: "Excuse me, miss," and bring out the strands from Rufus's collection. Don't need a microscope to see they're the same.

"What the hell?" she demands. "Is that my hair? Where did you get my hair?"

"Roddy Tebbit's apartment," I say. She tries to take it from me, but I put it back in its little baggie instead.

"It was a tutorial," she says.

"Off-campus?" I look at Bill. "That even allowed?"

"It's perfectly acceptable if everyone involved is content with the situation. Dr. Tebbit"—slight stress on the title—"felt it was important to separate learning from the pure academic context." From which I deduce that Bill doesn't love the situation but has no choice but to say he does. I look back at the kids and decide to throw some red meat on the ground.

"Did Dr. Tebbit offer you drugs?"

Bill's on his feet before they can answer: "Cal!"

"Did he?" Like it's the most boring question on earth.

He obviously didn't, because they're all staring at me like I've lost my mind. I pat my pocket. "Well, if that's a hard question, no problem. I can take a sample of Hester's hair today, and compare it with the one I have here from a few weeks ago. You met Dr. Tebbit in between. If her hair shows no sign whatsoever of drug use then, no problem."

And incidentally, would tell a lab her recreational life history for the last however many years, including any brushes with accidental procreation, any serious illnesses . . . With hair like that, everything since she was about twelve. All sorts of shit in which I have no interest whatsoever.

"Cal!" Bill says again, pissed as hell.

"Bill, I'm going to ask you to step outside." Bill is already starting to say no, he's bringing in a lawyer, probably more than one. I step right into his space. That is not something that academics do to each other all that much, and he's not used to it. "Bill, I am going to talk to these three adults about things they do not wish to discuss while you're in the room. You're not safeguarding right now, you're stepping on my case. Now scoot, or I'll feed you to Gratton and it can roll from there."

Bill looks at me like he's never seen me before. Figure he's right. He hasn't. He's only ever hired me, and that's not the same as seeing me working.

Probably won't be hiring me again, either.

He slams the door on his way out.

"Now, Hester. Where were we?"

But Richard is standing.

"Mr. Sounder," he says. "You should be talking to me."

Hester gets to her feet, too, but Richard waves her away. "It's okay, Hes. I know who Cal Sounder is. We all know."

We, with weight and finality. I look at him again, barely twenty and with those big feet.

"No fucking way."

He shrugs. "Yes, way. But maybe not like you think."

No one says anything for a second while Richard walks over to the window and looks out at the lake. He puts his hands on the glass. They're big, too. Not big enough to have cast the gunshot residue shadow on Roddy Tebbit's, but big enough that I should at least have wondered.

"You're a Titan," I say, and he nods. Now that I see it, it's everywhere on him. The collarbones are heavy under his shirt. The slouch isn't just teen slacker chic, he's heavy. If I had to guess, pretty new minted, his body still catching up with the weight.

"So, what, you lived a long life as a real short bastard and then you got dosed and figured you'd live the frat house movie? Anyone ever explain the concept of age-appropriate relationships to you?"

"I'm exactly the age I look, Mr. Sounder," Richard says, still looking out at the water.

"Kinda big-boned, then."

He turns around and looks at me with sharp, cool eyes. "You do that a lot when you talk to people, don't you? You make obvious jokes. I guess it makes everyone think you're stupid or crude, but you're neither."

"Fine, you caught me. Congratulations."

"And now you want me to think I'm smart for noticing."

I look at the other two. They're not talking. They're not even saying anything with their faces. Just watching. I look back at Richard and pay attention the way I should have when I came in. Writing bump on his finger. You only get that if you make notes with a pen, and these days you only do *that* if you want to engage theta rhythm and parietal lobe activity to remember more, understand faster and you're prepared to do the work. Richard cares about study.

"That isn't something you worry about. You know you're smart, but you want to be smarter. What were you doing at Roddy Tebbit's apartment?"

"I wanted him to tell me how he lives. He's—he was—not average. Not normal for a Titan. An outlier. Hes and Miles came with me because I was nervous. Because I'm ordinary. I don't know how to make sense of it."

"Yeah, you're just an everyday kid. Nothing weird about it."

"Touché."

I have never heard anyone say "touché" and not sound like a jackass before.

He looks away again. There's a little cluster of diving birds plucking fish from the still water about twenty metres out.

"Leukaemia," Richard says at last. "Some kind of rare variant, got everywhere in me. I used to be able to name it, but it turns out that doesn't impress anyone. Not even me. I wasn't doing well."

"They gave you T7."

"Deep radiation first. All the way in."

I think about that a while. I figure they all but killed him. They injected him with a high beta emission preparation. Without the T7 he'd have died in a few days. With it . . . internal burns, risk of septic shock, pruritus and vomiting. Organ failure, supported externally. Artificial breathing system. Pain on another order. And then recovery. Bone marrow transplants stimulated by the drug, cultured clone cells from all his organs, even the skin. Nerves waking up. He must have been half mad by the end, even if they put him in a coma for the worst part.

"Did you choose all that? Or was it chosen for you?"

"They tell me I'm Richard Wells."

I look at him and I can almost see it, somewhere in the shape of the head, the set of the eyes.

"Wells like Tessa Wells-Khayam; Khayam like Sonny Khayam. Whose father was Jacob Khayam and whose mother is Jeanine Tonfamecasca." Jeanine being Stefan's kid sister. Titan genealogy is half census and half population science.

Richard nods, counting off generations with me on his oversized hands. Note "they tell me," not "I am." T7 amnesia, and a lot of it. I wonder if he remembers anything at all, and what it would feel like to be that young and have no past.

Stefan takes family seriously, despite the inevitable proliferation of his name. He's not interested in keeping them all alive forever, but that's not the same as saying he's prepared to have his great-great nephew die from a treatable condition. He steps down from the tower, heals the sick and twists the knife in the others, and everyone remembers who's boss. Everyone, and particularly his children.

Stefan has three phases of direct descendants, all harnessed to the company one way or another, though the older ones are running overseas divisions. Athena is the most recent and probably the last unless he gets the urge to in vitro and have some more. I have no idea if he's still capable of sex—the first- and second-dosers can't get enough, mostly, and they're not shy about letting that be known—but the third dose changes things—the percentage increase in mass and volume starts to get significant, so they can only conveniently screw other Titans anyway, and there's not enough of them outside the family for that to stay exciting. After the fourth dose . . . well. Stefan doesn't seem to be interested any more, at least not like he was, but maybe that's just him. Maybe sex was only ever a way of keeping score.

So Stefan's children are special; everyone else in the family is peripheral, but important. Beyond that, frankly, in his understanding the world exists to service their requirements.

"How old were you?"

"Fourteen. The youngest, at the time, to receive a full dose."

"And it worked."

He shrugs and waves one hand vaguely at himself. "Took a while to . . . even out. But yes."

"And then Stefan lost interest. You had regular checkups. Money to burn on physio. Maybe to help with the PTSD."

Hester scowls at me, but Richard flicks her a little smile to say it's okay. He's right. I'm not gouging him. I'm seeing him, and he knows the difference.

"But they didn't have anything to tell you about what it all meant. Who the fuck you are now. And you thought Roddy Tebbit might be able to tell you."

"He was so . . . not a Titan. Like me. Except really tall and thin."

"Talk about anything in particular?"

He shrugs. "Just personal stuff. Survivor's guilt, I guess. But it did make me feel better. I told him about my therapy. He knew a lot about the T7 process. He helped me understand it at a granular level. What I am. What I can expect."

"You know what he was working on?"

"Sure. Freshwater biology stuff. Ecosystems in the lake."

"In Othrys?"

Robert is a nice kid and does not say "Do you know of any other fucking lake around here?" but I figure it's a close-run thing, and he's not wrong because that was probably the dumbest professional question I have ever asked in a long career of crossing all the Ts.

"He have some kind of grant funding?"

Robert shakes his head. "Full commercial."

And there it is. "You know who with?"

"He was reticent about money. About everything that wasn't science or—" Richard shrugs, waves at his own body. "This."

I think of Susan Green. "You watch the Marx Brothers with him?"

Richard stares at me. "What?"

"The Marx Brothers. The comedians, not the communist."

"Harpo, Groucho, Chico and Zeppo. I'm a college student, Mr. Sounder, I know who the Marx Brothers were. No, they never came up. Is that important?"

I honestly have no idea any more. "So Roddy Tebbit—"

"He was explaining it all to me. Like, not history, just . . . life. I don't fit in because I really am just a kid, and yet I'm also not. Right?"

He looks at me like I have the faintest clue what to say to that.

Shit.

I grab a piece of scrap paper and write Athena's number on it. "This is your—fuck it, I'm saying cousin—Athena. Dial the number and tell her I said you should."

He stares at me. "Athena Tonfamecasca is going to take my call."

"On that number, any time of the day or night. So make sure you call sometime around four in the afternoon, okay? Don't write cheques too big for me to cash."

"What do I tell her?"

"Anything you like. But she'll tell you . . . how to get on. Okay? She knows the road. You don't have to do everything the hard way."

I can see Athena throwing her hands in the air: for fuck's sake, Cal, you ever take your own advice?

Nope. Can't say I do.

But being with her, with what she is now, would mean toeing Stefan's line, and that would destroy us both. She doesn't agree, but she's standing in the other world and it suits her. She doesn't see what it would do to me. Or perhaps I'm wrong, and a fool.

Richard looks at the paper and folds it carefully into his wallet. Then he squares his shoulders. "I don't know what happened to

Dr. Tebbit, Mr. Sounder, but if you're wondering whether he was the good guy or the bad guy, I think he was the first."

"There's no good guys and bad guys. Not really."

He looks back at me without blinking from somewhere endless I don't want to go.

"Yes, Mr. Sounder. There absolutely are."

A re you quite finished?" Bill Styles says.

"You like the Marx Brothers?"

"Groucho and Harpo and the other one?"

"There's four of them."

"No, Cal, I don't, because I'm neither ten thousand years old nor twenty-two."

"Who was Roddy Tebbit dealing with?"

"What do you mean, dealing with?"

"He was fully funded to work on lake slime, and not by you. Who?"

"Jaybird Pharmaceuticals."

"I want an address and I want the contract."

Bill passes me a thin envelope.

"That's all you've got?"

"It's all I'm giving you. The university lawyers say you want more than that you can take it up with them officially."

"You tell them I was here to help?"

"I did. Sian Colbert expressed doubt and apprehension, as indeed I am doing now. She says you're to sling your hook."

"She's a good lawyer."

"Get out, Cal. If you come around again, bring a warrant."

"That how it is?"

"That's how it is."

He holds the door for me, which is as close as a guy like that gets to throwing you out.

———

go back to the office and call Jaybird Pharmaceuticals, but there's no answer. Then I call the building manager and it turns out their space is a postal box. I get the company listing from the city recorder. The company secretary is a lawyer in Fulbright by the name of Adler Givens. I call Adler Givens and get the runaround, so I send his name to Gratton and ask for some light police hostility. Then I call Floyd Ostby and leave a message. He calls back a few minutes later and says the old business stinks and Jaybird is the bridge between what happened then and what happens now.

"What kind of stinks?"

"Omnidirectionally stinks. The company only has one employee and one shareholder, who is also the director."

"Which is?" But I already know.

Alastair Rodney Tebbit.

Which means that Roddy was paying himself to work at the university.

I go down to the city recorder's office because they are short-handed and they do not appreciate voices on the phone giving them work. I take my badge, a chocolate collection and a gift box of scented hand cream. All three of those together buy me seven hours of passion with several hundred thousand filing boxes and all the dust in the northern hemisphere. By the time midnight comes around I look like I'm attending a Halloween party as lint, but an hour later I know why Bill Styles got shut down by the board. They let a ghost into their school.

Roddy Tebbit has filed taxes every year while he's been here in the city, but did not file in Burfleet, where Bill Styles's paperwork says he was before he came here.

I call Ostby back and he confirms. In fact Roddy Tebbit did not file anywhere.

Nor did he attend Burfleet, or hold a position at Burfleet.

Or any college or high school whose records are readily available.

In fact there is no evidence of his being born at all.

"Well, shit," I say, and Maryam the recorder's clerk says:

"Honey, it's like listening at keyholes. You come down here, you're never gonna find out anything good."

I call Musgrave.

"Fuck time you think this is, Sounder?"

"Sorry."

"No, you're not."

"There's no such person as Roddy Tebbit."

"Pretty sure he's in a drawer in my office."

"When you get in there, run a full genetic sequence, please, and find out what his real name is."

"You rang me in the middle of the night to tell me what to do in the morning?"

"Nope."

". . . Jesus fuck, Sounder, you want me to do it now?"

"Sorry."

"You're not even a cop."

"Sorry."

"No, you're not."

"No, I'm not."

"It's a fake name?"

"It's a fake everything."

"And you want to know now?"

I don't say anything.

"I'm getting dressed," Musgrave says. "But when you die, I hope they let me cut you open."

I'm tired, the way you can only be tired if you have a hole in you that should not be there, and when the car pulls up and a voice says "at your disposal, Mr. Sounder," I get in without really thinking about it. Then a man gets in next to me and I feel something hard and metallic dig in under my ribs, the muzzle finding an easy resting place right against the bone. The car pulls out into traffic and onto the expressway.

"Ow," I say, because the front sight is poking my putty lattice. It hurts, but it's also amazing because it's scratching the itch. It doesn't count as scratching if someone puts a gun in your stomach. My torso twists before I can stop it, pressing back and forth against the barrel.

"Aaaaahhhhhh thank you, that's good."

"What the fuck is wrong with you?" the gunman says. "Are you some kind of idiot?"

"Fuck you, too, buddy. You kidnap a guy, you can put the fuck up with his kinks. Otherwise go kidnap someone else and see what that gets you."

Mr. Zoegar twists briefly around in the driver's seat.

"Mr. Sounder, what are you doing?"

I tell him about the putty and the itching.

"There is an etiquette in this situation, Mr. Sounder. The gun is not a scratching post."

"I hear you, I really do. But did they ever use this stuff on you?"

"Do you know in the first four years that it existed the makers did not trouble themselves to make any variations in colour? They just assumed everybody would be happy with the one for white people."

"So that's a yes?"

"Once. In Monrovia."

"And?"

"After a week I all but ripped it out. Do not do that, by the way. It is satisfying but exquisitely painful."

"Maybe if you guys are going to torture me you could start with that? I swear to Christ I'll tell you everything you want to know from sheer gratitude."

Zoegar sighs. "We are not going to torture you, Mr. Sounder. This is not at all that kind of meeting."

"You know, most people just phone me."

Zoegar's face flickers.

"Mr. Sounder, it is extremely irregular that my employer see anyone at all, let alone someone connected both with the regular police and the Tonfamecasca corporate hegemony. It is my belief that our mutual interests align, but that the chances of our being able to work together are greatly diminished by the somewhat ticklish issues of secrecy and good faith which surround us. I therefore propose that we are all absurdly polite so as to reduce the risk of a poor outcome arising through word choice or unintended rudeness."

I look around the car. It's an executive saloon, serious luxe and all the trimmings.

"I'm Cal," I tell the gunman. "Sorry about that. Having a day."

"You said," he replies. And then, with a glance at Mr. Zoegar, "I'm Frank."

"Hi, Frank."

"Hi, Cal."

"You mind if I lean forward and check out the wet bar?"

There's a small refrigerated cubby between the front seats. Frank says go ahead.

The cubby does indeed contain one bottle of Falanghina and one of Japanese malt, both expensive.

"Nice."

"Would you like something?" Zoegar inquires.

"No, thanks. Just getting to know you."

"Then, in that case, you will forgive a practical necessity—for your own longevity, as much as ours."

He passes a small bag from the passenger seat. I open it and find a prisoner transport hood. I look at Frank, who shrugs, and I put it on. If you've never worn one, you won't know what it's like, but there's a seductive quiet in a transport hood. Sound is deadened and you can hear yourself more easily than anything else: your own blood, your heart in your ears. An expensive one—which this is—doesn't make it hard to breathe, just impossible to see. It's warm, and humid, and calm. When you're pretty confident you're not going to die, it's not so bad.

Zoegar waits until I've had a chance to relax. Then he says:

"We are professional lawbreakers, Mr. Sounder. Ne'er-do-wells for profit."

"I was guessing a cartel."

"Understandable, but no, in fact we are an independent concern, more in the vein of the original neighbourhood assistance groups or of the Sicilian clans which gave rise to that great name brand of organised crime."

"I feel like I should be concerned."

"There is no intention that you should finish this night in, ah, concrete boots."

I swear to god if he'd done the sleeping with the fishes thing I'd have laughed out loud.

"Please consider me reassured. So: assistance for who?"

"For whom. Indeed. Perhaps for you."

"Who do you work for, Mr. Zoegar?"

"You know who I work for."

"Maybe I'd just like to hear you say it."

"For Lyman Nugent, late of the municipality of Bizancourt and more recently of this sprawling metropolis. That is his legal name—for some years now, in fact, as I understand it. In the popular mythology of your remarkable city, he is known—inaccurately and with all manner of nonsense attached, as such names inevitably accrete urban myth—as Doublewide."

"The actual Humpty Dumpty of crime, huh."

Mr. Zoegar drives in silence for a while. Then he says: "Please, Mr. Sounder, be so kind as to remember my injunction to politeness. If even that is too much for you, think of the little pockets of propellant and metal resting under your rib cage, and consider it prudence to hold your tongue."

I do that.

———

We drive around and around for a good long while, and then we walk into a house. We're walking on plastic sheeting—I can feel it through my shoes. Maybe they're concerned I could analyse the mud and work out where we are. I hope it's that, and not that they don't want to have to clean up my footprints after they dump me in the lake.

Zoegar puts me in a lift, one hand on my shoulder as if I'm his old grandfather. I'm expecting to go up, but we go down.

When they finally let me out of the bag, I'm in a big triangular room panelled with expensive marquetry. It's lit by candles. It smells of roast meat, well caramelised, and potatoes. At the far end there's a dining table set for three, and sitting in a chair at the table is a man who cannot be real.

Green velvet suit, gambler's waistcoat stretched tight across the impossible belly; shoulders and chest a wide expanse of flesh. Mediterranean, but north or south is an open question. Say Sicilian if you love your classics, but you could just as well say Tunis or Tripoli and have as good of a shot. The arms, huge at the shoulder, taper and fatten in a caricature of ordinary musculature to hands like corpulent spiders. His reach must be more than two metres on each side, going on for three. Overall he looks less like Humpty Dumpty, now that I'm seeing him and not his shadow painted on the wall outside Victor's, and more like a fat mantis, or some sort of soft-bodied crustacean crawled out of its shell and adorning its vulnerable body with precious stones. The face is almost perfectly human, as if the head is exempt from this distortion, but the whole body is huge, carrying a weight of folded flesh which makes him disproportionately enormous while recognisably human.

"Hello, Mr. Sounder," he says. His voice is clear and fastidious, deep as a bellows.

"Congratulations, Mr. Nugent. I half thought you were a fairy tale."

"Even after our little brushes over the years? How gratifying."

"Oh, I knew there was someone, Mr. Nugent, but I didn't honestly believe you'd be . . . you."

Mr. Zoegar tuts, but Lyman Nugent—call him Doublewide, because if he isn't, he will for sure do until the original shows up—flicks the fingers of one massive hand.

"Mr. Zoegar, we can hardly spend so much effort on secrecy and then complain that our guest hadn't penetrated the veil. Mr. Sounder, did you really have no hint?"

"Sure, now that I know. Lots of people talk about you. But they talk about Santa too."

"Indeed, sir. Indeed, a lot of people talk. And those who do work for me know better than to say anything at all. Do you see?"

Meaning any time anyone goes looking for a connection, the lead dead-ends, because it was never a real lead. "Very nice. Now, though I adore admiration for my technique—do come and sit, Mr. Sounder, the meal is excellent and you've had rather a long week—we have graver matters to discuss. Indeed, sir, we do."

I sit. Zoegar does too, at the far end, and I wonder if he's there to shoot me if I lunge across the table at his boss. Doublewide nests in his chair, his elbows all the way out behind him and brushing the floor carpet so that his hands rest on the table as if he was just an ordinary fat man. If you don't look too hard, you can miss the strangeness of it, and then out of the corner of your eye you catch it again and realise that you're inside the circle of his arms, that he can reach you from there, with those remarkable spider-fingered hands.

I'm about to help myself to the food, but I see Doublewide looking at his man and waiting. Zoegar bows his head and he can't be about to do what I think he's about to do, but I follow suit, and he does. He says grace.

"Lord, our Father, bless this food and our endeavours. We thank you for all that you are, all things that have been and all that is to come. In your hands, O Lord. In your hands."

Doublewide looks up, and a smile lights his face. "Mr. Sounder, I'm proud of you. You see? You can be pleasant after all."

"Don't tell anyone. That's even more secret than you are."

"I'm not secret, Mr. Sounder. Just shy."

"Not for nothing, but a cop died today."

"Theirs is a dangerous profession. Laudable, of course, if sometimes locally inconvenient."

"This cop ate his gun. Turns out he was driving a certain vehicle. You saw it when you pulled my fat out of the fire."

"Ah, indeed."

"You have anything to do with his sudden feeling of remorse, Mr. Nugent?"

"No, Mr. Sounder, very much not. I should have preferred him discursive. I suspect his death is very much of his own engineering, though of course one always looks to the employer in such a context."

Always, and always assuming that wasn't Nugent himself, double games hardly being unknown in organised crime.

"Did you know Roddy Tebbit?"

"You ask a lot of questions for a dinner guest, Mr. Sounder. Please be so kind as to pass the baguette basket."

He can reach the basket, of course. Figure he prefers not to. I pass it along, and Nugent makes a little jazz hands gesture, palms out. "I adore French baking, sir. Adore it."

"Roddy Tebbit, Mr. Nugent. If you don't mind."

"I knew him a little. We were not friends, but . . . those of us who are not like the others . . . well, we meet, inevitably. You conceive that the attempt on your life was related to your investigation."

"I do."

"So do I."

"You turned up at a real convenient moment for me. How's that happen?"

"Good fortune on your part. We were rushing to protect Miss Green."

"And how did you know she needed it?"

"Oh, I deduced it, of course. With Mr. Tebbit dead, the possibility is plain."

"Did a bang-up job. She's worse than me."

"Alas, we may strive for omniscience, but omnipresence is somewhat more problematic."

"I hear Roddy had plans to survey Lake Othrys. Algae or some such."

"Yes, so I gather."

"It crossed my mind maybe you didn't want that to happen, what with your shyness and all."

Doublewide claps his hands duchess style, wrists close together, pat pat pat with his palms like flippers. "Oh, yes! The lower reaches are said to be a museum of gangsters murdered in the early days. But Mr. Sounder, I assure you, I've no bones to pick in that regard. No, indeed, sir. Did Mr. Zoegar not specifically advise you that concrete boots were not on the agenda?"

"I took that as a metaphor."

"It was, it was. You need have no personal fear. But as it happens, it is also literally true. The lake and I have no secrets together. Let the waters drain away, and I shall be unabashed. Apart from environmentally, of course. In that connection I should be quite upset. It is a rich and complex habitat."

"You brought me here to talk ecology, Mr. Nugent?"

"No, indeed. History. Or perhaps literary fiction. Eat, Mr. Sounder, and I will tell you a story."

"Can it be the one about the horse walking into a bar and the really small piano player?"

"If you like. Or if you prefer, it can be about murder and lies."

"That is a tough choice."

"Not for either one of us, I believe. Come now, sir. Please just eat, and I shall satisfy a curiosity you do not yet possess. And since you fancied me a fairy tale, I shall begin: 'once upon a time.'"

I eat.

Once upon a time—as Doublewide tells it—there was a boy named Peter who loved a girl named Lillian. He says a boy and a girl, because he is old, by definition. They were both adults in their prime, of course. She was a scientist, he was a doctor, they made science love and lived in a city far far away. He brought her flowers every day, and she made him cocoa in the afternoons, and that's how it was until somehow it wasn't. It was good fortune and hard work that destroyed them.

They were getting closer and closer to something, something brilliant and strange, and all the right people were interested and Peter and Lillian danced the dance of pharmaceutical funding, and were wined and dined. If Peter had developed an obsession, and a temper, and if Lillian had somehow lost the will to tell him to mind his manners, well, incautious couples can fall into habits that are not always conducive to happiness, and yet are not so awful as to require divorce. And they had the quest, which they shared, and which was going so well that Stefan Tonfamecasca himself had come at the last minute and stolen their company away from every other medical giant to keep it for himself. In-body reprofiling, was what Doublewide heard, so that if you were to combine it with T7 you could not only grow young, but customise yourself from an ever-increasing array of desirable genetic traits. Grant yourself natural beauty or tetrachromatic vision, or the relevant cerebral structures of a mathematical genius; effortless human perfection. The next stage in Titan speciation.

So they came here, to the city and to Chersenesos, to the nicest company apartment, the best building, the actual high life. They had the top tier of everything for the asking, and all the funding and assistants they could want. They weren't happy any more, by mortal standards, but they were content and enraptured, and on the brink of transcendent success. That has to mean something in this world, or what else is all of it for? It was a success story of science heroes and intellectual battles fought and won in the war on death.

But then one day, Lillian was gone. Gone from the apartment, gone from the lab. Gone from the country club on the Chersenesos point, gone from the summer place along the shore. Gone like butterflies in winter. No one could find her, least of all Peter. Her friends . . . her family . . . the police . . . no one knew where she was. They looked. They went to one another's houses, they brought in the police, they tried homeless shelters and refuges, convents and hostels. If she was alive, no one knew why she'd gone, whether she'd gone willingly. They waited for a ransom note, for a corpse. They walked the streets and called her name.

Did she die, then? Was she abducted? Was it personal, or corporate espionage? Certainly she was never seen again. Someone surely knew what had happened, but who? Perhaps Stefan Tonfamecasca, in whose palm they had lived, as his prized employees. Perhaps he knew what had happened to a beautiful, brilliant woman with an inattentive husband. Stefan, after all, was known for his appetite back then. He had a burning hunger to take mortal lovers, to wrap the tiny, birdlike women of the human world in his vast embrace, and delight them with his gentleness and his passion. But all his lovers—every one of them, and there were, oh, so many—all were paraded on his arm, documented and photographed in their triumph. It was part of their pleasure, and his, to be seen and envied. Sometimes even their most intimate moments were broadcast through strategic leaks and scandalous invasions of privacy, to the stunned admiration of the ordinary world, and to the onwards creation of secret and self-perpetuating lust in a million daydreams, among beautiful clubbers queuing at red velvet ropes. The Tonfamecasca parties were notorious, and rightly so. Stealing an employee's wife would hardly have been a blemish on such a record. So why hide her?

Peter came to believe that Stefan had murdered her.

The thought came upon him slowly, like a tumour in the heart. It fed on Stefan's generosity, on his commiserations, on his singular indulgence. Stefan said he wanted the research completed, that he had no idea where Lillian might have gone or what might have become of her. He said he was bending all his might to answering that question. He hinted that some competitor more bold than honest had stolen her away. Peter, furious, rejected the idea. He knew they were meant to be together, that whatever the present disconnect of their marriage, in the hothouse of Tonfamecasca Labs, it needed but a little time and nurture and all would be perfect again, and he knew that she knew that too. She would not go, so she must have been taken, and his eye turned upon the most obvious, most proximate threat.

He became a spy within his own life, within the Tonfamecasca company. The project languished, or perhaps it was always a mirage, but all the while as he worked, he was delving and discovering within the very heart of Stefan's fief. He began to roam the corridors, read other people's messages, snoop in other labs. He was famous, for a while, for solving their problems in passing, like a mendicant seer. Radical answers to unasked questions would appear on whiteboards, slipped into presentations amid the slides. He was a strange ghost in the new science, but not entirely unwelcome.

And then, taking with him his grief and his anger and his dark, dark suspicion, Peter, too, disappeared into the night. The company apartment in Chersenesos was searched again, seeking signs of man and woman. There was, perhaps, something, some hint of a struggle. A disturbed carpet, some trace of blood on a wall, but it might have been no more than a sneeze on a cold day after a walk. And who hasn't tripped on one of those long-haired rugs?

Peter was gone. Perhaps, in between times, he died of old age. It was long ago. But then, age is no longer guaranteed, so perhaps he did not. He knew, after all, as much as anyone about Titanium 7 and how it is made. Perhaps he brewed his own immortality: a kitchen-sink Titan, stirring potions in bathtubs in motels, injecting himself and screaming, conscious of every appalling second, in shacks in the desert far away from anyone. Perhaps he sought for a while to become a shadow alternative to Stefan's rule, a kingpin of illegal and dangerous rejuvenation. Perhaps, made young by his own knowledge, hidden as someone new, he will never rest until Stefan Tonfamecasca has paid for the death of his only love.

Or perhaps he's at the bottom of Othrys, or in a shallow grave in Stefan's roof garden, or lying on a slab in Musgrave's office.

Doublewide opens another bottle of dark red wine, and pours some for himself in a glass the size of a basketball.

I say: "Everybody loves a ghost story."

Mr. Zoegar frowns at me. Doublewide chuckles, and I feel it in my bladder. I keep thinking he must be a two-dose Titan. You don't get this big on just one. And yet I can't possibly know, because Titans don't look like this at all.

Unless I ask, but that would be rude.

"Peter fix you up, Mr. Nugent? You look a little irregular."

Zoegar is actually on his feet before Doublewide waves a hand, like a giant puppeteer. Zoegar shoots me a look: just wait till I get you home.

"An idiosyncratic reaction, I'm told, Mr. Sounder. Nothing to do with poor product. And, no, in fact. I acquired my T7 from a legitimate source, though I will confess there was an element of deception involved." The hand pressed to the vast expanse of chest in deprecation. "A sad mistake."

"It's not fixable?"

"I am alive. Magnificent! Different, yes, but not less simply because I do not look like an oversized matinee idol. I see nothing that needs fixing, Mr. Sounder. I do have an inconsequential request of you, however."

"Well, let's see if I can accommodate you. You'll appreciate that my time is my main professional resource."

"Oh, straight to the nub, very good, very good. I admire that in you, sir. In my observation of your career, it is laudably unblemished by inappropriate sentiment in the commercial setting. Though I must say, I believe your resources are not so limited. You have a keen mind and considerable nerve. So, indeed: I wish to commission you."

"To do what?"

"Nothing of great significance. Roddy Tebbit's liver and other organs are now the legal property of the Travis clinic, as I think you know."

"Yes."

"I would like them to get there, without mishap."

"And you think you need me for that."

"Stefan Tonfamecasca will not want it to. I'm concerned that he might . . . exercise his gravity, even just send someone to take them. One of Mr. Zoegar's many counterparts in his organisation. He might even go to court. But if, say, a man who functions as a damper on all things Titanic were to vouch for their destruction to Stefan while nonetheless delivering them to me . . . that would be an optimal outcome."

"That's not the same thing. You said the Travis. Stealing's another matter."

"It is the same thing, sir. The Travis and I . . . we are one, financially speaking. When all the shells are plucked away and the cockle is winkled from the rock. I can even prove it to you, though with that level of knowledge of my affairs would come certain constraints upon you. No, there's no need for that, Mr. Sounder. You can just drop them discreetly at the front desk. The staff will accommodate you as to timing and matters of . . . tradecraft."

"You want me to lie to Stefan."

"I offer you the opportunity to defeat him, in this one, small way."

"Why would I want to do that?"

"Oh, come now. Everyone who meets him longs to beat him in one way or another. Otherwise we must acknowledge we are outmatched, made secondary in our own world. If we do not defeat the Titan king, what is left to us but obsolescence?"

"You think that's going to persuade me?"

"I'm interested to find out. Who are you, Cal Sounder? I told you one story, will you not tell me another? Who are you?"

"I'm sure you did your research."

"I did, but you're an enigma, sir. A nobody, and yet somehow also a pin around which the city turns. Of course you're only a small businessman, but you are, undeniably, something of a figure in all of this, and I cannot for the life of me see how it comes to be so. You walk with giants. Are you on a mission? Like Peter, a grieving husband nursing a grudge? A son seeking vengeance? Is there some heroic story playing out here that I'm not aware of? Whatever it is, you may not be in the job much longer. I have my spies: Stefan is unhappy with you. He feels you have fumbled in this matter. And perhaps it means more to him than just a liver and some offal."

"What do you want them for?"

Doublewide steeples those long fingers. Long enough to go all the way around my head. The leverage on those arms would let him twist it off like the top of a ketchup bottle. "I think what I do with them once I have them is my business, Mr. Sounder."

"If you're going against Stefan, you're going to need a lot more than Mr. Zoegar here."

"Oh, not against. Never against. Around, beneath, beside. Orthogonal influence, dimensionalities of control. We are not in collision, for all that we occasionally abrade. But you? Do you think he won't pin you in a case like a butterfly?"

"I can handle Stefan."

The huge chest rocks, and the head lolls from side to side. "Oh. Forgive me. The idea . . . that anyone . . . least of all you . . . handles Tonfamecasca . . . your death wish must be of almost Titanic proportions. Or you have something special." The eyes glitter in the pouchy face. "Hence the question. I repeat: who are you?"

He really wants to know, and I really don't want to tell him, so I lie.

"Daniel," I say.

"Daniel?"

"Allegorical Daniel. I pulled a thorn out of his foot a few years ago."

"And now you believe the lion is your friend."

"I believe he doesn't want to eat me in case there are more thorns on the bush. I made sure to put a cutting in water."

"Blackmail? I wouldn't have thought you the type."

"Insurance. He wants to buy me off, but as soon as he does there's a risk he'll kill me, so we have a standing agreement instead. I get on with my life, he gets on with his. I do my best to keep Titan cases low-key. The department loves it because they get answers from the company they'd never get without me. Stefan gets a man on the ground whenever minor Titan shit hits the fan. New doser gets shitfaced with a bunch of models and burns down a bar, whatever, I tidy up. I sass him a bit and he smacks me down, so he knows he's in control. Stability in tension, and the longer it works, the less point there is in messing around with it."

Doublewide watches me across the table, hooded eyes dark in the white folds of his face.

"Admirable. And what is your exit strategy, when you are old and grey?"

"Retire to the sun. Go shark fishing. Open a bar and marry a windsurfer."

"How curiously specific. But Tonfamecasca will say that age makes you likely to die, and with that risk, his own risk increases. He won't like that."

"By then we'll have a working relationship. Mutual understanding. That changes the equation."

Eyebrows rise. "Oh, dear. I did not take you for a fool. Is it possible you have so thoroughly misunderstood the nature of the man you are dealing with? You're talking of half a lifetime for you, I grant. Thirty years, let us say. For him, the equivalent of perhaps five. He will not grow to trust you in that time. Nor will he forget the affront. No, Mr. Sounder, I am very much afraid your retirement will feature an altogether different relationship with sharks."

"Well, that's my problem, isn't it?"

Another contemplative pause. "You are a man of resolve. Perhaps you will improve your position and survive."

"I'm glad you think so."

"Or perhaps you will need another friend, in time. In which

case you might find one in me. I could prepare some sort of soft landing for you."

"I'm listening."

"The donor organs, of course, in the first instance. Tell Stefan you have arranged for their destruction, but bring them to the Travis."

"And in thirty years you'll help me out."

Laughter.

"That would be rather a lot to ask for a distant prize, would it not? Though perhaps you are the sort of man who would accept such a long-term proposition. No, I think I could arrange to sweeten the pot. Money, for example. Hmm?"

"I do like money."

"A very reasonable fondness, and one we share. So: I will give you a great deal of it in exchange for Roddy Tebbit's liver, lungs and other biological accoutrements, and in the fullness of time I will take the call when you need me. Which, I promise you, you will."

Too right, if that was really what was going on. I'd be stunned if I made it that far. Stefan would reach into every law firm and bank, every deposit box. He'd look under every floorboard and in every old mattress, starting in the city and spiralling out across the whole, entire world, until he found my leverage and crushed me to bloody pulp on the silk carpets in his receiving room. And then he'd make his next appointment get down on their knees and clean them, and they would.

"I don't love it," I tell Doublewide. "It puts me on the chess board. I prefer to sit the game out."

"Once, perhaps, that was possible, but not any more. You are connected. You hang in a web. Is it yours? Someone else's? I'm not sure. Perhaps this whole narrative exists to draw me into conflict on someone else's terms. Who is the spider, hm? You have friends. You have enemies. Even if they are a little hard to distinguish. You have disproportionate confidence, and even some effect. Is it bluff? Are you like the coyote in the cartoon, running over thin air until you look down? Or are you yourself some sort of weapon? Are you even sure which side you're on?"

"There are no sides."

"Of course, there are. Dozens. Perhaps we have mutual interests, you and I. Perhaps there is a deeper game being played which harms us both. Who profits, if you quarrel with him? If I do? This is what I wish to know."

"He does, Mr. Nugent. Always."

But I nod, and I take Doublewide's deal.

Zoegar puts me back in the transport hood and drops me in the centre of town. It's the deep part of the night by the time I watch him drive away, and even the party kids have gone home. The streetlamps reflect in sheets of black ice that were puddles eight hours ago, and the slush is turning hard where it's pushed against the buildings and piled up at the kerbs. I smell woodsmoke and cold coming across the lake, and then the wind changes and there's something else, hot and synthetic like burning tyres. A black cloud rising at the foot of Chersenesos, rising in a column, and fire engines blue and red and white crashing through the empty streets.

By the time I get there there's not much to see. The fire's out and the police building is wet and black at one corner. The firemen have everyone being checked out for smoke inhalation, because there's nothing they like more than bossing cops, the few times a year they get to do it.

I walk through the lines like someone else's ghost, everyone ignoring me. I see Felton and Tidbo. Two nurses up and one over, Kristoffsen J., the rookie cop from the hospital, has a nasty burn on her arm, but it'll heal. The guy next to her keeps saying thank you, over and over. Figure she pulled him out of something. Good for her. I keep going, looking, not finding. I see Gratton and he waves me over.

"Arson," he says. "Person or persons unknown. Fire bomb."

"Where?"

"My office," Musgrave says, appearing behind him. The medic working on her isn't happy she's walking around. "I'm fine, thank you," she adds to him, "I'm a doctor."

"You're a patient," he says, "in a post-crisis situation that may or may not be impacting your ability to make good decisions. Look up and to the left, please."

Gratton makes a phone gesture, taps his watch. Yeah. Talk soon. Musgrave waits until the nurse has looked in both her eyes and down her throat, then peels him off.

"I'm fine. Cal, my car's five minutes away. I don't want to be behind the wheel. Drive me home, please."

That's so unexpected I don't argue. Musgrave leans on me as we walk away.

"We need to talk," she says. "Right the fuck now."

"What about?"

"How much of a cop are you tonight?"

"You know exactly how much of a cop I am. What's going on?"

She sighs. "I burned down the lab," she says, and we turn the corner.

4

This is how much of a cop I am.

A long time ago when I first started working with the department there was a moment when maybe Musgrave and I might have had something. I'd blown in from—well, never mind. I did some fairly crazy things after Athena got her first dose, and I made some surprising friends. Musgrave and I were younger, dumber and hotter. We weren't dating and we weren't sleeping together, but we were thinking about it and we both knew that.

I went to Musgrave's house one night because she called me. It wasn't the kind of call that says to shower before you go. I went anyway. I found her ex's brain on the wall and the rest of him on the hall carpet. I found Musgrave holding the gun. She wouldn't call the department. She wouldn't say why. I found out later his brother was a captain in another town.

I thought about what to do for about five seconds and realised I didn't care. I liked Musgrave. I didn't know the ex. There was no way to tell what happened, even if she wanted to say. Could be she'd lie, she just killed him. Could be he tried to kill her. No way to be sure. Not for me, not for anyone. Not for a jury or a tribunal. Which would mean she got fired.

In the movies gangsters throw bodies into the lake, but in real life they swell up and escape unless you get that exactly right. You need a canvas bag and weights and a depth map and buying all those things at once can be hard to explain down the line. On the other hand there's a natural spa hotel on the far shore called the Alaric where rich lawyers take people they shouldn't, and kids from the bridge area think they'll have their honeymoon. It has indoor-outdoor pools in the main garden and wooden hot tubs by the cabins among the trees. Back another three hundred metres there's a section they don't put in the brochure where what comes up out of the rock is mostly acid. The pools there look every bit as beautiful, but you really don't want to bathe in them. A guy named Marlowe keeps the grounds and makes sure no one goes in.

Marlowe and I get along fine.

I never talk to Musgrave about that night and she never brings it up. Everyone assumes we slept together. Everyone assumes it was bad sex and we didn't want to do it any more. They mostly assume that last part was my fault.

I drive us to her house. I have only ever been inside that one time. Musgrave has a little remote on the dash and the garage door opens. I drive in.

Musgrave heats a tin of soup and we drink it outside on the swing set, wrapped in two separate blankets. She doesn't want to sit inside. I think maybe she's worried about surveillance.

"So are we going to talk about it?"

"Shut up."

"I don't mind, Musgrave, I'll sit here and drink soup. But sooner or later I figure you're going to have to tell me, because that's why you wanted me here."

"I burned down the lab."

"You said. I thought it was an interesting creative choice."

"Fuck you, Cal." But she smiles, just a little.

I think of Doublewide and the liver.

"Any chance you saved Tebbit's organs?"

"Every chance. All the evidence is intact."

"So . . . what caught fire?"

"The assay machine and the off-network drive. I had the results output set to local read, thank god."

"This would be the results of Roddy's genome scan?"

"It would."

"Who is he, for Christ's sake?"

"I have no idea. There's no record of a previous scan. But what there is, is data."

"What do you mean, data?"

"He was a biologist, right?"

"Yeah, supposedly. I don't know what the fuck he really was."

"Well he or someone he trusted jinked his liver DNA. He had an archival hard drive, basically, in his cells. It's not hard to do, just no one does it because why would you? Unless you're hiding a stash of documents you really don't want to get caught with."

"So what does it say?"

"It's encrypted."

"You burned down the lab because he had a porn stash in his liver."

"I don't think it's a porn stash, Cal."

"Why?"

"Because the stash is encrypted, but the folder name is in the clear. He wants you to read it."

She reaches into her pocket and pulls out a printed sheet with a single line of capital letters.

TONFAMECASCA MURDER

Yep. Definitely burn that shit to the ground.

"Drink your soup," Musgrave says, "and then get the hell off my porch. Oh, and get your shit from my car."

"What shit?"

Musgrave looks at me, which is as close as she's willing to get to saying, even here and now, that she's stolen Roddy Tebbit's organs from the police department.

"Your shit," Musgrave repeats, and pushes me off the swing set.

———

The doc box is like a freezer box for medical stuff. It's sterile and cool with a built-in battery, and if you fill it—which Musgrave has—with goop that comes separately in little sachets, it will keep body parts viable for twenty-four hours before it needs to recharge.

This particular doc box is not cool. It is the hottest item in the city right now by a mile. I'm going to be walking around with stolen criminal evidence which Stefan Tonfamecasca would kill for—maybe has killed for, maybe even personally—and Double-wide commissioned me to steal, which I now maybe can't do because he's a lying sack of shit.

He doesn't care about the organs. He wants the file to fuck with Tonfamecasca. I have some sympathy with that but depending what the file says something like this could create an actual problem. Or a war.

And if I'm going to deal with that stuff there is one thing I feel strongly and that is I don't want it to melt on my fucking shoes before I can figure out what to do with it.

The first thing I do is take the doc box home and plug it in.

When I was a kid, before I even really knew there was such a thing as a Titan, my grandfather gave me a wind-up toy. It was a little marching man in an old-fashioned uniform, the kind with lots of braid that halfway looks like a lion-tamer's. My grandfather was a severe old bastard with bad memories and bad hips, so we did not have a great time together often, but any time he came around after that I would get out the soldier and we'd watch it march across the table. For as long as neither one of us said anything and he drank his coffee, we had something. I don't know you'd call it love, but maybe it was, or the nearest a man like that and a kid were ever going to get. The little soldier would march and march and finally walk right off the edge and my grandfather would catch him every single time, one-handed. It got so he'd look the other way and drink his coffee, but still his big hand would go out and catch the soldier before it could fall more than a few inches off the table top. That soldier walked in a straight line, one foot in front of the other, and nothing was going to stop him following his orders.

There's an obvious thing here that I'm supposed to believe and it's supposed to guide my thinking. It goes like this: Roddy Tebbit was Peter the scientist and Stefan killed his wife. Roddy's been trying to prove it ever since and recently he found something that means he can. Stefan found out he was back and killed him, but didn't realise that Roddy had made his own body the messenger. Now all I have to do to bring Stefan down is give Doublewide the liver, or indeed just bring the case myself. On the face of it that would make me some kind of folk hero or some kind of dead idiot. Likely both. If Stefan ever went to jail—and that is a big if—I'm not sure he would actually notice. The first thing he would do—the obvious thing—is buy the whole company that owned whatever facility he was in. How does jail work, exactly, when one of the prisoners is also the boss? And if you assume he'd need protection in there—from what? Do they have rhinoceroses in jail now? Do people get jackhammered in the lunch queue?—you name for me the criminal kingpin who could resist the bribe Stefan would offer on day one? T7 changes what jail time even means.

Taking Stefan down would be a national effort. Even a multi-national one. But you can never tell how fast a wall like his will crumble, how many people have been waiting for the moment. Perhaps, with the right moves, it could be done.

So maybe I'm supposed to go through with it because I hate everything Tonfamecasca, or maybe someone knows me a little better than that and they think I'd want to put Athena in the top job. Maybe the world actually would be better with Athena in that job, or maybe she'd be worse. You never can tell.

Maybe I'm supposed to call Athena right now, mix her up in this, so someone else can take her down.

Maybe the whole thing is a hoax; Roddy Tebbit had some other reason to hate Stefan and he decided the only way to beat him was to make himself look like Peter and fake up a bunch of files, then force Stefan to overreach and kill him—in which case you'd expect Roddy to have laid a trail for me.

Maybe Doublewide is Peter and he faked the whole thing up, or he didn't, and he's laying a trail.

Maybe maybe maybe and if I had another one I could start a farm. I hate political cases. Which is a shame because they're almost the only ones I get.

Coffee, then work. And hope like hell I can see the edge of the table before I walk right off it.

Good morning, Nicky, how are the poodles today?"

"I'm not talking to you, Sounder, get the fuck out."

I make like I'm going to slap him and he cringes. I don't feel great about it but I don't have a lot of time and he's a terrible human being.

"Nicky, I asked after the poodles out of politeness but what I meant was that you owe me a number of favours owing to my historical forbearance and this is when you come through."

Nicky is notionally a vet and to be fair he is qualified in veterinary medicine, but his real strong suits are having sex with the owners of small dogs and prescribing pills for mysterious dog ailments which coincidentally have enjoyable effects on humans. That is to say that Nicky is a sleazeball and a drug dealer who is also a vet. I really do not give a shit about the second one but I have occasionally in my off-season been hired by angry spouses to discover the identity of their wives' boyfriends. It is always and exclusively wives, and in fact he has a type, which you can imagine as the kind of person who walks a poodle through town in what is effectively swimwear plus a coat. Simultaneously: the kind of person whose husband has particular opinions about what he will do with the guy who is showing his perfect girl a good time behind his back. Which, when it's Nicky, I don't reveal, because everyone needs an off-book medical opinion from time to time.

He grumbles, but mostly for tradition. Then: "What do you want?"

"I have a doc box full of human organs and I don't want them to go off."

"Fuck. Fuck! Did you finally crack and off someone?"

"Yes."

"Yes? Are you fucking serious?"

"Yes."

"You murdered someone and you're keeping their organs in a doc box and you don't want them to go off because why?"

"I don't have time to do any cooking until the weekend."

"Are you fucking serious right now?"

"Yes."

"Are you?"

"The fuck do you think, Nicky, of course I'm not serious. Do you actually want to know what's going on?"

"Will I sleep again?"

"No."

Nicky swears as he walks around his office picking things out of drawers. The whole place smells like dog hair and strippers. He puts five or six pouches of goop in the compounder and it spits out a vacuum bag the size of my head.

"Put this in the box feed chute and add distilled water."

"Yeah, I'll just fix up a still in my lounge."

"You can buy it, asshole. From drug stores. They even deliver. How long are you going to keep your dead person parts running?"

"A week maybe."

"If you're fucking lucky. Those boxes are not high spec."

"How will I know if it's getting tricky?"

"Best scenario a little orange light comes on. Less best it's a red light."

"Worst case?"

"You know it's gone wrong because of the smell."

"That's just great."

"Don't look at me. Serial killer support services is way down at the bottom of my CV. I'm thinking next time I go for an interview I won't even include it. Now if you're finished freaking the shit out of me I have a ten o'clock with Mrs. Leydoux's Bichon."

"With her what now?"

"For fuck's sake, it's a dog."

I take the goop back to the doc box and pick up some distilled water on the way for cash. Then I go up to the roof of my building and rip the cover off the main electrical board up there. I patch the doc box power in, fill it up with what it eats and seal it twice, then drop the whole thing into the grey water tank behind it so that it disappears except for the little rubber duck on a rope tied to the handle. Then I go downstairs and hope like hell I did it right and Roddy Tebbit's liver does not explode and end up in everyone's grey water.

Then I go down to the lake.

I walk along the bank and wonder what Roddy Tebbit wanted in there. Did he think he was going to find Lillian's body, mummified by the cold? That Stefan would be such an amateur?

What else, I wonder, might he have seen in the depths that someone might want to hide? Illegal dumping? Am I chasing round after ghosts, while some two-bit garbage operation finishes cleaning up their mess? That's the trouble with this city. It's hard to know what's real.

I sit by the food truck and look away from Chersenesos towards the farther shore. The menu, on a metal board, swings in the breeze, and I read it even though I know it off by heart. The breaded shrimp is awful because they bring it overland. The lake fish tastes of lake and in the winter there's always something grimy about it, as if the fish get dusty when the soil flows down the mountain-sides. Maybe they do: there's green chalk water running in a great plume from the Vidderfluss under the Tappeny Bridge. But people don't come here for the food. It's an outdoor speakeasy. Liam will service alcohol at any hour of the day or night, to anyone.

This is where Donna plays backgammon: a blind old woman with steel-white hair raking in the money from anyone dumb enough to bet her. She says she can smell the dice, that she's like the Pinball Wizard, except she makes it pay. I think she runs the odds in her head and knows the board like a fox knows geese.

"I need a solve."

"Take me out to dinner."

"You don't eat."

"But I drink, Cal. I drink plenty."

She does. It's like watching an old sailing ship drown in flat water.

"How about I buy you a starter and you have a look at what I've got?"

Money changes hands. Not much. Not enough, for what I'm getting. She knows that. She knows what she's worth, but that's not how she sees it. She calculates against the next drink. She won't take more. I try to bargain her down, then I subtract what I've spent from a fair price and use the rest to buy food. I send it to her home. She eats whatever she can stomach and gives the rest to the kids who play in the stairwell, because they don't get enough.

Donna sips and I read her the problem off the sheet: the prompt from Roddy Tebbit's liver in Musgrave's stolen file. On paper, it looks like a grid for a crossword puzzle, or maybe a game of Battle-ships. I tell Donna that, expecting her to laugh at me. It's a stupid description of a complex thing, but it's what I have. I used to bring documents in Braille when I wanted her advice, but her hands shake so much half the time she can't read it.

Donna doesn't laugh at me at all. She just nods, like a doctor seeing a bruise. "It's a matrix password," she says.

"A what now?"

"A passphrase which has to be arranged in a particular physical relationship. Some of them have a time constraint too, or a keystroke rhythm. That's called a 'fist.' Don't laugh, those are the hardest to crack. Matrix passwords are a way to get reasonable security out of easily memorable terms." She makes a face. "It's fashionable."

"How do I get past it?"

"Buy me another."

I do. I smell it as I pass it over: Pflümli, Swiss white brandy, like alpine vodka. It burns going down, makes you feel warm, but the tail end is sweet.

"Get your hands off."

I do.

"How do I get past it, Donna?"

"You could brute force it."

"Which would take how long?"

"Depending on how hard whoever locked it was trying, and assuming you're using your usual level of computing power . . . between a hundred hours and about ten thousand years."

"That's not going to work for me."

"A hundred hours isn't that long, Cal."

"And maybe I've got a hundred hours, but I don't have two hundred. I need faster than that."

"Where was the file held? A server?"

A liver. "Somewhere a bit unlikely."

She doesn't care about the deflection.

"So you've already got a layer of security by obfuscation. That's good. That means it's likely not that hard-core. You don't hide something if you think it'll hold up."

"Unless you're paranoid."

"True."

"Can you open it, if I bring it here?"

"No."

"Donna—"

"Not any faster than you. Actually breaking it—that's fiddly. Boring. I'm sure someone can do it. I'm not interested."

"Not interested why?"

"Because I'm fucking lazy, Cal. I'm lazy and I'm an addict and I like it that way. It would take days of sobriety. Long enough for my hangover to catch up with me. Long enough to remember all the things I drink to forget. Maybe even long enough that I'll start thinking about stopping. And it's not necessary. They'll be perfectly simple words. Tricksy, maybe, but simple. They'll be memorable and meaningful. Who hid this and why?"

"I'm not sure."

"Did they want it buried forever?"

"Very much not."

"Was it someone's insurance? Were they scared of it getting out before time?"

"I think they wanted someone to carry on where they left off. Contingency."

"Then it'll be guessable, won't it? All you have to do is be the person they want, not the person they're hiding from."

"That's what I wanted the file to tell me."

"Well, then you're shit out of luck, aren't you? Buy me another."

"No."

"One more, Cal."

"What do I get?"

"My gratitude, of course."

I buy her another because otherwise she'll cry. Then I go back to the office and send the food order before I forget.

I sit at my desk and think about Peter and Lillian until it's time.

The Heraklion is the biggest tower as you walk along the Chersenesos east shore, the one that gets the sun in the morning. On the west side, where people love sunsets, there's the Perseid. It's the same building facing the other way, except that the Heraklion is where Athena has a penthouse. The security is a lot better than it is on my apartment.

"She dropped by my place," I tell Ken the doorman.

"Yes, sir," Ken says.

"It was a movie scene. She sat behind my desk. Surprised me."

"That must have been very dramatic, sir."

"I figured I could pay her back. Just head right on up."

"Yes, sir."

"You're good with that?"

"Of course, sir."

"So I can go right on up?"

"As soon as she confirms, sir."

There are sixteen Tonfamecasca apartments in this building. Figure Ken has seen some shit. Figure Ken is not remotely interested in mine.

I wait for Athena to confirm.

Come on in, Cal," she says. She has a shoe in one hand, something from that Portuguese designer, custom-made for her. The heels have to be flared just before the stiletto tip or the weight of her body will put them through most engineered hardwoods. "I'm just getting ready."

"I don't mean to intrude."

"You're not. Come on in. I've got about forty minutes."

She's wearing a blue silk thing that looks like she stole midnight and wrapped it around her shoulders. I go to sit down in the living room.

"I'm not getting dressed out there, Cal."

"I thought you were done."

"This is a bathrobe. Don't be an ass, get in here."

So I get the chair in the bedroom instead. Athena glances over one shoulder. "Okay, what's up?"

"I need the history."

"We did this. It's not really my thing. You need—"

"Maurice does not like me."

"He's offended on my behalf. It's not that he dislikes you."

"Kinda is."

She picks something out of the wardrobe in silver sequins and dumps the blue thing on the bed. Too late, I shut my eyes. The afterimage of her flashes on my retinas like a shadow cabaret: perfect silhouette stretching. I hear her chuckle, and the sound of something sheer on skin.

"It's safe to look now, Cal."

"I doubt that."

I'm right. She's dressed, but I don't want to touch her any less. She turns her back on me and indicates the zip.

Goddammit, Athena.

I zip her up. I try not to notice the heat coming off her, but I'm clumsy, and the nape of her neck is higher than it was when I used to do this. My fingers brush her spine. She doesn't move at all, or make a sound. The stillness makes it worse. We stand that way, my arm out holding the zip at eye level, knowing it can go down as well as up, and that if I exert the tiniest tug in that direction I will begin something which cannot be stopped.

I can smell her.

I step back. She turns around.

"You're very disappointing, Cal Sounder." She doesn't look disappointed. She looks alive and bright, like a hunting dog seeing a rabbit.

"I know. Will you tell Maurice to behave?"

"No, because he won't. But I'll tell him I don't care who you are, I want him to answer your questions to a reasonable and usable level of detail."

She's his boss. I keep forgetting that.

"If it doesn't work—"

"It'll work."

"If he can't help."

"Okay, that."

"If he can't help, I need to talk to Elaine."

She sighs. "Now, there's someone who really doesn't like you."

"Yeah, but that's fair."

"Why is that fair?"

"She's your mother. She thinks I took advantage of you."

She snorts. "You should try, see what that gets you."

It comes out before I can stop it. "I know what it would get me." Truth. I do. It would get me a life on the far side of the mirror. It would get me Athena, and everything as it was, but in a penthouse like this one, working for Stefan one way or another. Sooner or later I'd be like all of them, and then a little later so would she. The traitor part of me always asks what would be so bad about being a Titan. Everyone wants it. Why not? But I know the answer: there wouldn't be anything bad about it at all. Not for me. I could do good things for the little people forever, for as long as I wanted to.

One lifetime, perhaps. Not two.

Stung, Athena leans down and touches her open lips briefly to mine; not a kiss, but the forerunner, the hanging instant in which you know what's happening, but it has not yet become thing itself. I taste her breath in my mouth. Then she draws away. "I'll talk to Maurice. And yes, Elaine too. Now get out of here. You're testing my resolve."

And mine.

I get out.

The voice on the phone is deep and precise. "Mr. Sounder. You know who this is?"

I do.

"Mr. Nugent."

"Mr. Sounder, I hear there was an unfortunate incident last night."

"Yes. Very unfortunate. I was quite shocked."

"It has caused me some concern. I thought perhaps I wasn't the only person bidding for your services in this matter."

"Funnily enough, I had a similar concern. I thought maybe you'd reached out to a third party. That would be hurtful."

"Yes, of course, if you had nothing to do with the unfortunate situation now evident, you might well think in that direction."

"Now, your Mr. Zoegar thinks we can't work together, you and I. Says there's no trust." I want to ask him about the genetic file stash, but even assuming he tells me something I don't know enough to recognise another lie. They say an investigator should never ask a question they don't already know the answer to, and no doubt that's hilarious but it doesn't make any damn sense.

"Mr. Zoegar is a cynic, sir. I am an optimist. If I extend you my trust in this matter, will I be disappointed?"

"No, Mr. Nugent. I think you will find me extremely effective. But turnabout is fair play. Is there anything you want to tell me about this little commission of yours?"

That's as close as I can get without giving it away.

Doublewide doesn't say anything for the longest time. Figure he actually doesn't like to break his word, which is interesting.

"There is nothing I want to tell you, and in the narrowest sense nothing more you need to know. Do the organs still exist?"

"I have no information for you on that matter at this time."

"I see. Well, then, when you think you have an answer . . . come back to me."

"And if you should think of anything that might assist me in my inquiries—peripheral information of relevance to the case—do please let me know. Anything at all."

"Oh, I shall, sir. I shall."

I don't feel like eating alone, so I go across town and get more Hungarian-Goan takeout. I sit in the back office of Roddy Tebbit's building with Jerelyn the commissionaire, and we eat it and talk about movies. Then we talk about love. Jerelyn has loved a great deal in her life. She has been dumb enough about love that she's wise now. I tell her about Athena without explaining the specifics. She doesn't offer a solution, she just nods and says it's hard. Then we talk about other stuff. Whatever stuff. Two working people making friends on a dark November evening in the city.

If there was any justice, Jerelyn would be on the list to be a Titan. A world full of women like her who lived forever would be a hell of a lot different from this one.

"Everybody thinks that," Jerelyn says when I tell her, shaking her head.

"But do you know, I think I would be every bit as vain and self-ish as the next girl."

"Maybe. Or maybe you'd be about half as vain and selfish, and that half would make a difference."

She threatens me with a spoon. "You are supposed to say of course I wouldn't!"

"You're supposed to say I'm wrong."

She raises the spoon even higher.

In the morning, I go and see Maurice Tonfamecasca. Athena took his job because she's smarter than he is. People tend to dismiss him because he's angry and he's ridiculous. It's worth remembering that angry and ridiculous people can do bad and effective things just like anyone else.

Maurice has an office in Tonfamecasca Tower, right at the tip of Chersenesos. It's a middle-floor office which shares an elevator with any number of ordinary mortal offices, but it's a one third section of the round tower's window space, so he looks out across Othrys and east towards Tappeny Bridge. It's a serious office, with expectations he doesn't meet.

Security makes me walk into a tube door so they can scan me on entry: no explosives, of course, no guns, no chemicals, no biologicals. Rumour has it the bottom disc of these things is like a trapdoor that goes right down into a blast chamber, so that if you're wearing a suicide vest they can drop you and then clean up later. The rumour is true. I've seen the room—though not when in use.

I wince as the guard clamps me: micro-injectile recognition chip, self-limits after twenty-four hours, breaks down into a vitamin shot in your bloodstream. In the meantime the elevators will work and the lights will come on if I use the bathroom. Oh, and if there's a fire, they won't leave me behind during the evac.

"Follow me, please."

Everything in Maurice's office is mahogany and leather; there's barely enough light to see by. He makes the staff wear soft-soled shoes so the whole of his floor feels like a library, and the cleaning crew finish each night shift by rubbing an artificial scent into the furniture: old paper, sealing wax and cigars. He dresses like a newspaper baron or a president, tailored suit with suspenders, Savile Row shoulders, double breasted and single vented. There's an actual baseball bat on the wall, like he stuffed and mounted Al Capone. Visually he's about perfect for the gig: slick hair, broad shoulders, clear over seven feet. They dosed him early, at sixty, because he had some kind of arthritis. He still moves stiffly, but that's probably just the suit.

"Hi, Maurice. You look well."

"And you're still you. I'd offer you a drink, but I don't have any pond water."

"That's okay, I'll serve myself."

There's a jug of fresh orange juice on the bar. I help myself and offer to fill him up with his own booze, and he sneers.

"I don't understand why she continues to tolerate you, Sounder."

"Honestly, nor do I, but she's your boss and she told you to answer my questions."

"Is that what you think?"

"I don't get a whole lot of satisfaction out of talking to you, either, Maurice, so I'm just going to ask and if I don't like the answers I'll go back to Athena and tell her you're ignoring her instructions. Figure she can use that to move you down a few floors and then I'll ask again."

"Get lost."

"You ever meet a Titan scientist named Roddy Tebbit?"

"I did not ever meet him. I hear he was nuts."

"Where'd you hear that?"

"I spoke to Bill Styles. I gather you harassed my cousin Richard."

"Who went to Tebbit because no one in the family gave a shit about him, by the way. How did the good doctor come by his T7?"

"He was on a contract. It was part of the deal."

"Sure, I hear that's completely normal. Say, did you know there's a woman in the typing pool who's like four hundred years old?"

Maurice waves a hand.

"A few decades back, Stefan was a little more relaxed about it. Tebbit had a promising line of inquiry, and Stefan lurched. He's prone to enthusiasms. And sudden disaffection."

"I need detail."

"I don't have it. T7 makes us young again, Sounder, it doesn't make us into savants. You want the detail on Tebbit's contract, talk to HR."

"That's not his name."

"Isn't it? How distressing."

"It wasn't his name when he was working here, either, so if you know enough to tell me the terms of his contract, you know who he was back then."

"Unfortunately, I was lying. Executive bullshit: never admit you don't know. I haven't a clue who he was. Like I said: HR might be able to help."

"What about Peter and Lillian?"

A flicker, deep down in his eyes. "Peter and Lillian who?"

"Researchers. She died, he vanished. Rumour is she and Stefan were stepping out for a while."

"No doubt."

"No doubt they were?"

"No doubt that's the rumour. It's always the rumour. If Stefan is involved, either he or someone else brings sex into it."

He says it like sex is something they only do in the cheap seats.

"So were they?"

"Stefan fucked everyone for over a hundred years. How could I possibly know? When are we even talking about? My lifetime? Before?"

"You're the family historian. You tell me."

He smiles like a dolphin. "All right, I'll get someone to look into the files and have an answer for you as soon as possible."

"Is that supposed to mean tomorrow or next year?"

"Well, let's see: on Roddy Tebbit, I'm just working with a physical description. No names, no time frame. That could be a little vague for anything quick, I'm afraid. And Peter and Lillian, well, at least her name is uncommon. We probably haven't employed more than a dozen of those globally. But a lot of the early records are formatted for a different system, so it'll be a manual job. Still, I should have something for you in a couple of weeks, with a fair wind."

"Athena—"

"Is welcome to take it up with me. I'm sure she wouldn't want to burn significant corporate resources on a favour for a friend. That would be in violation of her fiduciary responsibilities. No, I think she'll just make some noise and get on with polishing my office chair with that ass you can't bring yourself to actually touch any more, however often you manage to kiss it when you need something for your little detective sideshow. No, Sounder, you're a lapdog. Go foul the streets. I have a call."

"Thanks, Maurice. Always a pleasure."

I get in the elevator and push down, but it goes up. I feel my stomach get left behind somewhere around the fortieth floor. When the doors open, I look into a room like a madman's cathedral.

I step through onto a dark wood floor covered with Isfahan silks. The walls are made of faceted smoke crystal. The ceiling, triple height, is a single domed piece of the same stuff polished en cabochon. It must have been custom-made. There are cherry trees growing in pots the size of a compact car, and I can hear birds singing, sweet and high and clear. In the sunken lounge area there's a fountain and a circle of sofas, and away by the wooden doors that lead out onto a terrace that's almost as big as the room itself there's a piece of solid granite cut into the shape of an enormous desk.

I walk down to the fountain. When he speaks, I realise he's been there watching me all along, and that I knew it because I could hear him, but he's so huge my brain simply didn't process him as alive. Stefan is twice the size of a normal human, almost four metres high and broad in proportion. Baseline, he was thickset, a wrestler rather than a dancer; after four doses of T7 he gives substance to the word his process made famous. For now he looks fifty years old, olive skin weathered like a Tyrol mountain climber or a wandering god: cragged and honey-haired and vast. He wears a pair of slacks in dark grey with a white shirt open at the neck.

His voice hurts, even when he whispers: notes of infrasound, like they use for riot control, produced naturally in his chest.

"Hello, Cal," Stefan Tonfamecasca says. "I think it's time we had a little chat."

Something to drink?" The decanters buzz when he speaks. I wonder if he can still get the tops off with those fingers. It must be like taking a splinter out using your nails.

"I'm good."

"Have something. I'm going to."

He is, too; a pint mug of whisky, and it looks like an eggcup in his hand.

"Now, Cal . . . now that we're comfortable. I'm not feeling the love. You've forgotten me, here in my tower. Or you're too busy to call. Normally, you'd come and see me immediately with something like this. Mm?"

His voice is just so huge. He's a four-time doser, twice for age and twice more for serious injury, one time in a racing car on his private track and once when a hired killer actually got line of fire and put three .505 Gibbs rounds into him. The gun was just powerful enough to break through the density of the ribs and reach the meat. Now, I don't think it would even trouble him. He moves like something geological more than human. It doesn't matter how vast his muscles are, the bones are too heavy, and his heart's expansion can't match the sheer scale of the body. If he gets dosed again, he'll be effectively paralysed, but right now, he's the largest human being alive. The pitch, when he speaks, reverberates in your lungs and makes it hard to breathe. I'm timing my inhalations to his pauses.

"You're talking about Roddy Tebbit."

"I am. The fire at the police building, Cal. Very distressing. Particularly for me, having to find out that you were investigating the murder of a Titan. And not just any Titan. A rogue of some kind."

"I should have come to you sooner."

"I thought that was our deal, Cal."

"I wanted to get some things straight first."

The impact from the laugh is awful. A big wave on the beach, hitting you unawares; standing too close to an artillery cannon, or the speaker at a rock concert; the blast from a bomb. It's not just the ears, it's the whole body that hates it.

"Such as whether his donated organs were a medical miracle, perhaps? You weren't indulging your knightly fantasies for some sick child, were you?"

"As far as I know, T7 organs are just big."

"As far as anyone knows. I go out of my way to avoid speculation on that topic. Can you imagine if the common man came to believe that a Titan pancreas might heal grandma's Alzheimer's? Or daddy's cancer? Some misguided soul would inevitably try to haul one of us off for vivisection, and there'd be all kinds of outcry over what I did then."

The long speeches are like holding the bag for a heavyweight with fast hands. Wham wham wham. Whamwhamwham.

"That's under control."

"The organs were destroyed, then?"

"I can't confirm that yet."

"It seems to me there's a great deal you can't confirm these days."

"Ain't that the truth."

The laugh, again, genuine and no less agonising.

"Athena didn't give you up, Cal. I happened to talk to Maurice and hear you were coming in. I can't believe she has time for you right now. She's managing a very tricky negotiation with Beijing. I'm always amazed by how many plates that woman can keep spinning. Why don't you just marry her and make her happy? It'd be a weight off everyone's mind."

"Weight's exactly the problem."

"I never met a man so determined to do himself down. Billions of souls on the planet begging to be admitted to my house, and here you are like a cat in the doorway. Don't want to go out, won't come in. Why did you really wait so long to get in touch?"

Classic interrogator's switch, bringing the topic back to where he wants it, but Stefan does it with a Titan twist: the long speech and then the pause so I can breathe. Once, Twice. Stefan shrugs: humans. So fragile.

"You were cutting the ribbon on an Atlas Suite at St. Helen's that night."

"Oh." As if that had not occurred to him. "Yes, I suppose I was. Filthy, petty occasions. I go along, fiddle with a pair of human scissors like daddy playing with dolls." He holds up his hand, huge fingers, peers at them. "Then the hospital board wants to talk about what good work they do and perhaps I'd like to endow a wing or something. Like building an extension on an anthill. They trot out some pretty doctors. Maybe in the hope that I'll want to fuck one of them, or feel some kind of nostalgia for the time when I would have, and sign a cheque with my erection."

More laughter, louder. Instinctively I keep putting my hands up in front of me, trying to push it away. Stefan pretends not to notice, but his eyes are big enough that I can see the glint of satisfaction even though he's trying to hide it.

"But you didn't hang around. You left early."

"Did I?"

"Yes. You got a call and you left. It looked urgent."

"Gosh. Then presumably I raced across town and beat your man Tebbit to death with a baseball bat."

"You know he was shot."

"I do. You can't seriously imagine I killed him."

"No."

I can hear him exhale as he leans towards me, feel the sheer density of his body blotting out other sounds as he comes down on one knee to look into my face, and the vast arm, as big as I am, reaches to the ground to support him. His mouth is big enough to engulf my face.

"I don't really give a shit whether that's true, Cal, but it's nice that you're still smart enough to say it. No, I didn't kill him. Tebbit was a researcher for me for a while. Long time ago now, in your terms. When his contract ended, we gave him his money and sent him on his way."

"Tebbit's not his name. You know that, too."

"I don't remember, Cal. Perhaps that's fragmentary T7 amnesia—you know how we old ones get—or maybe he just wasn't very important. If I wanted to, I could look him up. If a friend were asking, as it were."

"Or a judge."

Stefan can't exactly twitch. His muscles contract and very

slowly his head rocks back, like a giant tortoise touching something it doesn't like.

"Feeling your oats, Cal? Whatever has got into you, all of a sudden?"

"You may as well tell me, Stefan. I'm going to find out."

"Perhaps I don't feel like helping you. You don't help me, any more, it seems."

"Okay, I'll ask Maurice again. Put the screws into him."

"Cal," Stefan sounds delighted, "have you got something on my nephew? Come on, let's gossip. You can tell me. He's so achingly up-tight I sometimes think he's had some sort of surgery. Is it shameful? Does he stand on street corners in Tappeny Bridge selling himself to all comers in the hope of just once feeling he's finally done an honest day's work? Do you know, if he did, I'd actually have some respect for that. No, Cal, it's no good. Maurice doesn't know. He'll try to cover that up, of course. Waste a lot of your time. Did he give you that line of shit about file formats? We made a weasel into a Titan with that boy. Jeanine's fault entirely, my sister dotes on him. I'm hoping that the passage of time will change him into something more interesting, but honestly I think he'll just mummify in his own sense of entitlement."

"So I'll ask Elaine."

His head comes around so fast I can hear the muscles strain to hold it.

"That won't do at all, Cal."

"Then you tell me."

"I don't really take direction from the quick, Cal. You want to remember that. Athena likes you, but even if you married her I wouldn't expect it to last more than a few decades. You're inflexible. Time will grind you down. She, on the other hand, is perfect. Made for immortality. In three or four lifetimes, she'll be better at this than I am. But you . . . by then, you'll be a distant memory. She might still have a photograph of you, but she won't really care. She'll remember one time you had sex, and that it was good, but not why; she'll remember one time you fought, and that it made her sad, but not what it was about. If I kill you, she'll remember being angry with me, but that will wash away in time. I'm her father, and you're a mayfly. When everyone else your age is gone, she'll feel differently about it."

"You're full of shit."

"I don't think I am, Cal, and nor do you."

"Peter and Lillian. Who were they?"

Stefan's head cocks to one side and he almost smiles. "A fairy tale. There was a Lillian, of course. Pretty girl. She had the same last name as one of our scientists at the time, but they weren't related. There was a tabloid story, and as usual they got it all wrong. The wicked Titan and the married genius. All so very meaty, below the fold. For my part, I mostly remember some pneumatic fucking. That woman was a delight. She crawled all over me, called me her god. Brought friends to play. Vice can be like that: it enjoys seeing the place where its degradation is indistinguishable from its triumph, and ecstasy swallows them both. And then one day—did she get bored? Or did I? She lived happily ever after, anyway, and I—I barely recall her face, or whether I liked her, just as Athena will forget you. Hmm? Well, it's not important. Find out about the organs, Cal. Destroy them or hand them over to security here. Give my regrets to the Travis. Tell me when it's done."

"I'll let you know if I have any further questions." I get up to leave. Stefan's hand stops me, like walking into a glass door.

"I gave you instructions, Cal. You need to understand that. I wasn't asking a favour. I was telling you what you need to do."

"I don't work for you, Stefan."

"Of course, you do. Everyone does. Let me remind you who you're talking to." The laugh again, long and loud and so close, and I realise he knows what it does, how much it hurts. He leans down into my face, and the waves hit me one by one. He carries on, battering me backwards with just the sound of his contempt until I fall onto the carpet and he stands over me and roars.

"I am STEFAN TONFAMECASCA!"

If the laughter was bad the shouting is like a kind of death. My ribs flex and my heart skips a beat on each word. The world goes silent, and red: blood vessels breaking in my eyes. I see him watching, face peering into mine as the world falls in around me from the edges, and I go away.

The world comes back slow. I can smell perfume: jasmine mixed with something sporty. Someone's looking in my eye with a torch.

I say: "What?"

I hear noise and it hurts, like when you're a kid and you get an earache. I turn my head and there's that bubbling sound, and more pain. Low-grade damage, from excessive volume.

I say: "Shit."

Speaking hurts too. In fact everything hurts, but nothing hurts the bad way, when you know you're broken. It just hurts like it fucking hurts.

The person with the torch speaks again. They tell me to stay still. They have kind hands. I let them do kind things for a while.

"Athena?"

"Don't try to talk, Cal."

Not Athena. A man's voice, kinda ticked off.

"Is she here?"

"Cal, it's Marcus. From St. Helen's."

Marcus the nurse.

"Am I in hospital?"

"No, you're in your apartment. You're also an idiot. What did I say about washing the lattice?"

"Am I going to have a sphincter mark?"

"You'll be lucky if we don't have to start over, the state of you. Stay still."

I stay still. Marcus works on the putty lattice. I don't even have enough energy to sass him. Damn it.

"Hold this."

I reach out.

"Not you, Cal."

"Got it." A woman's voice.

"Sporty jasmine," I say.

"Is he delirious?"

Marcus laughs. "No, honey, that's you he's talking about. Keep your eyes closed, Cal, I'm using the curer."

A flash of white purple, long and hot. Bullet hole itches again, feverish, then a hiss as Marcus sprays something topical over the top.

"Don't inhale that or you won't be able to smell anything for hours. Just let it clear away for a second."

I hold my breath. It's hard.

"And you're done. You want to open your eyes now, Mr. Detective?"

I open my eyes. Marcus looks tired and grouchy, which I figure is where he lives. There's an open medical bag resting on my night stand and I'm lying looking up at my own ceiling, my sky. Over by the door is a woman in a business suit which must be bespoke because it fits perfectly and there's no off the peg place that sells for that shape, not even here, and not even now. I look at her face and try to place it, and then I do.

"Well, hi."

"Hi, yourself," says Mini the wannabe.

"What's she doing here?" I ask Marcus.

"Search me, Cal, it's your apartment."

"Who called you?"

"She did."

"What the fuck is going on?"

Marcus just looks down at me like he's really tired, and then starts to laugh. It's a good laugh, with no malice in it, and nothing happens to my body when it touches me.

"I really do not know the answer to that one. You two kids talk out whatever is going on. I am going home and I am going to bed."

"Can I get up?"

"Do you want to?"

"No."

"Then yes you can, so long as you are sensible."

"I'm always sensible."

"I don't actually think you know what that word means. You're fine, by the way. You're bruised and you may get some nausea, but there's no serious damage that wasn't there already. Take it slow, but yes, you can move around if you feel like it."

"Great."

"Oh, but if you rip that thing out again you can just put some tape over it, I am not doing this a third time." His eyes close for a moment. "Cal, are you . . . okay for some bad news?"

"Yeah." He's going to tell me it'll scar. I can live with that.

"Susan Green died."

"She what?" My witness. The singer.

"She died, Cal."

"No, she was stable." She was nice.

"Yeah. She was stable and then she deteriorated, and she died."

"She died?" I can hear myself repeating the words.

I know objectively that it happens—I see it happen all the time—and yet death remains incomprehensible: the line where the meaning of things just stops, and the universe carries on. The root of all Stefan Tonfamecasca's power is not a lie: he defies this moment. He's not wrong.

There are words that you say because they are the closest humans have ever come to encompassing death.

"I'm sorry."

Marcus nods. "She wasn't mine."

"Like you don't take it personally anyway."

"I don't."

"Nor do I."

Liars, lying to one another badly for comfort in the face of something that just is.

———

Marcus leaves me alone with Mini.

I say: "So, hi."

Mini says "Hi."

I wait for her to say something else.

She says: "Do you . . . want coffee or something?"

"Yes. Coffee. Exactly."

I roll on my side and let my legs drop down to the floor. I feel the lattice tug and figure that would have hurt if the whole area wasn't asleep for now. I walk into the kitchen and Mini doesn't try to prop me up. She just trails along behind like a puppy. I pack the jug with ground coffee and put it on the stovetop. Someone's searched the kitchen, but pretty professionally, so they've put everything back.

Great. I look at Mini.

"How're your eyes?"

She looks at me blankly. I get the feeling Mini has a lot on her mind.

"What? Oh. Fine. Dirty trick, though."

"I didn't want to get nasty."

"That wasn't nasty?"

I tell her the truth. "No."

I give her a cup of coffee and we sit in my kitchen at the little pine table.

"Mini short for anything?"

She looks away. "Taormina."

"Okay, then, Taormina. What are you doing in my apartment?"

"I came to your office. I was leaving, but then you arrived. You weren't . . . in great shape."

I do, I think, remember the stairs, the walk from the car. I made it to the first landing and there wasn't anything left in my legs. Did I throw up? No idea. I sat there and leaned my back against the wall and—yeah. Someone came.

"You saw the discharge sheet from St. Helen's. You called and got Marcus."

"Yes. I hope that was okay."

"Lady, why don't you just say what you came here to say. We

did not get off to the best start and now you're here in my apartment and I'm all kinds of fucked up. Just . . . get to it. Please."

"I wanted to make a deal."

"If it's a plea deal, you're talking to the wrong guy."

"It's not a plea deal," she snaps, but she looks brittle and maybe
even scared.

"If it's a sex deal I'm not interested in that either."

"You made that clear, thank you."

"Well, sorry. Now I'm just being an asshole because I feel like
hell. Come on, Ms. Denton. What've you got?"

"I know something you probably want to hear. I want—I wanted
something in exchange."

"What's my end?"

"I wanted you to train me." She turns her head away.

"To fight whom?" Zoegar the grammar freak would be pleased
with himself.

"An opponent bigger and stronger and heavier than I am. In a
confined space."

"But now you look at me and you're not sure."

"Someone messed you up pretty good, Mr. Sounder."

"I got shot."

"That was before. When you came to Victor's."

"Marcus told you?"

She stares at me. "Are you kidding? Everyone knows that. Victor
ran the security footage over dessert. It was basically the first thing
I saw after I got the lipstick out of my eyes."

"Gee, thanks, Vic."

"I guess you guys are friends or something. I feel kind of stupid
for what happened."

"Yeah, you ought to. More than stupid. That was some coercive
shit."

"I know."

"You're fucking lucky Victor didn't just cancel your sub-
scription."

"She never has before."

That's a surprise, sort of. Maybe they've been escalating. Maybe Victor's getting a little bit less picky in her old age. I hope not. The club runs on a high wire between vice and horror, and she's what keeps it up there. If she slips, it'll get really bad.

"How long have you been going?"

"A few months. Mac got us in. Business thing."

"What you tried on me . . . If that's your jam I'm not teaching you shit."

The brittle look again. "It's not. Who did this to you?"

I tell her the truth. "Stefan."

For a cold minute, I swear, she's about to ask "Stefan who?" and then she gets it.

"You fought Stefan Tonfamecasca?"

"No."

"But you said—"

"He laughed at me, Ms. Denton. He got right up in my face and he laughed hard enough to cause bruising. That's the track you're chasing so hard. That's what it means that we have Titans in the world. It has nothing to do with your aerobicised ass muscles, however great they are. A four-dose Titan isn't just a big guy with a nine-figure bank account. When they talk about the speciation rich that's not a political metaphor. It's just the truth."

"So they're unbeatable."

"No. Titans fight at Victor's from time to time. Sometimes they lose. First-dosers, mostly. You want to beat a Titan like Stefan, you drop him in the lake without a breather pack."

"What?"

I shrug. "Titans past the second dose can't swim. Too much bone, not enough flotation. What do you care, anyway? You want to impress them, not smack them down. Seriously, catch your Titan with honey."

"Did you try that on Stefan Tonfamecasca?"

"Oh, well, nothing works on that bastard."

Not even saving his favourite child from certain death. Not any more, evidently. And on that note why isn't Athena here? She must know what happened. Why isn't she here? Is Stefan keeping her away?

Or does she not want to come?

"Will you teach me?" Mini says.

"What's the tip?"

"Mac fessed up this morning. Someone put him onto you. He . . . set me up. I don't feel great about that."

"Pretty sure he's done that before."

"Oh, shut up," she snaps. "Don't fuck me around. Okay? I can go anywhere and get fucked around. I can go home if I want that. Just fucking say yes or kick me out."

Oh.

I can go home if I want that.

"That kind of depends, Ms. Denton, on what you want me to teach you."

"I just told you."

"You asked if it was possible to beat a Titan and I said it was. Is that what you want to learn? Or do you want to know how to deal with your asshole husband?"

She stares at me, and then she turns and runs.

I think I may be the asshole in this picture.

A new voice says:

"Am I interrupting?"

I turn around and find Athena in the doorway, making it look low and narrow. Today I can't help but see the line of Stefan's cheek, the sharpness of his gaze in hers, but Athena still moves as if she belongs in the world. She glances back after Mini.

"Who's the gym rat?"

"Is that nice?"

"Don't tell me that's my competition, Cal. I'd be a little offended."

"Athena . . . I am very tired and very bruised. Mini Denton is—not even a client. She's a source. I think she wants me to help her stand up to her husband."

"What makes her think that's your thing?"

"I guess she's met me."

Laughter, like lake water more than thunder. "That is fair."

"She's the wife from the fight cage at Victor's. Mac Denton being the husband."

"She's the one you lipsticked? I heard about that. Would it have killed you to use the cheap shot on him and treat her with a little respect?"

"I did. If I'd gone the other way around I might have lost. She's much smarter than he is. And then I would have been on the hook to have sex with her."

She snorts, coming into the room. "Fate worse than death."

I think about Susan Green, hanging in the air above the car that ran us down. The sound of the shots that went into her. "Not really."

It turns out I'm crying suddenly, which detectives do not do.

Athena puts her arms around me and rocks me gently from side to side. Her hair smells of a plain, ordinary shampoo, something with fake melon and honeysuckle. It's the one she's always used.

"I'm sorry, Cal."

"Not your fault."

"I mean I'm sorry about Stefan."

"That's not your fault either. In fact kind of the opposite, if you think about it."

"He's just—"

"No, he isn't. He does what he does. He means to do it. The whole world deals on his terms. I don't have a problem with that."

"Yes, you do."

"Yes, I do."

But not so much of one that I'm gonna give him up to Double-wide, not yet—because who the fuck knows what damage that guy is carrying around that he'd make us all sit for? Better the devil you know.

Better no devil at all, but that's just crazy talk.

"Why did he leave the party?"

"What?" She cocks her head. Her hair falls differently now, from that slightly bigger head. Still beautiful, but changed.

"At St. Helen's. He was cutting the ribbon on an Atlas Suite, and he left about the time Roddy Tebbit was killed."

"Did you ask him?"

"He fobbed me off. I can't exactly make him tell me things."

"Nor can I."

"I asked him about Peter and Lillian, too."

"Who are Peter and Lillian?"

"Supposedly Lillian was Stefan's lover."

"Then she probably was. When?"

"Sometime."

"Jesus, Cal, that's specific. This is what you wanted to ask Maurice?"

"Maurice doesn't know. At least, Stefan says he doesn't. He says I also can't ask Elaine."

Athena looks away. "My mother's difficult right now."

"Difficult how?"

"Just difficult."

Which is a little terrifying, because it's not like she's ever been easy. Athena's playing cat's cradle with her fingers. I wait.

"That's why Stefan left that night. She was upset. Maurice couldn't calm her down and he couldn't get me."

"Where were you?"

"On a date."

"Oh."

"You asked. I didn't get the message until later, so he called Stefan."

"Everyone calls Stefan."

"Yes. You did."

I did.

"He thinks she may need an early T7 dose. Some kind of dementia. Not a side effect, even. Just the old-fashioned kind."

"I didn't think that happened."

"If it can happen to a normal person, it can happen to us, Cal. You know that. We just have a cure-all that costs the moon and takes us out of the world."

"How far out of the world?"

Because I'm never sure, and I've always been afraid to ask.

She reaches out to touch my face. I should move away, make the point. I don't. I try to put my hand over hers, and realise, again, that my fingers aren't that long.

"Cal?"

"Yeah."

"It was a shitty date."

We sit like that for a while until I remember I'm a detective.

"Can you ask her to talk to me?"

"Elaine?"

"Yes."

"I can try."

"Without Stefan finding out?"

She pulls back her hand, tilts it this way, that way, and I wonder what Stefan will do to me if the coin comes down tails.

I say: "Ask."

Athena leaves with a promise that she'll check in on Elaine and maybe ask about Lillian, or maybe not, depending. I lie in bed with sporty jasmine on one side and Athena shampoo on the other, and sometime in the dark I lose track of both of them, and I see Susan Green again, just before the car hits.

"Harpo," she says, quite clearly, as if it's important.

I wake up sure that it is.

Groucho, Zeppo, and Harpo, and people who think they're funny throw in Karl.

I put on a coat for a dressing gown and go to my office. Someone's been in here, too, less discreet but still professional. They don't care if I know, but they're not in a hurry and they don't want me to get any clues from what they're looking for that might take me to what I'm looking for.

Round and round we go.

I fire up the terminal and the file from Roddy Tebbit's encrypted liver. I slot the names into the matrix, and it doesn't work. There's no drama about it, the file just doesn't open.

I really thought that would work.

I try juggling them around and then I fire up an anagram maker and try that.

Go carpophore hobo

And so on.

I fall asleep again there, in the chair, and if I dream again, when I wake I don't remember.

S tanding in the lobby of Roddy's building waiting for the elevator.

"Jerelyn?"

"Yes, my darling."

"Roddy ever talk about old movies with you? The Marx Brothers?"

"I don't think so."

Someone's holding the elevator on floor six. Jerelyn says the Millers are going away for a long weekend. "Mr. Miller never learned to pack light."

The light doesn't move.

"How about Rufus?"

"How about him, what?"

"You think he could have done it?"

"Why would you think so?"

I tell Jerelyn about the hair. She makes a face.

"That is disgusting."

"It is, isn't it?"

"That man."

"You think he did it?"

"Yes. Absolutely. Arrest him."

"You think?"

"No, but now I absolutely wish that I did. Hair. Oh my god. My hair?"

"Everyone's hair. But probably women he finds attractive."

"Now I'm offended as well as revolted. Personally and on behalf of the sisterhood."

"You don't need to take a vote?"

"There is a mystical democratic connection which binds all women together. Also: do you hear what you just told me?" She shudders, then laughs. "Collecting hair. Eeeeyuch."

The elevator arrives, and I step in.

I walk into Roddy Tebbit's apartment and look around. I look for old media: discs and optical storage, even tape. I look for a backup hard drive. Something more accessible than the genetic stash, something for every day. Usually when you do this you're looking for the disreputable collection, the ordinary things someone doesn't want you to know. The cheap bikini snaps, the long-cherished personal nudes with old lovers. Sometimes it's a fetish. Sometimes it's darker than that.

Roddy Tebbit doesn't have much of anything to be nervous about, that I can find. I go into the bric-a-brac again looking for pictures, for history. Postcards from Italy: a bronze boar from Florence, the Vatican in Rome. An appallingly erotic Psyche and Eros. Three or four of Canova's Perseus Triumphant, holding Medusa's head in one hand and that weird hooked sword in the other. I remember the picture of Roddy in Susan Green's sketchbook. I was wrong: not Achilles. And not Medusa, in Susan's drawing, but a bearded Zeus. Figure it's a stand-in for Stefan. We've all felt like that from time to time.

Roddy Tebbit had lost his wife. Everyone says so. You'd think he'd keep something. But when someone dies—especially when someone dies and their spouse is going to live for a whole other lifetime—often the survivor doesn't need or want to be reminded. You think of widows' houses as full of pictures of the dead, but many times they're not. Many times they look towards the future as if the past is just last winter's snow.

I keep looking. Some arthouse snaps of another city, could be anywhere, just as easily Istanbul as Denver. Come to that it could be both: holiday snaps all jumbled up. Friends. Group shots, low def. Good enough for a facial match maybe, if not Roddy then someone he knew. Maybe I can triangulate. But that's the trouble with all that technological crime solving: it costs money. It costs energy and heat and time, and there's always someone—usually a government—that has a higher-priority ticket than you do.

Nothing else. No Marx Brothers. No clues—or maybe they're all clues, and I'm just not much of a detective.

I sit in Roddy's lounger and look out at the city.

Be the person he wants, Donna said. Not the person he's hiding from.

Who are you, then, Roddy?

Are you Peter?

Are you someone else?

What did you really want here?

Why are you dead?

Well, why is anyone?

Money.

Sex.

Power.

Same thing, in the end.

5

The car comes at midday and it's long and black. I still feel like I've been holding pads for Jimmy Sledgehammer Givens but I get in and try not to make a noise that sounds like "oof." Athena helps me with the seat belt, and I let her because I need the help and I can pretend I'm just inappropriately enjoying her body brushing against me for a few seconds while she reaches for the clip.

I'm persuasive enough that she lingers for a second, and when she turns away I feel her smile.

The driver doesn't say anything, but you can tell he wants to.

The road winds on and around to the north shore, up into the foothills at the edge of the forest. I'm expecting a gate and a palace, but I'm wrong. There's just a dirt track, and green trees all around, then a wood-frame zero-impact house half hanging over a gorge, and in the house: Elaine.

She looks different from when I last saw her. Older and stranger. She's still beautiful, like a movie star whose smile always fills the screen. She must have been small originally, because she's still only big: broad in the shoulder and thin as if she doesn't eat enough, long chestnut hair down around her shoulders. She's wearing army surplus and for a wonder I'm pretty sure it actually is, not something from the Chersenesos military chic which was popular last year. Just a black T-shirt and a green jacket, and a pair of trousers with those giant pockets. Military pattern boots, too, but those are a little less spartan. There's a flash of red at the ankle and I can see padding.

She puts her arms around Athena and glowers at me.

"What's he doing here?"

"I brought him," Athena says.

"He's like Maurice. Always hanging around."

"No, mother. That's me. Cal runs away."

Ow.

Elaine gazes at me or through me for a while, then up into the sky. The moment stretches. I wonder if she's going to fall asleep, or just stand there until she gets moss growing on her. She doesn't seem to be aware of us at all. Athena waits. You can't see anything on her face that says she hates this moment, fears what it means, but she does.

Elaine turns around and stomps inside. "Come on, then."

The last time I was in her house, it was a different house and a different Elaine. It was a pool party and she wore a swimsuit with cutaways around the belly button and hips, and huge black sunglasses that made her look half like a rock star and half like an alien in an old movie. Maurice Tonfamecasca was there too. He could barely take his eyes off her, palpable sexual desire radiating from him as he watched her walking around, assembling a map in his mind of the body under the suit. She was Stefan's unattainably glamorous ex, giddy and hugely popular survivor of years of Titan-style debauchery. There was a feature in *Time,* and rolling coverage in *Paris Match.* That was years ago.

It occurs to me to wonder whether she's had some work done on her face—just enough, and expensive enough, so that you might not think of it. That Elaine might have. This one . . . I don't think so.

Athena nods to the doorway.

"Let's go."

She waits a moment, and when I don't move, she shrugs and leads the way.

Inside the house is like the apartment you always thought you'd have one day: clean lines and ample space for furniture that looks comfortable and yet perfect; wide windows looking out over the forest and the lake. There's a fire pit for actual logs, so well done you can barely see the extractor and the filter unit, the long pipe down to the plant room where the carbon gets molded into little black bricks and taken away once a week by the service company. I can smell pine smoke lingering in the air, the way it used to when I was a kid in the mountains. It's like being ten years old again.

Athena's mother makes gin cocktails and pours them into thick earthenware cups. She leads us out onto the rear deck, which looks down into a canyon, water rushing down towards the lake. There are birds here, lots of them, and a late season bug drifting up from the spray to bother Athena's hair and bumble away again when she shoos at it with her hand.

"How have you been?" Athena says.

"Pretty good."

"How are the bears?"

"Fine." Elaine sips at her cup, then again, harder.

"I heard they got interested in your garbage."

"I talked to them. Now we understand one another."

I see Athena tense, and realise Elaine's speaking literally. She went out and had a conversation with the local bears. A third-dose Titan could probably do that just fine. Stefan, at four, could pat them around like cubs. Elaine's not there yet. I picture her standing in a circle of bears, making bear noises she thinks are words, and the bears trying to figure out why the fuck they haven't eaten her yet, and then the moment when they just do. Athena is seeing the same thing.

"Just like that?"

"Yes. Just like that." Another swallow. I try mine. It's strong. She's drinking faster than I would. She's bigger than me, but not that much bigger.

"Next time, let's maybe get one of the wildlife rangers to help."

"Oh, those people." Elaine shrugs. "They think bears are just animals."

"Mother, that's what they are. They're animals. Big and very beautiful, but dangerous, too."

"What the fuck is he doing here?"

The change of tack comes seamlessly. Maybe it's not a change at all, and there's a perfect connection in her mind, clear and crisp.

"He wants to ask you something."

"Yes, of course he does."

"I said he could try."

"Making promises for me?"

"Just for me. I didn't promise you'd answer."

"Please tell me he's at least using you for sex as well." Athena's face doesn't change, but I know that hurt.

"Just . . . will you listen?"

"All right, then, boy. What is it?"

"Lillian and Peter."

She sits very still for a while, looking out at the canyon.

"You . . . have some balls to ask me about that." She almost sounds approving.

"I don't know anything about it. There's been a murder, and it keeps coming up."

"It would."

"Stefan doesn't want me to ask you."

"Hah. No. That old bastard would much rather never hear those names again. What did he say?"

"That she was wonderful. That they were lovers. Then they weren't. That there was a tabloid story, because she had the same last name as one of the scientists working at the company."

"Well, then you know it all."

"I don't think I do."

"All of that is true."

"But not complete."

"If you want detail, I'm sure there's a sex tape somewhere. There's always a sex tape."

"Did he murder her?"

She lifts her eyebrows up very high, like I'm a dog that juggles. "I've changed my mind about your friend, Athena. He's more interesting than I remember. Darker and colder."

"Please. Did Stefan murder Lillian?"

Elaine doesn't answer for the longest time.

"No, boy. He saved her. Until he didn't."

"Saved her from what?"

But Athena's mother closes her eyes and drops her head back onto the cushion, and a moment later she's asleep. The earthenware cup rolls out of her hand onto the deck, and doesn't break. The gin pours away between the boards. I wonder if the bears come up in the night and lick it from the stones in the canyon beneath.

In the car on the way back, we sit carefully folded away from each other, as if Elaine is still watching.

"Thank you," I say, as Athena drops me off.

"That's fine, Cal."

"She'll be okay."

"Yes, she will. Her next dose will take care of it, and she'll be herself again."

"Don't wait too long."

"I thought you didn't like T7, Cal."

"I don't like what it does to the world. But she's sick and that makes you unhappy. I don't like that, either. I can't fix the world. You can fix Elaine. I don't have a problem with that."

I get out of the car, and she waves, and then we're going different ways again.

There's a reason the word is "gumshoe." I turn my back on Chersenesos and put one foot in front of the other, heading south and east. The farther you get from the lake shore, the older the houses get, and the darker the streets. In this city, the old town is whatever's left in the hinterlands, where it's not worth spending the money to knock something down. There are pretty townhouses here you can get for a song, because no one rich wants to be this far from the water, or from the towers on the point. If you're going to live in the city, you live in the neon, not the dark. Out here, some of the original Othrys and the original people still live something like the way they did. And also out here there's a bar that used to be called Lacarte's.

When I first came back to the city, Lacarte's was a cellar with aspirations, but like a lot of things those aspirations have been around for a while without getting any younger. The original Lacarte was a gnarled French Canuck with a gambling habit, on the run from his ex-wife and maybe some bad smuggling decisions somewhere between Jammu and Sierra Leone. I don't know, I didn't ask, and for a wonder, no one ever told me. He died anyway, of bone cancer, about five years back, and for a while Lacarte's looked like going with him. The nephew who took it on fitted it out nice in pursuit of one of those property booms that's always just about to happen in Tappeny Bridge, and when it didn't come he took the operating account and moved on, leaving nothing but some stained nubuck seat covers and an unpaid staff.

Then one of those things happened that they write about later in local history books. A sullen long-hair named Marto Costanza who worked as a washer-up and daytime cook was in the kitchen when a bunch of construction guys came by for eggs. One of these guys, it turns out, was Marto's brother Matias. Marto made them eggs and told his tale of woe, whereupon a conversation between the brothers took place about fucking landlords and fucking bosses generally. Marto and Matias's friends got pissed and righteous that the Lacarte was going to close, like that was the line. This crappy, gentrified, failed little day drinking spot was the Rubicon that capitalism was no way going to cross.

They just flat out occupied the place. First it was a protest, then an illegal squat for a hundred days, and then a bunch of families got together and bought the nephew out. Marto Costanza got his hair cut and put a red bandanna around each arm, and now he runs the Lacarte Free House and Working People's Hostel. The smoke comes out the door and down the road, and on Saturday nights they sing the "Internationale" at closing time. More dirty communist sex is had in the upstairs rooms of the Lacarte than anywhere else within three thousand miles, and that includes the university.

I know the downstairs scene a little. I don't even hate it. I'm an investigator. You can't do the job without occasionally thinking the whole world is a crime scene. Plus there was one time I had a divorce case—I do have to make money between when some Titan steps in burning shit—and the guy told me after I followed him around half the city that, yeah, he'd been to bed with a woman who lived there on and off, but only that one time, because as they were doing the deed he realised she had a tattoo of Vladimir Ilyich Lenin and it was winking at him every time she moved.

But if you're looking for the Marx Brothers on the shores of Othrys, you could do worse than try the place where Marto and Matias's picture hangs over the bar, and the beer runs red.

I stand across the street for a minute. There's a tricker kid practicing flips under a streetlight, her boyfriend filming. Three steps, kick off the wall, land solid. Go again. Sometimes she does a twist instead, rolling along the chicken wire and coming down like a dancer.

I realise I'm in their shot.

I've always watched them, like birds flying. Now I wonder how many of them scout for Doublewide, how much he sees. How close an eye he's keeping on me.

———

Doorman looks me up and down and throws me some revolutionary socialism like it's a shibboleth. Maybe it is.

"What is to be done?"

"Well, fuck Bernstein, for a start."

Guy laughs. "I like Bernstein."

"You put a gun to my head, I guess *West Side Story*'s okay."

His face wrinkles for a second. "Wait—"

"I'm screwing with you, man. But I gotta be honest, I don't really love the vanguard concept all the way to the top."

He stretches out a fist and knocks it against mine.

"I hear that." And he opens the door.

Inside the place is blue with honest-to-god tobacco. There's a disclaimer about lung cancer and emphysema next to the sign that says they don't give credit. Technically tobacco is illegal now, in a workplace, but the people here aren't exactly the type to run to the cops, and the cops aren't exactly all that interested in busting Lacarte's for a health violation that's only gonna buy them ass ache. It's the house crop, grown in greenhouses outside the city and the workers get a cut of the sticker price rather than being paid for their time. Most of the patrons take it in cheap white clay pipes, so the whole scene looks like a Dutch painting with hippies.

I go to the bar and order a Caledonian red ale. It really is red, too, not cherry but there's no other word for it. It tastes fine, sharp and full of earth. The woman who pours it wears an eyepatch, with a scar running down onto her cheek.

"I don't know you," she says. "I'm Tony."

"Cal."

"You just moved here, Cal?"

"I been around awhile. Too lumpen to come for a drink, maybe."

She laughs. "Long live the revolution, then."

I drink for a while. There's a guy at the end of the bar reading a book. Figure it's going to be more a political text than pulp. Two tables in deep conversation, not looking for company. I get Tony to bring me some bread. When it comes, it's Russian black rye, with oil and pickles and a shot.

"You looking to meet new people?"

"Honestly, I don't know what I'm looking for. One of the brothers around?"

She looks guarded then.

"You got a complaint?"

"Naw, I don't want to rile anybody up. Figure it's polite I talk to one of them. I need something, Tony, and I could not tell you what. But it has to do with this place, maybe, and maybe they can help. If that's a problem, I'll just eat my rye and get the hell out."

"You spoke to them before?"

"One time they had a query. I was able to help out with that." Shortest case of my life: missing person, turned out to be drunk on the roof. "Cal Sounder."

"I'll ask." She retreats into the back room to use the house phone, and the man at the end of the bar sighs and turns his page. I was wrong. It's not a pamphlet, it's poetry.

Marto doesn't have a desk because desks are for fuckpig capitalists. He has a workman's trestle table covered in papers.

"They have machines for that now," I say, pointing.

"Yes, they do," he agrees. "But the automation of labour is a conspiracy of de-humanisation. Work is of our nature. Giving even our chores to the machine saves time at the expense of self."

"Okay."

"What can I do for you, Cal Sounder?"

"This—listen, man, I am not here to make fun, okay? I have a bunch of dumb questions and I don't want you to think I'm messing with you."

"You don't strike me as someone who makes fun."

Man dresses like the bass guitarist in a skiffle band, talks like a priest.

"You know what I do."

"You're the shock absorber. From the Titans' point of view, you stop the masses from realising the extent of their subjugation. You relieve them of the need to exercise raw financial and political power in the protection of their interests where those interests collide with the law. But . . . you also protect ordinary humans from the consequences of that subjugation as best you can. Yours is an equivocal profession. But I hear you're not entirely an asshole."

"That's a five-star review, where I come from."

He chuckles. "Ask your dumb question."

"Does anyone ever call you and Matias the Marx Brothers?"

His eyebrows go up. "I'm sure they do. It's pretty obvious. But not like I know about it. It isn't a thing."

"That doesn't mean anything to you except—"

"Groucho, Zeppo—"

"Yeah."

"No."

"You ever meet a skinny nerd Titan named Roddy Tebbit?"

"I don't meet Titans much at all."

"Roddy Tebbit was some kind of recluse. A doctor at the university. Then he got dead. I heard he was into the Marx Brothers. It might be important."

"He wasn't into us, for sure. You say this guy was tall and thin?"

"Crazy tall, not so broad. Still not little. Yeah."

Marto shakes his head. "I'll ask around, but a Titan, in here? I'd be all over it. The moral rightness of our position persuades even our natural enemies. Or maybe it's the beer. All that shit. You get me?"

I do.

"Used to be we liked stories of the Titans' misdeeds. We would put them out samizdat, shock sheets. Fucking manifestos of condemnation. We were going to wake people to the injustice inherent in the system. All the things you smooth over, we try to highlight.

But those stories don't catch fire any more. Not that no one cares, but they got fatigue, you know? How many times can you read how rich is Stefan Tonfamecasca, how many hospitals that money could buy, how many schools, before you just expect the world to suck that hard? So now we like good stories about how we do, how our way is better, how it's natural. It's slower and less angry, but it works. Little by little, it works."

I don't think it does, but what the hell.

"Thanks for your time, Mr. Costanza."

"Do you like the place?" He gestures.

"Well enough."

"Come back sometime. Bring a friend."

"And if that friend happens to be Athena Tonfamecasca?"

"Then she'll have to sit down very carefully. I don't have any special chairs." But he grins again. "I'll tell the door: Cal Sounder is welcome. You'll find it much more relaxing here than at Victor's, you know."

"Ain't that the truth."

I think about what he said about stories of the Titans' misdeeds. And I think of Elaine: *he saved her.*

Figure you don't get if you don't ask.

"Hey Costanza?"

"Sounder?"

"Who are Peter and Lillian?"

He comes back and sits down. "Ghost story," he says.

Once upon a time—according to Marto Costanza—there was a woman of surpassing beauty who was married to an ordinary man. She was brilliant, he was diligent. They worked for the Titans.

"Because, I mean, it's the only game in town," Marto points out, "Like if you make a success, get crazy rich, the first thing you buy is your dose, isn't it? So any company boss ends up a Titan. Any boss ends up owing his immortality to Stefan Tonfamecasca."

"The house always wins."

"The house doesn't even need to win. There's no game because the house owns everything. The money you bet with, the air you breathe. The myth is that when the wheel spins it's any different from when it's standing still."

Cheery.

So Lillian and Peter worked for the Titans. But that's not right either, because it was all her. Lillian was the driving force, and Peter stood beside her and did the hard work. He was so proud of her, so very proud.

And then Lillian met Stefan Tonfamecasca.

"It was obsession for both of them," Marto says. "Immediate love, like fire that consumes. Peter never had a chance. One day he was the husband, the next he was gone, just out of her life. He was angry. Little bit crazy, maybe. He tried to kill Tonfamecasca."

"How?"

"He hired a gunman. It was a good attempt. Tonfamecasca was wounded. He had to take more T7, before he was ready."

"I know that story."

"Sure, you do. Everyone does. But it's the context that matters. Tonfamecasca grew again. Peter began to think he could force his rival out of humanity that way, by killing him over and over until he was so big he could not survive, or at least, could not function in human society."

"Yeah, a lot of people think that. They don't factor in how much harder it gets each time."

"Ordinary people always underestimate the complexity of revolutions. Revolutionaries, too, of course, but they learn the hard way. And Peter did, too. He tried again."

"He missed."

"Oh, no, he was very much on target. A long gun, this time. He fired from half a mile. Maybe more. The first shot missed, but the second was perfect. A golden shot, like the hand of God."

"Didn't think God had much to say to a socialist."

"God has been a socialist since 1848 when Karl Marx explained things to him. Ever since."

"Did not know that story."

"But Lillian had seen what was happening. It was impossible for her. God is also a romantic. She stepped into the path of the bullet. Perhaps she leaped up to embrace Stefan, perhaps she pulled him down with her ordinary human strength! And he, so used to responding to her commands, bent his head. Surely he would not have done so if he had known what was to come. The bullet . . . struck her. The impact was terrible, the power of the gun, the shot intended for the Titan king. She lost an arm, just torn away at the shoulder, like that. Blood and horror. Peter saw it, through the gunsight, saw her face. He went a little bit mad at what he'd done. He could have taken another shot, but he did not. He fled, his mind burning with remorse and self-hate, so he did not see the next part."

"She didn't die."

"No! Exactly. Tonfamecasca saved her life, of course. Lillian became a Titan because of what Peter had done. She was forever beyond him now. He fled into the night. Fled and disappeared so that even Tonfamecasca could not find him to finish him off. The rage of the Titan king was endless and deep, but even the lightning cannot strike what is not there."

"And what happened to Lillian? He got tired of her? She got to know him better?"

"She married an Argentinian rancher, an old man who just wanted someone to talk to, and did not care for the idea of immortality. He was content that she make love to his gauchos and dance in the moonlight, so long as he was not alone. An amicable reconception of bourgeois heteropatriarchal monogamy."

"And Peter?"

"Peter killed himself and sank into Othrys. It's a human tragedy, is it not? A brilliant scientist ceased to work in her field and was nearly killed; a dedicated husband became a monster and then despaired; a monster became only more himself. This is the meaning of the Titans, Mr. Sounder. Beneath their feet, the fabric of the world is torn, and everything of worth flows into the cracks and drains away, leaving only them, and us, and the stained residue of good things burned in their fire."

"I think if we didn't have Titans we'd just have one another." Athena, talking through my mouth.

"Yes. And you believe that would be just as bad, whereas I believe it would be a miracle. Probably we are both wrong, and it would be something in between. But that is still better than this."

"I feel like you put that together so it would come out that way."

"I did. I'm a propagandist, not your fucking babysitter."

I get tired fast. Subsonic injuries do that, and maybe the beer isn't helping. I still don't have the key to Roddy's file, and I still don't know shit about the whole Peter thing. It makes great mood music, but no one knows—or wants to tell me—where it touches the real. Maybe it's the true and honest history, in pieces. Maybe it's nonsense. Time to find out.

I go back to my office and make the call.

"Hi, Felton."

"Ah, shit. Is that Sounder?"

"It is."

"Sounder, what do you want? Cops are working."

"You got a rookie on shit detail right now?"

"I got your friend Kristoffsen going through the Desk Sergeant's in-tray."

"Fuck she do to get that?"

"She's injured. Got heroic in the fire."

"So now she's doing the worst job you got?"

"Maybe she'll learn something from it about how to not die. Isn't that right, Kristoffsen? You're learning how to not die?"

Something indistinct from Kristoffsen.

"She's peppy, Sounder. I can't decide if she thinks she's in the Marines or what."

"I need her."

"Yeah, I don't think I can just tell her to come over there and satisfy your needs."

"I need a list of women who died or were seriously injured near Stefan Tonfamecasca. Anyone who worked for him and disappeared. Married scientists working on the T7 project, one or both missing. All and any going back—shit, just all of them. Cross-referenced, any two together."

"All of them means searching like a bajillion files, Sounder."

"That's why we have computers, Detective Felton."

"If we put a search like that into the system it's going to make some bells go off in Chersenesos."

"Oh me, oh my! Whatever shall we do, Felton? Someone might notice us doing our jobs."

"You think that's funny, Sounder, but you don't know what it is round here when the eye looks down from the mountaintop."

"Is it doing that right now?"

"After the fire? You fucking bet it is. You got anything on that?"

"You think it's my case?"

"One freakish fucking thing and another freakish fucking thing happening the same week? Yeah, I think it's your case, and so do you. What have you got?"

Nothing, because I know exactly what happened. Shit. "I trawled some firebugs and came up empty."

"I coulda saved you the trouble, you'd asked me. This wasn't professional. Distinctly amateur."

"Ooh, amateur. Then maybe it was me."

"Yeah, except you've got an alibi."

"I have?"

"You mean you haven't?"

I was across town with an urban legend who runs a really low-key but very connected crime syndicate. Unless he's lying about that. Oh, and he literally asked me to arrange a fake fire and steal evidence, which I have, it's in a box at my place.

But you already searched my place. Or someone did.

"I was polishing my guitar collection. You mind getting your flunky on the question I asked?"

"Of course, I mind. Kristoffsen, get over here, Sounder wants you to do something. Come listen so you can tell him very specifically to fuck off."

I say it again and Kristoffsen does not tell me to fuck off. She says she'll get right on it.

"You want it as it comes in, or in one piece?"

"How long will it take?"

Kristoffsen makes a noise to indicate: anytime between now and summer.

"Shit, nothing works in this city."

"That is not my fault, Mr. Sounder."

"Sorry. I know that. Thank you, Officer Kristoffsen."

Felton comes back on the line. "Did you just apologise to my rookie?"

"Yeah."

"Don't do that, Sounder. I don't want you setting the bar so high the rest of us can't reach it."

I call Mini Denton because I feel guilty. She doesn't answer. I leave a message telling her if she wants my help she can have it, and here's my daily rate.

I call Athena because I want to. She doesn't answer either.

I sit until my feet stop hurting and the itch gets warm under my rib cage. Then I get my coat and go down to Gull Town, the worn-out, lower-rent business district inland and a little west of the point. It's the place some start-ups are born, but mostly it's where companies go to die. In a brownstone that really is brown, organic and mossy from the alpine dust, a guy called Orhan runs a business doing credit and background checks for schools that don't want to hire someone with the wrong sort of convictions. On off days, he runs searches for people like me. Orhan's a grinder, not an artist, but I can't lean on Floyd Ostby all the time; he'd push back.

I give Orhan two names: Mac Denton, and Roy Mullen.

"What do you want, Cal? What are you looking for?"

"Denton, you're gonna find all kinds of shit on him. Bullying, light assault and some harassment. Make a list but don't foreground it. I want to know if he's been lucky recently. Maybe a distant relative died and he inherits twenty thousand. Like that."

"This relative attach any kind of conditions to so generous a bequest?"

"Maybe to beat me down in public."

"Always nice people we deal with, Cal."

"I hear ya. The other one, Roy Mullen, he was a cop. Tread light, but I'm pretty sure he took money to drive over my witness and shoot her in the chest. She died. He got me pretty good, too."

Orhan raises bushy eyebrows. "How'd that work out for him?"

"Not well. Figure you've got a few hours before they shut his accounts."

"You seem like you're having a time, Cal. I'll do you a solid and check your man Denton for outgoings in the same amount, in case he maybe sends someone to let you know he is unhappy."

"Thanks, Orhan."

He shrugs. "Got to protect my revenue streams. It's not a favourable economy."

From Orhan's I head north again, then take a waterbus along the shore and duck inland to Victor's. She's not there, which is fine, because I want to talk to Sam.

"How's your chef?"

"I am not discussing that with you."

"Come on, Sam, it's just small talk before I ask you what you really don't want to talk about with me."

"She's fine, Cal. She has doubts about me as a long-term partner."

"I don't."

"Well, that's great, let's get hitched right away."

"Come work with me. That gets you away from Victor's. You can bootstrap to respectable security professional."

"Yeah, sure, because just everyone thinks you're respectable."

"Athena does and that's all that matters."

"So I hear. Also that you keep stepping back, which I understand conceptually but for the record: you're an idiot."

That is probably true.

S am, if you were going to make a first-dose Titan put a gun to his own head, how would you do it?"

"I got an alibi."

"And what is that exactly?"

"If I'd killed your guy you'd have never found the body."

"Not really how those work."

"Yeah, also I was here." He shrugs. "What do you want?"

"I want to know—"

"First thing people think of is knock him out. Drugs, obviously."

"Tranquilisers."

"Sure. An absolute shitload of them, maybe, and even then it would not be my first choice."

"Why not?"

"Because of what's happening right now. You'd find it and then you would go: 'Huh, this guy was unconscious when he shot himself, I wonder if that's legit?' And then you would go 'what the fuck am I saying, of course that's not legit, it's fucking ridiculous.' But also: why not just overdose him on ketamine? He'll be just as dead."

"So you would go with—?"

"If I wanted to make it personal—which I assume is the point of the whole drug-and-shoot thing—maybe with the right person and the right information you can use a hostage."

"Nasty."

"And unreliable."

"What else?"

"If it was a proper covert operation I'd go with carbon dioxide. You leave him breathe a while after, there's not much left to find in the body. Then he's unconscious, you pull the trigger. Fine line, but it's conceivable no one would ever know."

"And physical force?"

He shrugs.

"Maybe, Cal. I mean seriously maybe, not anything like a certainty. Someone like me. I could maybe do it."

"That's why I'm asking how."

"Well, you know this, maybe not consciously but you've scrapped with a couple of first-dosers in your time. It's not even that different from your match the other night, just more extreme. Titans have big muscles and big bones, but the nervous system isn't any different. You hit it right, you still get a knockout. Multiple inputs in short succession. Rotation, disorientation, shock, and . . . Blammo. Out he goes and down. Figure if you got it just right, you wouldn't even leave bruises, or they'd be real faint. Covered up by pooling. Maybe figure them for perimortem."

"Look at you with the lingo."

"I watch TV."

"Could I do it?"

"You mean could I show you how?"

I think of Mini Denton.

"Yeah. Could you tell me and give me a reasonable shot at pulling it off?"

He shrugs. "I guess. But at the same time . . . it'd be pretty amazing if you did it perfectly first time out of the box. You're not subtle."

"Imagine I was."

"I'm sorry, Cal, there's a limit to what I can imagine."

"Shit, Sam."

"You brought it up."

"Give her flowers."

"What now?"

"The chef. Give her flowers."

"I'm not an idiot, Sounder, I know to give her flowers."

"Have you done it yet?"

"No, but—"

"Give her flowers. And think about coming to work with me."

"Go away now, Cal. You're a ball ache."

"I'm just saying we'd be great together."

He eyes me without enthusiasm. "But you didn't think to bring me flowers."

I go back to my office. The tricker kids in the condemned lot opposite have found a new route over the rubble, running up a section of concrete pipe and flipping back over it, then turning and going on up into the open structure. They're having tea in a green kitchen halfway up, all lined up along a table like something between a dance party and a magistrate's bench. I wave to them, but they don't wave back and the putty lattice tugs in my side, so I leave them to it.

Orhan has answers by the time I get home.

"You're right, they're assholes," he says.

"I know that, man."

"I'm not kidding, Cal, you need cases with a better class of suspect. These two are . . . tcha. Like if I would villain—which I would not, because I am quite law-abiding, but if I would—I would not villain with these guys with someone else's dick."

"I hear you."

"Denton is a total shitbag. Always fighting, suing, swinging it about. You know this."

"I do."

I'm about to say more but I hear a creak outside. I keep talking, plenty loud, to Orhan.

"What about Mullen?"

"I got more on the shitbag."

There's a loose board in the hall but it's not that loose. I worked pretty hard to get it right. It creaks when someone steps on it, but only if that person weighs in excess of one hundred and fifty kilos. I listen, and I hear the faintest whisper. My visitor is standing right on the board, very still.

"We'll come back to that. Mullen."

Creak.

Orhan says: "The other kind of asshole. Sad story."

"Oh yeah, how so?"

Creak.

There's a Taser in the top drawer of my desk, and next to it a five-inch knuckle knife, like vanilla brass knuckles grew a single sharp tooth. There's a real gun, too, but if I use that I can't ask questions later. Hanging on a wall hook there's a megaphone. Figure I can summon assistance with that and it'll be here in an hour or so. If I dump the call with Orhan and dial emergency, or tell him to call the cops, Gratton will be here in twelve minutes, give or take, but the person on the other side of the door will hear and things will kick off. Twelve minutes is a long damn time in a small room with a Titan.

I take the Taser and the knife, make some "uh huh" sounds to cover the noise as I turn the carpet over and run the Taser cable from the lamp stand to the wall by the door, then flip the carpet back on top.

Orhan is still talking about Mullen. "I think he was a good guy. Like we all could play pool together. Drink tea."

I hear the board release, like a sigh. Still can't hear the footfall, but now I can hear the shape of a body in the hall just outside, the shadow in the room tone.

"Orhan, he absolutely shot me."

"Yes, obviously, we cannot play pool together now. He shot you and also he shot himself. But still basically I think he was a decent fellow."

I go over to the door, crouch on the far side from the hinge. My door opens to your left because for the majority of people that's weird and uncomfortable.

I say: "That is a flexible fucking definition of that word."

The door smashes open. Huge fucking shape in black, two and half metres high and proportionately broad. Superhero big. He's wearing a ski mask over his face and executive tactical gear: black camo slash-stop trousers with a non-conductive chain weave boxer built in to stop anyone stabbing or electrocuting you in the private parts. Steel-toe boots and some sort of gi-inflected combat jacket in the same ballistic fabric Susan Green's shawl was made from.

I fire the Taser before he can look around. The current goes straight into the desk lamp and makes it explode. The guy flinches back from it: flying plastic and stink, but he's smart. He tucks and goes into a punch combo in case someone's coming for him, puts his fist through the wall about where my head would be if I was standing there. A great big chunk of dry timber frame and brick goes crashing into the hall.

I twist my body out and round as hard as I can and put the knuckle knife into the side of the knee. The blade punches through—the chain weave stops too high on the leg, fashion over form—and in. I twist it forwards, and lean.

Titans are strong and heavy. Their bones get so thick that they're like armour plate. It's not just a question of scale, it's also density and structure. Eventually they get so big, like Stefan, that they're slow, but all kinds of new dangerous that you can't predict.

This guy hasn't got there yet. He's big, and hard, and tough, but in between the bones is just meat. The kneecap pops out nicely. He screams, but it comes out like a roar, and he tries to get ahold of me as he goes down.

He doesn't manage it or I'd be in serious trouble, but clips me in passing and sends me sprawling through my own door into the hall. I scoot back, crabwise, grabbing the megaphone as I go. He tries again, lunging and the yelling, then throwing up, and lunging again. Damn me, that is some serious resolve. The eyes in the ski mask are batshit crazy with pain and fury. Figure no one has done anything like this to him ever in his life.

In fairness very few people have been exploded with a desk lamp and mutilated in the knee, which is—also in fairness—why I did it that way.

Titans don't care about physical injury, because they know they can get it all back. They fucking hate it, and they hate pain more than anything, maybe, except wounded pride, but they keep coming, because as long as they win, they can always just get bigger and younger and dance on your grave.

When he comes again I let him go by, then scream into his ear as he passes with the megaphone volume at maximum. Bad enough for me, in the closed environment of the little room. Shit for him. He claps one hand to his ear and howls. I can see blood under his fingers. I drop down into a crouch and use the knife to take the tendons along the back of the other leg. He goes down onto his front, and this time he's not getting up anyway because there's nothing left for him to stand on. I jump on his back, run up the spine stamping all the way, then kick him in the side of the head. It's not as scientific as Sam's version, but it's the same principle: overload the senses and the brain shorts out.

Blammo.

I sit behind the desk and take a breather.

"Orhan? You still there, buddy?"

Turns out that whole thing was so fast he hasn't hung up.

"I am. What the fuck was that?"

"Yeah, sorry about that. Animal control had to come in. Guy in the next apartment had a cougar in a cage. Not the sexy kind. It got out, you believe that? I think it ate a dog."

I can hear Orhan not buying that for one second. Figure the fight didn't sound real cougar-ish even over the phone.

"Listen, Orhan, this is a distracting environment right now. I'm gonna call right back, okay?"

I hang up on him and then I go over and put about a hundred

layers of duct tape handcuffs on the unconscious man on my floor. When that's done I figure it's time to pull off the ski mask and see who he is. I'm all kinds of hoping it's fairy-tale Peter, because then I'll have a whole gigantic clue right here on my floor. When I pull off the ski mask I wish that even more, but it's not.

"Oh, hi, Maurice."

Which sounds a lot calmer than "oh, shit."

Figure a stranger breaks into your home and tries to end you, and you straight away end him, that is actually a tolerably simple outcome from a cop point of view. There's broken furniture and all manner of evidence of a struggle. If maybe then it turns out that you're an investigator, that's worth writing down, because it wouldn't be unknown for a person like that to step over the line somewhat. Did you poke the bear? Well, even so, it's not too complex.

Then let's suppose it now turns out you knew this guy and you didn't one hundred percent get along. Maybe you went to see him recently and came back all fucked up, so much so you needed medical attention. You say it was someone else did that, but the fact remains you went to his place of business and got fucked up, and now he's in yours and he's dead. To a cop, the symmetry is uncomfortable. Your first responder at this point is calling his boss to let them know that this evening will not be a good one for a movie and a long bath.

Finally we get to where we are: the guy who broke into your place isn't dead, and he has his own story to tell. In that story, the whole thing was you trying to kill him under cover of whatever. Now you've got a problem because the hinkiness of the whole thing makes the bad guy's version look only slightly more bullshit than yours. Maybe this guy with whom you don't get along, who is in love with your ex-girlfriend's mother, maybe . . . something. More people get dead because of families and love than anything else.

And that something space, that itchy feeling of backstory, that's where the money comes in. Money is a weight on the fabric of the world. Good things flow towards Chersenesos; they flow away from Gull Town and Tappeny Bridge. Justice being one of those things. When something is complex, a whole lot of money has a tendency to make it go away, or turn it inside out.

Short version, Maurice Tonfamecasca, with his patella in his coat pocket, is Maurice Tonfamecasca only a few hours away from release into the care of a private medical facility, and it's like I told Mini Denton: this isn't how you impress a Titan. It's not how you make friends, most particularly not with a guy like Maurice.

This is a real problem, because Maurice is by any ordinary standard very, very rich. He's connected and low-grade untouchable, and if he decides to go pro on dealing with me instead of trusting his own artisanal chops to cut my throat, I will have to go on the run or I will very much die. If I stay anywhere near Othrys, a guy like Sam will shoot me in the street from a moving car, or in my living room from a tower three quarters of a mile away. I'll wind up in one of the pools where I disposed of Musgrave's ex-boyfriend, or I'll die in a fire.

Stefan would regard it as natural attrition, or the providential removal of a distraction. Athena . . . would never forgive Maurice, but even if she killed him back, that doesn't do me any good at all.

Just how bad is the friction between those two?

While I'm thinking this, he wakes up and starts swearing at me. I tape up his mouth and call Orhan back because we didn't finish our conversation.

"Tell me about Denton."

"Throws his weight around, thinks that's how Titans do," Orhan says.

"In fairness he's sort of right about that."

"Your guy got a bonus from a consultancy contract he had. Corporate hospitality account. I'm looking at it now but I can already tell you it's a shell."

"Was it a big bonus?"

"Depends who you are. But for you and me, it was fucking huge."

"You got any kind of sense of what lives in the shell?"

"Another shell and another. But the lawyers are Dietrich Hellawil in Chersenesos."

Right around the corner from the Tonfamecasca company. Figure if I go there and lie to them they will show me their exterior security tapes and I will recognise Maurice coming in that day.

I say goodbye to Orhan and sit down behind my desk. I look at Maurice.

"Who was Roddy Tebbit?"

No answer. I get myself a glass of water and sit down again.

"What happened with Peter and Lillian?"

No reply.

"When I got beat down the other day, Stefan said he just noticed I was coming in, but I don't think that's true. Did you play him, Maurice? Just happen to drop my name?" A thought occurs to me, really late in the game. "You were trying to use me to score points against Athena." There's something in my throat. Figure it must be rage.

Maurice looks back at me through narrow eyes. He's full of the same thing, viscous and violent. There's a lot of fight hormones in this room. A lot of inhalable bad decisions. Get smart, Cal. Think.

I drink some water and say some affirmations in my head. There's a yoga class across the street, and in the summer, with the windows open, I can hear the things they murmur as they salute the sun. *I am a calm person. I am not governed by negative emotions. Rage and pain wash over me as the river washes over the stone. They polish the surface of my serenity, but I remain as I am.*

To pass the time while I wait for the surface of my serenity to get all shiny, I talk to Maurice a bit more.

"From where I'm standing it looks like you paid Mac Denton to fuck me up at Victor's and when that didn't work you made sure

Stefan saw I was coming in so he'd do it for you. I'm wondering whether I'm gonna find out that Officer Mullen was yours, too, and Mac was just to distract me. Was it all to knock Athena off her game, Maurice? Get your job back?"

Two dark eyes staring at me from the floor. Dark as Othrys, and as deep. There's a hint of Athena in that resolve, that certainty. I know him better than I thought.

I look at Maurice and I realise, fully and for the first time, what some part of me has known all along.

From the moment he came through the door, one of us was dead.

The phone answers on the first ring.
"Yes?"
"Hey, Zoegar, it's me."
"Me, who?"
"I know you know."
"I assure you, sir, that I am at an entire loss."
"I want to talk to Nugent."
"There is no Nugent here, Mr. Sounder."
"I knew you knew."
"I fear you are mistaken. Goodbye."
"It's Cal Sounder."
"Why, hello, Mr. Sounder, how nice to hear from you today."
"I need to talk to Nugent."
"I will inquire if Mr. Nugent is available."
"You said he wasn't."
"That was before I knew it was you."
I take a couple of slow breaths so that I don't yell.
"You and your boss are very particular people, Mr. Zoegar."
"We are admirers of formality."
"Is he there?"
"Indeed, I am, Mr. Sounder."
"The weirdest stuff has been happening, Mr. Nugent."

"It does, Mr. Sounder, all the time. So much more often than people choose to believe."

"Would it surprise you to learn that someone very politely ransacked my place looking for Mr. Tebbit's organs?"

"I am quite amazed."

"So that's the first weird happening, right, because I one hundred percent thought that was you."

"I should never do such a thing. It would be a breach of the close bond of trust we have built from our long acquaintance. I can trust you, can't I? You would not lie to me?"

"No more than you to me, Mr. Nugent."

"We understand one another perfectly, Mr. Sounder."

"And then this evening—how shall I put this—you remember the lion we discussed? I took a thorn out of his paw?"

"One does not easily forget a lion, Mr. Sounder."

"Well, then I'm guessing you know all the cubs and such that follow him around."

"Oh, intimately."

"So would you be surprised to hear that one of them—let's say the greyest one—just paid me a visit, and he was not in a talking mood."

"The greyest, you say. By which I take it you do not mean the oldest, but the most drab."

"He's bidding fair to upset that assessment, but yeah."

"Quite so. And quite remarkable—your continued vitality, too. I'm so pleased I did not underestimate you. Where is he now?"

"He's alive. He's lying on the floor in my kitchen with his patella in a cup. But you see that presents me with a kind of a problem all itself."

"Oh, dear me, yes. I see that it does."

"So I thought to myself that a man of your resources might have resources just for moments like this."

Doublewide doesn't say anything for a while.

"That is unexpected. You would deliver this . . . cub . . . into my hands."

"Yeah."

"You understand that once he is in my keeping, your control of his ultimate destiny will be limited."

"I do. I need to talk to him in a quiet place, Mr. Nugent. A full and frank discussion is necessary between us. We're past the point where we can just hug it out."

"And after?"

"I would not expect to socialise with him any more."

"This . . . is not an inconsiderable request, Mr. Sounder."

"Let's be straight, Mr. Nugent. You and I don't make inconsiderable requests of one another, now, do we?"

"I ask you for a liver, you bring me a man."

"He does include a liver."

"I am not sure that I wish one quite so entailed, sir."

I take a breath and I let him have it.

"Mr. Nugent, I may or may not know where that item you are looking for is, but I will tell you up-front that I do know why you want it. I know what it means."

Silence.

"Your friend Mr. Zoegar, he was of the opinion that you and I could not trust one another. I took that to mean you would never trust me, but now it seems you sought to have me do something with consequences far beyond what you led me to believe. That is not the act of a friend, sir. Now, this situation we are all in is complex and delicate, and right now I feel a broad disaffection with almost all parties to the negotiation. We can proceed on that basis into the next stage, or you and I can step together a little more. I'm right here offering you the opportunity to restore the goodwill between us. What do you say?"

"Mr. Zoegar would use the word 'consilience' to describe what you propose, Mr. Sounder. A jumping together of destinies."

"Well, for the next half hour, I won't make any firm decisions about which way my destiny is going to jump. After that, I'll figure I'm on my own, and things could get untidy."

There's a pause during which I assume Lyman Nugent considers the state of my affairs before they become untidy: a scientist murdered under an alias, a cage match, a gunshot wound, a dead lounge singer, a dead police officer, an exploded police station, stolen internal organs containing encrypted nuclear grade kompromat, and now my would-be murderer, my ex-girlfriend's cousin and by definition one of the most powerful men in the world, mutilated, bleeding and pissed off on my office carpet.

Figure Nugent likes all that even less than I do.

"I shall be delighted to accept your kind invitation, Mr. Sounder. See you in twenty minutes or so."

"See you then."

He hangs up, and I turn and look down at Maurice Tonfamecasca.

"Fuck you, Sounder."

"Maurice, you came to my house. Now you've got nineteen minutes to persuade me we can forge an eternal friendship. After that it's out of my hands."

Maurice smack-talks me for eighteen straight minutes and ten seconds. When Zoegar and a few friends arrive with a stretcher and carry him down the stairs, he smack talks them, too.

When he sees Lyman Nugent in the backseat of the car, for a moment I think he's not going to react at all, and then he looks at me, at Nugent, at me again, then he stares at Nugent and he starts to make a weird noise, like a bull choking. I figure that is the sound of a man who is used to counting his lifespan in centuries remembering what it feels like to be ephemeral.

There's no room for Maurice in the car, and in any case the lowing noise he's making doesn't sit well with Doublewide, so they put Maurice in a trailerbox, and Zoegar offers me the front passenger seat.

"Well," the fat man says. "This certainly is a how-dee-doo."

The trailer bounces on its wheels, and I can hear screaming. Doublewide waves like he's the Pope.

"Drive on, Mr. Zoegar. Drive on."

———

*Z*oegar takes us out of town fast, over the suburbs on pillars of concrete and steel and beyond the city limit, to that weird transitional space where you can still see the city and already smell the farms. Pig country, and if Maurice can smell that too, I hope he gets what it means.

Pig country. If you've got enough pigs, body disposal is quick, and within a few days every single piece of trace evidence is gone. They'll even grind up teeth.

Zoegar shifts to the back roads, and ten minutes later pulls into a gas station. The trailer gets hooked up to a common country flatbed and the saloon car vanishes back the way it came. A big, genial woman in overalls takes the wheel of the truck and tosses the keys of a minivan to Zoegar. This time there's room for me in the back with Doublewide.

"Well, Mr. Sounder, it is very good to hear from you again. I confess, when you did not deliver those organs, I came to believe you had chosen to throw in your lot."

"Stefan and I had words. I didn't like what he had to say."

"What was that?"

"He laughed at me."

Doublewide's pouchy mouth bends downwards. Yes. He knows exactly what that means.

"You're not concerned that your assailant's sudden absence would be traced to you?"

"I figure he made sure not to leave a trail. Maurice has a house on Syros; flying time is a few hours. You can have one of your boys call and try to make an appointment. I'm guessing he left this afternoon and won't be back for a week, so he cannot possibly have been murdering me an hour ago. All sorts of people will confirm that."

"Yes, I quite see. Conferring upon us a similar liberty. Well, we shall soon be at the venue, Mr. Sounder. You said you wished to converse with Mr. Tonfamecasca."

"I have questions."

"As do I, though those must wait on yours, since you are my guest. I have a preference for the more sophisticated forms of interrogation. The soft touch, let's all be friends, more flies with honey. I take it that is acceptable?"

Doublewide's lips open in a little smile. I can see his teeth.

Titan teeth can be very alarming. They grow new ones during the dosing process, in scale with the head. They are fresh and white and sometimes just a little feral. Doublewide's make him look like a salamander seeing a particularly juicy bug.

"It is."

We get to the farmhouse half an hour later and it's a fine old timber-clad place with a water tower. There's a couple of open shelters for tractors and ploughs, a converted stable that looks like a guest house, and some modern cabins I figure are probably Swedish pre-fabricated, put together in the factory with all the infrastructure already in the walls.

Watching Doublewide walk is strange. I realise I haven't seen it before. His body is formidably strong, like you'd expect from a Titan, and his legs are thick as trees, but by the same token he can't really move one thigh past another. When he's going slow, he rocks from side to side like a sailor in a black-and-white movie, but when he's in a hurry he turns diagonal and throws himself forwards, vaulting along on one hand and then the other like he's doing parkour on the flat. It's eerily fast. In human-scale rooms, he's awkward: too big—and too embarrassed, maybe, to let you see that he doesn't move like an ordinary man. Out here he's at liberty, and better suited than I am.

They get Maurice out of the trailer. Somewhere, out of sight, the pigs have heard the engine and make little noises of delight.

Zoegar cuts Maurice out of the duct tape with the kind of long knife that has implications. It's got a spine so thick the section is almost a triangle, and all three edges look sharp enough to make you wish you were someplace else. The back end has a fat, flat pommel on it like a mushroom, where you can lean in.

It's a knife for penetrating an abnormally resistant rib cage, say, or the skull of one of those dogs bred to hunt bears. Maurice's eyes track it as Zoegar slices through most of the tape around his arms, then steps back to let him finish the job himself. It still takes a minute or two of straining, because Zoegar is a conservative sort of man.

I give him a little fuck-you wave.

"Hi, Maurice, it's me, Cal."

"Sounder—"

But then he doesn't have anything to say.

"You sure that's it?"

Maurice looks away.

We're in the living room of Doublewide's hobby farm. It's big and rustic and cosy, with thick rugs all over the walls and a fireplace in the middle with a stack of pine logs. A few hours and some red velvet and you could make Santa's Grotto in here, no trouble at all.

I look at Maurice, his legs bandaged quite professionally by Zoegar. They haven't bothered to restrain him in the leather high-back love seat because he can barely stay upright without holding on to the arms.

"I suggest you start with sorry. 'I am sorry I came to your office to kill you, Cal. It was personal and I understand you're upset.' I mean, I don't imagine it gets said a lot in this situation. You could try an actual apology. They're free."

Nothing.

"Mr. Nugent, do people generally apologise at this point?"

"You shock me, Mr. Sounder, with the implication that I would know such a thing. This experience is quite entirely new to me."

I look at him. He does the salamander smile again. Zoegar rolls his eyes. Apparently this is too fey even for him.

I tell Doublewide I'm sorry I asked.

He beams. "You are forgiven!"

"You see, Maurice? That's how it goes. You want to try it?"

Maurice isn't looking at me. He's looking at Doublewide. Titans always think other Titans are in charge. They're also almost always right about that, even when the appearance is against it.

"Who are you?"

"Lyman Nugent," Doublewide says. "Beggar king. Big fan of your uncle, though perhaps that's the wrong word. Let us say I admire his . . . reach." He flexes one mantis arm, reaching two metres to lift an apple out of the fruit bowl and take a bite. He's dainty with it, but half the fruit disappears into his mouth. Maurice watches him. They say that Stefan Tonfamecasca's arm reaches anywhere in the world, but they haven't met Lyman Nugent. Figure Maurice is right now thinking about that.

Finally he looks at me and says "I'm sorry."

"Traditionally, there should be a 'for.' What are you sorry for?"

"I am sorry I came to your office and tried to kill you."

"That is what you were doing?"

"Yes."

I look at Doublewide.

"That sound about right to you?"

"I thought it palpably sincere. Shall we eat?"

"By all means."

Maurice stares.

"Why, yes, Mr. Tonfamecasca, you too. You are fallen among civilised thieves today. It is to everyone's advantage that we resolve this matter without unpleasantness, yes?"

"Sure."

Zoegar opens a door, and the same big woman who drove the truck comes in with a tray of barbecue and a syringe. Maurice looks warily at the last.

"It's a nausea shot," she says primly. "So you don't throw up my fine food. There's anti-tetanus and a painkiller in there too, but don't get the idea you can walk on those legs just because they stop hurting quite so much. You put weight on those, especially that knee? You're going to experience all kinds of bad things. Now, hold still."

He does, hissing as the needle goes in, and then leaning back. The woman smiles. "All better. For a given value, I know. Lyman, he needs some time on my table soon, so nothing bad happens at the joint."

"Understood, Priscilla. Quite understood, and thank you."

She shrugs, and bustles out.

"Barbecue," Doublewide says, "is the only food apart from lobster where a grown man is permitted to wear a bib without criticism. It is intended to be messy, sweet and bad for you. Wine is hopeless in its company, so we shall have the local beer."

And we do.

When we've eaten together—even Maurice manages a plate of ribs and slaw—Doublewide leans back and steeples his fingers.

"My dear Mr. Tonfamecasca, I'm afraid we must return to the issue at hand. Mr. Sounder is wroth with you for what I take to have been a premeditated but under-planned attempt upon his life. Is that right, Mr. Sounder?"

"I don't know about 'wroth.' I'm pissed, I guess. But I'm a working man, Mr. Nugent. I'm tired of getting the runaround, to the point where I just want some answers. I can put my personal issues aside if I get answers. Some assurances, too, of course."

"Indeed. There can be no peace without guarantees of future security. I, on the other hand, have no emotional dog in this fight at all. Saving your presence, Mr. Sounder: I like you, but I can't just kidnap and murder a person because he offends against someone I like. I'm gregarious! Within my limited circles, at least. There'd be no end to it, sir. This farm would be entirely fertilised with the dead. However."

He looks over at Maurice.

"I am private, Mr. Tonfamecasca. Deeply private. I have devoted considerable effort to ensuring your uncle knows little or nothing of my affairs. I have no desire for his close scrutiny. Now our paths have crossed, I am concerned that you will be unable to remain discreet about my existence, my appearance. My name. Like Mr. Sounder, I will require assurances from you. Earnests of goodwill if you are to leave this place. But before we negotiate that, you must satisfy Mr. Sounder, as I have promised."

Maurice goes to say something, but Doublewide, from the other side of the room, holds up a hand in front of his face. Again the mantis articulation, the eerie foreshortening of distance.

Doublewide glances over at me. I look at Maurice.

"Tell me the true story of Peter and Lillian."

Again I see something flicker in his face. He hides it, but it's recognition. Guilt, even.

"Yeah, there it is. You know. Stefan told me you didn't know anything, but you obviously do. Now . . . how would you know something like that? Elaine. Elaine told you, didn't she? Are you two . . . dating, by the way? Athena says not."

He glowers, then shakes his head.

"So you go where she goes. You're her walker. And you're in love with her, but she's not buying. Is that it?"

"She's cautious. She's had some bad experiences with romance."

"Well, she married Stefan, so yeah."

Maurice just looks at me like I'll never get it, whatever it is.

"Does Stefan ever murder people? Personally? I mean obviously people who get in his way have accidents. But up close? You'd think he would, but I've never been able to work it out."

Maurice shakes his head. "I don't know."

"He ever make you think he might murder you?"

Maurice looks away. "Yes."

Yeah. You'd expect that. I would. It still makes me feel sorry for Maurice, like we're a little bit the same. Then I think: he better not do that to Athena.

Better not have done it.

But that's a problem for another day.

"Peter and Lillian. You can start with a name."

"It's a tabloid thing. It's not real."

"That's fine. Tell me the tabloid version you know. I heard Stefan's when I came to the tower. Couple of others over the last week. Elaine told me hers, too."

He scowls. "You upset her."

"Maurice, you need to adjust your way of thinking right now. You're used to a situation where saying 'you upset my friend' is enough to make someone quake, but you just tried to kill me and you blew it. I'm not scared of you. Your family is screwing around. Titans are having some kind of internal discussion and real people are getting hurt. I don't really give a fuck whether she was upset or not."

Doublewide raises his eyebrows. "Your prejudices are showing, Mr. Sounder."

"I'm sorry, Mr. Nugent. You're quite right, that was rude. It's just that the overwhelming majority of people who get T7 get it because they've spent a mortal lifetime being an asshole, and sadly the process does not change that about them. You're about the second Titan I've ever met that behaved like a person and I figure that's because you know what it is to have a bad day."

He shrugs. "Undeniably."

"So Maurice, this tabloid thing? This whole Peter and Lillian narrative in all its versions? I kinda like it. I'm going to write all the different stories down and publish an anthology. Chersenesos Folk Tales or something. You think it'll sell?" He's about to answer but I can see it's gonna be more bullshit, so I change direction. "Oh, wait, tell me this, instead: where were you at nine in the morning last Thursday?" The morning after Roddy Tebbit was killed. It's hard to lie in reverse order, and I have to ask myself whether perhaps he's on a spree. It happens, even to ordinary humans.

"I . . . went to work."

"What did you have for breakfast."

"I don't know. Cereal. With yoghurt. That's what I usually have."

"Thursday last week. When did you wake up?"

"I had . . . yes. I had the Trinsom meeting. I had breakfast at home, I woke up early so I could read the notes."

"Sleep well?"

"Yes. Fine."

"How long, do you reckon?"

"Eight hours. I always try to get eight hours."

"And the night before, what did you do?"

He looks away. "You'd say I was a walker."

"You were out with Elaine."

"Yes. She had tickets for a talk at the science academy. Debenture, of course."

"Oh, of course. VIP and champagne with the boffins. What was it about?"

"Afforestation and habitats."

"Bit dry."

"She likes it."

"Not your perfect romantic setting, though."

"It's not like that. I'm not trying to romance her. I love her. She loves me. She's just not ready yet. She'll come to it in time."

This stupid fucker is so far out of his league he has no idea the height of the wall.

"You should have taken her to an old movie. The Marx Brothers, maybe."

He stares at me. Figure he genuinely has no idea why the fuck I would say something like that. He looks almost grateful. "Does she—does she like the Marx Brothers? Did she say that to you when you saw her?"

"Yeah. She loves the Marx Brothers, and she talks to bears."

He winces. He knows about the bears.

"She not well, Maurice?"

"She's fine."

"I'm not sure she is. Athena doesn't think so."

"Athena has no idea. She's hardly ever there. She just waltzes in, like a teenager. I'm surprised she doesn't bring her laundry."

"Bit of a problem for you if Elaine gets another dose, isn't it?

You're not due for decades. She'll overmatch you." In her bed, not that he's ever going there. I'd put money down he's wrong about her.

"Hardly your business, Sounder."

"Man, you were happy with the Marx Brothers thing, when you thought I had the inside track. Maybe I'm just looking out for you."

Doublewide chuckles. I ignore him.

"Afforestation chat. All night, was it?"

"Yes. All evening, anyway."

"What time did you get home?"

"I'm not sure. Late."

"Elaine can verify all this?"

"I don't see why she should."

I don't see how she could. Lady talks to actual bears. Court would probably not be hugely impressed, whoever she used to be married to. But Maurice doesn't see the problem. Can't see it. So:

"Because it forms part of a criminal investigation I'm undertaking officially on behalf of the police, Maurice."

Priscilla the driver-cook comes back. I wonder if she's brought sundaes, but she hasn't. Doublewide raises his eyebrows at her.

"Maurice Tonfamecasca is right this second en route to Syros," she says. "I spoke to his PA."

"Well, now," I look back at Maurice. "Well, now. First you better tell me about Peter and Lillian, and then anything else I want to know that Stefan might be keeping from me, and then you and Mr. Nugent will have to work out how to reassure him that you won't blab. Otherwise it seems to me you'll never come back from Greece, on account of being eaten by pigs right here. Stefan will look for you for a while, but not for ever." I shrug, and let the truth of that sink in.

"Stefan takes pride in not really giving a shit, doesn't he? In outliving everything, even his own emotional attachments. Assuming he ever liked you in the first place. Do you think he likes you, Maurice? Because he gave me to understand he did not. Like I think it's possible he likes you even less than he likes me, and he really does not like me." Maurice won't look at me. Yeah, he knows what Stefan thinks, all right. Old bastard probably tells him on a regular basis. "And Elaine will never know why you abandoned her."

In Maurice's version of the story, Lillian met Peter Antonin when they were very young. He was smart, she was smarter, but people didn't always get that, because people are assholes and he was louder and brasher than she was. They teamed up, and shared credit, which basically meant he took some of hers. But they were a team, all the same, until Stefan came along, and then it was over. Lillian was free of Peter's ego and Peter's career, and Peter took his money and went off into deserved obscurity. Lillian and Stefan had a gay old time and then it ended. Like Stefan's version, it's perfectly in character, perfectly anodyne. Probably, the same PR team made them up.

"So what was her name, Maurice?"

"Whose name?"

"Before she married Peter. What was her name?"

"I don't know."

"Lillian Brown. Lillian Beauregard. Smith. Jones. Klassen. Hatchard. Odunayo. Nespoli. Come on, man, throw something in here."

"I never heard it. I'm sorry, Cal."

"Why *did* you try to kill me? I honestly have no idea."

"You were annoying Stefan."

"Bullshit, try again."

He slaps his hands down on the arms of the chair. Zoegar twitches upright, hands moving to the small of his back. I figure pistols, twinned, with heavy ammunition. Maurice doesn't see him but subsides anyway, and Zoegar doesn't finish the draw. Maurice scowls at me.

"I was just fucking tired of you, okay? Of your fucking snooping and your shit. I was tired of Athena crying about you, Cal! I don't like that she has my job. That is bullshit. It's bullshit and fuck Stefan for even thinking that fucking infant can do it better than I can. Okay? So yeah, sure, I hope she dies in a ditch. But she's still family. When you hurt our family, when you reject our family, that's all of us, and who the fuck are you? You're no one. Some ant with ideas of humanity. Fuck you. You can't even let her move on, you just keep her on the hook year after fucking year. You're a prick. I was tired of it. And you upset Elaine."

I wait.

"You upset Elaine," he says again.

And after that it gets pretty quiet in the room, because Double-wide is trying to look like he hasn't heard anything and that's the loudest silence I've ever heard.

I didn't tell him about Athena, and there's no reason he'd know. I told him I was Daniel and Stefan was the lion. Now he knows better. Well, it was always going to happen, and it's not like we don't have new reasons to trust one another, what with kidnapping her cousin together.

"You going to do it again, Maurice?"

But he will. I already know that.

He looks at me, and something settles in his face that I've never seen before, not even when he was trying to kill me. I can't place it for the longest time. There are flavours of disdain and contempt, even boredom, but something deeper, like looking down from a satellite. And then I get it. It's the Titan look, the one Stefan has all the time, like I'm a very long way down and he's just watching me crawl around in the dust. His voice changes to something like perfect calm, like now, at last, he's finally figured out who he is, and he's speaking from the soul.

"Yeah, Sounder. I will absolutely kill you. And you—" this to Doublewide, "you I'm going to catch and I'm going to bring you to my ranch—which is not some check shirt lumberjack fantasy that stinks of pigs, it is a real ranch—and give you a ten-minute start, and then I'm going to hunt you like a deer, and when you're dead I'm going to stuff your ugly corpse and keep it in a glass cabinet. I'll have wine tastings in front of it. Smoke cigars with all my friends who didn't end up looking like freaks when they got dosed."

Doublewide's hand flicks out. I'm right, it does look like a mantis, that unfurling: eerily fast across the distance, and the weight and angle inhuman. The slap takes Maurice across the side of the face and the noise of the impact is like a gun going off.

"Rude," Doublewide says, the hand still making the return journey, much slower.

Maurice flops. His jaw's broken, maybe his cheekbone as well. He's shaking, and I'm pretty sure he's laughing. Whatever else happens, our conversation is done.

"Mr. Nugent?" I say.

"Mr. Sounder."

"I'm all finished here. I wish you the best of your own discussions."

"You have no . . . views . . . on the resolution of this matter?"

I think about it a while. I say: "No."

"Very well. Mr. Sounder . . . regarding that liver . . . I shall either receive it, or I shall not, and I shall understand our relationship accordingly."

I put my hand out for him to shake, and he looks at me, waiting for me to realise, but I wait with my arm extended towards him, until he folds himself into his mantis shape and drapes his fingers into mine as if waiting for me to kiss the papal ring. He squeezes briefly to emphasise the tiny, unhuman shake, and as I let him go, I see something between bemusement and respect.

"I don't do that very often, Mr. Sounder."

"Nor do I, Mr. Nugent."

One of Zoegar's boys drives me back to the gas station and we trade cars again, and in a little while I'm back at my apartment as if I never left. They've even cleaned it for me. I can smell the bleach.

I spend some time replastering. I know how to do that because I have done it before.

Then I go to my bedroom and I lie down on the bed, looking up at the cold grey sky until it turns out I can't sleep.

Hello?"

"It's me."

"Hi, Cal."

"Are you okay?"

"Of course! Are you?"

"Yeah. Yeah. Athena—"

"Yes?"

"Do I keep you on the hook? Should I stop?"

"Yes, you do. And no."

"I miss you."

"I miss you too. You could just knock."

"I'm at my place."

"No, you're not."

"No, I'm not."

"Well, then."

"There are things I need to tell you."

"No, there aren't."

"Things I should tell you."

"No, there aren't. You should come to the door. Right now, Cal. Otherwise I'm coming down there to get you in my pyjamas."

"You don't wear pyjamas."

"Which is why you shouldn't make me come down."

I don't.

Her mouth on mine is like breathing. She tilts my head up and holds me there, and then slowly falls back onto the wall until I'm taller than she is, until I can lean down onto her. She makes a noise in her chest that sounds like a motorbike starting. I don't remember getting to the bed.

I remember every single thing after that.

———

Athena's gone before I wake up. I let myself out. I can smell her all over me. I have bruises from her fingers, because at the end she forgot to be careful, and I didn't care.

I'm extremely ashamed of myself.

And I still don't care.

Maybe this is doable.

Maybe I can be with her.

I go back to my office and smell bleach.

I sit in front of the terminal and try "Antonin" along with the Marx Brothers in Roddy Tebbit's file. It doesn't work.

I go up on the roof and refill the doc box. The green light has gone out; the orange one hasn't come on. I don't know what that means. I don't know how much these pieces of meat matter, any more.

I don't know what Doublewide wants to do with them. Maybe this. Maybe he's doing it.

He knows I'm involved with Athena now, if he didn't already.

Stefan is waiting for me to tell him I've destroyed Roddy Tebbit's data.

Gratton is waiting for me to tell him what the hell is going on.

It's getting to the point I have to pick a side.

Or make one.

I look out across Othrys. It's oily black all winter long, then azure blue all summer. There's a public beach by the Tappeny Bridge, and since last year, when they moved all the junkies on and combed the needles out, it's a nice beach. Out beyond it, the sun comes up over the mountains, and on days like this it just sits there in the crack of the Typhon pass. If you go all the way out there there's a tunnel for the railway, and the two huge statues they put up that mark the edge of the greater city boundary: Gaia and Cronus, metal skeletons coated in white composite that tries to be marble. She holds the earth in a sling, and he carries a sword with two blades, one coming off from the other two thirds of the way up like a leaf or a curved tongue.

I think about Roddy Tebbit in Susan Green's sketchbook. She

drew him as Perseus, the mighty warrior holding aloft the head of a monster.

In kids' books, Cronus always has a sickle, or sometimes even a scythe, but he didn't in the original myth and he doesn't on the statue. Like Perseus, he has that weird two-tongued sword. The design is not some whimsical Ancient Greek lifestyle choice. It's a chopping weapon for an ugly kind of war: a working man's tool that pierces like an axe when you need to cut armour, or a butcher's hook when you want to gut someone. It's nasty and unromantic and functional.

That kind of sword has a name, because nasty, unromantic functional things do.

It's called a harpē, and that's what Susan Green tried to tell me in the second before the car threw her in the air. I'm an idiot from my toes to my hat for thinking she said "Harpo." I've been wasting time.

I go downstairs to my office and bring up the matrix password screen.

It takes a few minutes to get it right, but I open the file. Or, actually, files, because there are hundreds of them.

6

Hundreds and hundreds of documents, sprawling across tens of thousands of days and dozens of lines of inquiry, like a nest of string and pictures, tied together with nothing but obsession. Roddy Tebbit was, indeed, looking for evidence that Stefan Tonfamecasca murdered someone. He had a million separate clues, pages of notes, endless theories; files with the faces of women who might be the victim, picture after picture of the smiling dead of decades, pretty and smart and unsolved. He had lists of their connections, however tenuous, with Stefan, how they met, or might have, where and when. He spent seven years trying to find the one, true corpse. He actually came across three others, unrelated to Stefan or to himself, and called them in anonymously to local police. He wandered parks, forests, backwoods and construction sites with a chemical sniffer, like a mad nighthawker looking for treasure in all the wrong places. He broke into farms and sampled pig shit, dug up graves looking for second bodies hidden under coffins. Once, in a vintage clothing store, he came on a jacket he thought was hers, and a week later he tried to buy an entire plot of land from a developer. When the man wouldn't sell, Roddy signed on as unskilled labour so he could be there, and he came every day, even though he only had a few shifts. He got in trouble with the union, was thrown off the build, and kept coming night after night after night. The guard dogs got fat, he fed them so much steak. After three months, they'd dug up every single square metre of that place, and found nothing, and Roddy drifted on with the jacket packed away in his suitcase. The scanned images of hand-written notes are jagged, stained with tears. *Not here,* underlined again and again. *I was so sure.* I picture him sitting in roadside motels and rooming houses, alone at night, just him holding the jacket on his knees, looking down at the collar and listening to the sound of the rain.

I follow Roddy through his maze, his winding amateur inves-tigation, watching him miss obvious avenues and chase off after rabbits he'll never catch. He drives me crazy with his bullshit, his pride, his need. His stupidity. For a smart guy, he's appallingly dumb. I want to grab him and yell at him: there's nothing here.

But that's because Roddy doesn't put things in their proper order. He's not building a case, he has no thought of prosecution. He wants to know, first. He thinks detection is the business of find-ing the one right clue that reveals everything, and that it ends in a living room, where you put your hands in your waistcoat pocket and explain why you've called everyone here this evening. There are no prosecutors and no penal codes in Roddy's movie of his life; there's no budget ceiling, no awareness of Stefan's defence team, the fog of reasonable doubt they would summon over anything touched by Roddy after this mad quest. There's no real world, only justice.

Justice for what?

For this, this one file, separate from all the others, which I almost miss because it's so small and so long ago. Roddy did not need this file, because he knew it. It was burned in him. The root of his mania and the banner he raised high.

It is a medical history for Lillian Jana Antonin, and it is cold, hard reading.

The preamble is three years of cosmetic surgeries. Lillian changed her appearance incrementally. She added an inch of height first. They broke her shinbones and vised them as they healed, ran electric current into her to stimulate bone growth. Old-fashioned and painful, only for the very determined. In a world used to Titans, she must have looked elfin, slender to the point of fragile. Vulnerable. Standing next to Stefan, she would have looked like air and glass.

After that she worked her way up her body: ass, belly, ribs, breasts, shoulders and face. The first consultant in the history noted that she was good-looking and physically fit. He did not feel comfortable performing these surgeries. He advised a period of reflection and counselling. He was replaced. Lillian Antonin was fitting herself to a template, to her lover's ethereal, impractical dream. Was he paying? Was he demanding? The history has nothing to say. When it was done, there was a gap of six months which reads as contentment, and then things changed.

The new pages are not from the cosmetic clinic. They are triage notes and emergency room reports. Perhaps Lillian couldn't adjust to her new height, for she became clumsy. She bruised her lower legs and hips slipping in the backyard, then another time ran full on into a glass patio screen. She got caught in the closing door of a public bus and twisted her shoulder. She took up dancing but almost immediately suffered a spiral fracture in one arm, consequence of an over-enthusiastic twirl. She graduated to escrima, and seemed to like it, but couldn't learn to keep her guard up, so black eyes became a weekly occurrence. Through it all, she smiled, and smiled, and reassured everyone that nothing was wrong.

It was wrong, of course, and they all could have known, could have chosen to know, if just one of them had been prepared to push a little, to ask shameful questions. To pry into her private affairs. It's easy for me, because I don't like people very much, and because it's all right here in front of me. It's in the file, and when you put it all together, it has every warning sign and diagnostic signifier.

Lillian was not clumsy, and for that matter she was never unhappy with how she looked. She was locked into a relationship characterised by coercive and violent control, and her partner was spiralling. The pattern of abuse is obvious; the escalation is plain; and the outcome, inevitable.

One night in lonesome October, however many years ago, it came to a head, and Lillian nearly died. She didn't die because she chose not to, because she was a fucking hero, now and forever, and if there was a wall of stars for weaker, smaller people in bad situations who survive, and escape, or even manage to win, Lillian's name would be on it. Somehow, after years, when he came that night, she hit back, and she did it well. What happened next wasn't a beating, it was a fight: the princess taking on the dragon. She stabbed him eleven times, but the blade didn't penetrate his ribs. He got the knife from her and used it, and all that extra weight in his arms made for a different outcome. At last, she hit him with a sharpening steel, a rod of heavy iron with a cross handle. She went up his arm twin-stick style, broke it twice, and finished with a shot to the front of the head that put a bleed in his brain. He fell, and she fell down next to him, and they looked into one another's eyes as things went as dark outside as they had been inside all along.

Roddy knew all this, but he kept it separate from all the rest. It was the source of his rage, the certainty that Stefan had done all this, had first seduced his wife, then made her change her face and her name, and then brutalised her.

It doesn't take very much effort to confirm it. Musgrave for hospital records; Gratton for police reports. Roddy built quite a case, in a way.

But because he never put it into a timeline—or perhaps because he couldn't—the story wasn't what it appeared.

He saved her, Elaine said.

Yes. He did.

Lillian's injuries predate her arrival in Chersenesos. The hospitals, the doctors . . . none of them is within a thousand miles of the city until long after the pattern is established.

Stefan saved her, all right.

He saved her, with T7, from the violence of her husband.

Roddy Tebbit was hunting the man who killed his wife.

He never realised she was still alive, and he never realised that the man he was looking for was Peter Antonin.

When you have dates and names, and when you know someone was given T7, you can fill in the blanks, even if Stefan Tonfamecasca doesn't want you to.

I go back to the city recorder's office. Maryam the clerk gives me a little smile and makes mint tea in a tall pot, and serves it in glasses while we work.

"Family history?" she asks me, and I say yes, but not my family.

Unless I end up marrying in. Then I inherit all this, and all the players, all still alive.

Except Roddy, I suppose.

There are no deaths recorded in the Antonin matter. Lillian survived, and obviously so did Peter. She disappears off the radar, which must have been weirdly simple, because the T7 process would have given her a new face—or rather, her old one back. The body's self-image would have been reset, shifting bone and rejecting plastic, kicking against the intrusions of Peter's design.

Figure it hurt like hell.

I call Athena—Maryam gets little dimples when she hears the change in my voice—and ask her to send me all the T7 emergency deployments for that year. It's so long ago, neither of us was even born. The software grinds its way through the archive files, and for a while I wonder if it's going to be like dealing with the city, but the Tonfamecasca company can afford to move data from old formats to new ones as the technology changes, and after a few minutes the system spits back answers. Not good ones, of course. I guessed that already. I tell Athena not to look until I tell her. I tell her there's a story she needs to hear in sequence. She says okay. I wonder if she'll say that when I tell her about Maurice, and Doublewide's farm. That's part of the sequence too.

Maryam shows me to a little nook between marriages and land registry, where there's a comfortable chair and the light falls just so from one of the high windows. I sit and I read and I wish I'd never learned how.

When Lillian Antonin was lying on the floor and paramedics broke in and put her on a stretcher, and she was taken direct to the T7 unit of Demeter Mercy under the eaves of the cathedral, Stefan Tonfamecasca personally handled the infusion, and paid for it, and held her hand through the painful months that followed, as her renewing body spat out implants and screws and laid down new bone over the old cracks.

He went out in the evenings and drank and screwed up a storm. He wasn't a saint, to carry all that horror—but carry it he did, in his own way. He came back every morning, and he made his calls and did his deals from the hospital meeting room. He had food brought in and in the end even a bed. For five months, Stefan didn't go home except when he was so high and horny he had to cut loose, and then he'd use the place for fornication and a shower, and be gone before the dawn. There's a trail of tabloid stories and lurid pictures, one notable sex tape. And in all that time, no one went to the T7 ward. No one thought of it, wanted to know who was in it, or maybe they did and Stefan just cut them down.

Lillian Antonin disappeared. When she was healed, she bought a house outside the city and Stefan stopped screwing every available rock violinist and cam girl and paid court to her as if he'd just discovered his one true heart.

Perhaps he had.

But he lied to her, all the same.

I leave the recorder's office behind because I've pretty much run out of questions. I walk down Thermopylae Street to the board-walk, then across to the little park where people fly kites at the weekend. It starts out at ground level and then rears up to be four or five storeys high, so you're level with the top floor of the French Quarter apartment blocks and their blue Parisian roofs, with their views out onto Othrys. If you stand here on the right day you can catch just enough of a breeze to get a kite up and out of the brown glacier dust that hangs over most of the city, and then coax it higher and higher until it catches the mountain winds off the lake and it can go all the way up into the blue. I stand on the top of the hill, thinking about everything in the world, and I wish I could do the same.

On the boardwalk there's a Finnish coffee place where cops go for coffee and breakfast lörtsy. Gratton sits at the table on the far left as you look at the lake, and there's a free chair for me. I glad-hand him like an old friend, leaning over to put my arms around his shoulders as I sit down.

"When the fuck did we start hugging?" Gratton says, smiling as if he's telling a joke. We drink coffee while the waiter comes over with Gratton's lörtsy. It smells like pork and apple. He hasn't got one for me.

"You ever swim?" He points across at the little crowd.

"In winter? No."

"You ever think about it?"

"Yeah."

He nods. "You would."

"You?"

He nods. "Once or twice a year."

"And?"

"And every time I ask myself why I'm literally freezing my balls in a lake."

The waiter drifts away. I get out my wallet.

"You really must let me pay for coffee."

"It's fine, it's on the department."

"I insist."

I pass him the thumb drive like it's a mid-denomination bill. He takes it the same way, shakes his head, but puts it in his pocket.

"And why does that feel like I just took delivery of a burning sack of shit?"

"It's the murder case our victim was building against Stefan Tonfamecasca."

Gratton chokes on his coffee.

"Unsuccessfully," I tell him, now that he's breathing.

"You're not funny, Sounder. Where did you get this?"

"I got it from where Tebbit hid it, which you don't want to know about."

"How much do I not want to know about it?"

"Probably slightly more than you don't want to know any of this."

Gratton looks at me like he really wishes he was a kite, too.

"All right, Cal. Tell me what's coming down."

I tell him everything, except about Musgrave burning down the lab, and Maurice trying to kill me, and me handing him over to Doublewide. I also don't mention sleeping with Athena. So really not everything at all.

When I've finished my coffee with Gratton I go up onto my rooftop and get the doc box, then walk it across town to Tonfamecasca Tower. Doublewide will be pissed as hell, but that's too bad. This isn't leverage on Stefan, and he can't have it.

I tell the security guy I want to see Stefan, and he laughs.

"Not happening, my man."

"Sure," I tell him. "I'll wait."

Security guy is about to tell me I won't, but that's as long as it takes. The call comes through to let me up. He wants to scan the doc box, but I flat palm his chest and walk right on by. I get into the elevator and don't push a button. It moves anyway.

Stefan is sitting at the enormous desk. He doesn't get up. I walk across the room and put the doc box down beside him.

"You're an idiot," I say, and Stefan nods.

"You would feel that way. I'm sure you think I should have told you the whole story at the beginning."

"No."

He raises his eyebrows.

"No?"

"No. It's private business. You could have saved me some time, but . . . whatever. Time doesn't mean that much to you, does it? You're an idiot because you saved *him*."

Dr. Lillian Antonin, a researcher at the Tonfamecasca company, was first treated with T7 at Demeter Mercy on September 9th. But on the same day, according to the company files, Dr. Peter Jens Antonin was admitted to a private room at Asclepius General and treated by an external team. He also received T7, which healed his broken bones, increased his physical mass, and left him screaming for day upon day until the regular staff broke in and anaesthetised him.

Stefan shrugs. "He was a resource, Cal. He really did understand the drug in some special instinctive way. Had a knack for it. I wanted to keep the scientist and lose the man. I failed, of course. I got Roddy instead. We've done a lot of work on T7 amnesia since then; perhaps today he wouldn't be such a patchwork of lost pieces and inventions. Although after she hit him with that steel, the bleed probably did a lot of the damage. And I rather enjoyed Roddy, over the years. He was so achingly persistent, so honest and determined. It was like my very own serial television show: the wronged drifter moving from town to town in search of evidence he will never find, doing good along the way. Falling in love, even, from time to time. And all that, with a delicious wash of irony that only I could see: compulsive viewing. Well, I suppose all things must end. Except me, of course. Is that his liver?"

"No, I brought you steaks."

"Ah. Bathos. Very good, Cal. Well done."

"Did you kill him?"

Stefan rumbles in his chest, and I realise it's a chuckle. He's keeping it in, because he's in a good mood.

"Don't be absurd. Think of the algal perfusion or whatever it was, and the benefit to the lake ecosystem. Not to mention the entertainment value. No, no. I told you, Roddy was no problem for me."

"He was for Lillian."

"Peter was. He really did die that night. She really did kill him, and it really was self-defence. And Roddy wouldn't have recognised her if he saw her, even if he could remember. That weird little doll Peter wanted so much, that he turned her into . . . she doesn't exist now. Not for decades."

"And you're not together any more."

"No. By our mutual choice. Good times, though."

I look at him looking at me, daring me to ask.

"Who was she, Stefan?"

"That's a very muddled question, Cal. I think you mean who did Lillian become, after? You already know that. You must do. You'd just rather pretend otherwise. I kept her alive, I fell in love with her, and I married her. You tell me who we're talking about. You know the time frame now."

I do, and there's only one answer.

"Elaine."

Stefan nods.

"Elaine."

Athena's mother.

"Did she ever find out that you kept Peter alive? Is that why you broke up?"

"No. No, we went our separate ways because life is endless and we grew tired of the same conversations, the same gestures of affection. But we're still friends. You might even say we still love one another, as family. Perhaps one day we'll get married again. It's really too soon to say. That's part of the meaning of who we are. It's always too soon to call an end."

"You're sure?"

"That she doesn't know? As sure as I can be. You might ask Maurice, if you can stand the sight of him. He clings to her like a mollusc. Which is about his level, I suppose. If anyone knows whether she ever realised I might have done such a thing, he would. I think he keeps notes on everything she ever says, in case it helps him say something clever."

"What was she upset about? The night you left the St. Helen's opening?"

"I never did find out. She was inconsolable for about twenty minutes. Then she was herself again. She's ill, as you know. Her cognition teeters one way and then the other. She'd pass a competence test, so I can't force her into T7 therapy, and when she's not well she doesn't want it. Both Elaines think they have perfect clarity. But Athena will get her there. You're helping, incidentally, with your burgeoning new romance. I didn't expect that. I may have to revise my understanding of your uselessness."

"Well, thank you, your highness."

"Maurice, again, was fluttering around Elaine that night. He can't grasp that when she's not quite herself—and that is all it is—the things she says don't track real-world objects or events. He sees this architecture of significance and pays close attention. I think he's looking for signs of love."

"I have to talk to him anyway." Guessing he won't be in the office. "If Elaine is Lillian then Maurice is a suspect."

Again the chuckle, like water in the depths of a cave. "I suppose he is, Cal."

"If I want to search his place, am I going to need a warrant?"

"You mean, since I own it."

"Yes."

He smiles at me, as if I'm catching up with something everyone else has known for ever.

"No, Cal. Knock yourself out."

How the other half lives: Maurice Tonfamecasca's apartment. It's not like Stefan's alien cathedral, with its implications of post-humanity. It's just the nicest apartment you can imagine. You go through a quietly solid door into a space that's just the right size, the right shape. The ceiling feels airy but not coldly distant; the furniture is casually elegant and comfortable. There's no gold anywhere, and no granite, just Italian pale wood and a throwback fire pit for a centrepiece. Beyond that, a garden terrace and a private pool. There's even art on the walls, some old van Biervliets in mixed media, what looks to be a Hockney over the dining table. Everything is exquisite and expensive, but none of it particularly advertises. It just happens that things this nice cost a lot of money.

If I'd met Maurice's apartment before Maurice, we might have gotten along better.

I look for the place he sat, and I almost can't find it. It seems strange that someone so desperate to make a mark on the world couldn't even imprint on his own home, but I suppose that's part of the point of Titan-grade furniture, and part of the truth of Maurice's life, because this was his home, but it belongs to Stefan.

I sit where there's a book resting open, and a view of the city rather than the lake, and I wonder what it means about someone that they choose that angle: the humans on the streets below rather than the water, deep and cold. Maybe that Maurice wanted to see the little people. Maybe that he wanted to be down there, part of the life of the world, but didn't know how.

The book is about cooking.

I go and stand behind the bar and imagine I'm making a drink. I pour water into water in the cocktail shaker, then pour it out into a glass. I drink the water and it tastes artificial. I carry the glass into the bedroom.

This is the room where Maurice wanted to bring Elaine, so this room matters. He would have had it ready, always, just in case. He always believed she was just waiting for the moment.

I have to be careful thinking of him in the past tense.

The bed is large and solid. The label on the mattress says the springs are alternating titanium alloy and carbon fibre. I'm not sure if that means you can hide behind it if someone shoots at you, or just that Titans can screw on it as vigorously as they want without breaking it. Maybe both.

There's a single upturned water glass on one side of the bed. The other side has a glass too, waiting. I open the closet and there are a few clothes in Elaine's sizes next to his suits. For a moment I wonder whether they were sleeping together after all, but the tags are still on. These aren't her clothes, they're offerings laid out for her, in this secret and unwanted temple.

I walk across the hall: guest room. I don't know what I expect to find. Did Maurice take lovers, from time to time? Did he feel the need either for sex or just contact? Did they look like Elaine, or as little like her as possible. No answers here. If he did, he purged the apartment of them after they left.

I sit down at the terminal in his office and open it up. There are no passwords: the door only opens to Maurice or Stefan, or now, to me, because Stefan says so.

I open his bank accounts and look through. There's the payment to Denton that Orhan told me about, clear as day.

I look for Mullen, and there's nothing there.

I open up the correspondence file, and do the same, searching for Mullen's name. There's nothing there, but I wouldn't expect anything. That's a hit. You pay for that a little more discreetly.

I search for my own name and find Maurice's broadly expressed opinion to Elaine, to Denton, to Athena. I already knew he didn't like me. I find his arguments with Athena about the Tonfamecasca company, the way she's doing his job. They are polite, but she let him know she was in charge.

I search for Susan Green, Roddy Tebbit, Peter Antonin, for Lillian.

If Maurice had anything about any of them, he didn't have it here. Maybe he kept all that in his head.

I search for Elaine, and find her everywhere. Drafts of letters, notes, lists of gifts.

I wonder if he killed Roddy to impress her.

But it doesn't really make sense.

Say you're Maurice Tonfamecasca and you just found out that Peter Antonin is teaching at the university as if he wasn't a monster. Maurice probably doesn't much care about monsters generally—he sort of is one—but this monster is different. Maurice just tried to kill me because he thinks I upset Elaine. What would he do to Peter Antonin, if he could?

Figure he'd put on his executive tactical and go ninja the little motherfucker to the point of death. But that makes for a crime scene that does not look like our crime scene. If Maurice broke into Roddy's place and beat him to death with a stapler, how did Roddy end up shot just once in the side of the head? That is a controlled, quiet sort of crime, not a crime of rage. It's almost merciful. It doesn't have anything like the flavour of the man who broke down the door to my office.

But all right, that man and the man who lived in this apartment are not the same, and we all contain multitudes. Picture Maurice, in that moment of discovery. He has time to be colder than he was with me, he plans it out. Peter's sins are so appalling that they merit thought. He drugs his target—let's assume, even though it doesn't show up later on Musgrave's machines—and he puts his big hand around Roddy's smaller one and he holds the gun to his head. It's righteous and satisfying to dispense long overdue justice, and he has no idea that Roddy no more remembers Peter than any of us remembers being born.

Bang.

He slips away into the night, unseen.

How does he do all that?

Let's say they're friendly somehow, or Maurice makes Roddy think they are. Let's say that for now. He puts something in Roddy's drink and away we go. Okay, fine, but Maurice has to get past the front door first, doesn't he? Let's say he comes in with the after-work crowd, he's still a foot and change taller than the tallest of them. He literally stands out. Say he gets close enough to the camera that the height issue isn't obvious to whatever rookie Felton has reviewing the tape. Jerelyn may not notice everyone, but she'd notice Maurice because he's a fucking Titan. He is not your average bear.

Does Maurice come in pretending to be Roddy? Does that make any sense? From the corner of your eye, maybe, if you didn't look, two very tall men might become one, but Maurice walks with a swagger, like he owns everything. Roddy for sure never did that. It doesn't play.

For this to work, Maurice has to buy Jerelyn.

I want to say she's not for sale, but everyone's for sale at one price or another, and when your name is Tonfamecasca you can generally meet it.

I walk back to Maurice's computer and look for Jerelyn. I look for the building, for her address, for family. I look for anything that puts Maurice near her. Then I look for anything that puts him near the apartment where Roddy died, or near the university. I use his terminal to track his phone, and he—or at least, the phone—is never, ever there. But then right now, the phone is in Syros, having Mai Tais on the beach, so Maurice knows how to hide, if nothing else.

But my instinct says he didn't buy Jerelyn, because he wasn't there.

Maurice tried to kill me—probably twice—but I don't think he killed Roddy Tebbit.

Hey, Floyd."

"Hey, Cal."

"I'm sorry I pissed you off."

"Yeah, well."

We don't get along. That doesn't mean we can't get along. Ostby pours me a glass of whatever horrible health drink he is drinking.

"This was really good laundering. It's been a privilege."

"I guess I'm glad I've been able to help with your professional development."

"Peter Antonin, as it turns out. I gather you know that already."

"Yeah."

"A lot of tax fraud and undeclared money. A lot of stuff moving on and off shore. I think the point, actually, was to maintain the identity, rather than dodge the tax. Set up to be permanent and user-maintainable. Fire and forget."

"Yeah, I figure he didn't even know where the money came from himself. Who it came from."

"Life is long, I suppose. One sees a little of everything. Like, your man here was a nature nut."

"He what?"

"Right? At first I assumed it was just another shell. But it's legitimate. I would not have thought him the type."

"But he was."

"Evidently. Made a large donation to a wilderness charity a fortnight or so before he died. Trees and buzzards and bears, oh my."

I'm awake now, like Ostby's office was just flooded by the cold water of the lake.

"You . . . want to know which one?" He looks a little alarmed. I'm guessing there's a lot going on in my face.

No. "Yes."

Ostby reaches into his papers and pulls out a single sheet, but it doesn't matter, because I already know what it's going to say.

Roddy Tebbit made the threshold donation to attend a top-drawer fundraiser for local forest wildlife conservation three weeks ago. The keynote speaker and guest of honour was Elaine Tonfamecasca.

Elaine, whose house in the woods has a fire pit where the smoke gets sucked down to the cellar, and Susan Green told me Roddy was impressed because the carbon capture was expensive.

Elaine.

am not Maurice, so I do not go and talk to Elaine. Instead I go to Roddy's building and I wait until after the lunchtime rush.

Then I put a picture of me and Athena and Elaine right there on Jerelyn's desk.

"I know her," I say.

Jerelyn looks at the picture and closes her mouth.

"I know she was here and you helped her get in."

Nothing.

"I'm guessing she came in through the freight doors, and you zoomed the camera to look somewhere else. I'm guessing you did the same thing for her on the way out. Figure she didn't even tell you why she was there until after."

Jerelyn doesn't say anything for a while. Then: "And what are you doing in this picture, Cal?"

"Athena and I dated, back in the day. Maybe again now. It's complicated."

Jerelyn snorts. "I should say it is, if you're about to arrest her mother."

Maurice could never have met Jerelyn's price. Elaine probably didn't even have to ask.

"I'm not a cop," I say to Jerelyn, but maybe mostly to myself.

get a cab to drive me to the house. I flag it on Saturn Drive, right in front of the department stores and all their cameras. I make phone calls the whole way, like a little trail of breadcrumbs: Orhan, Ostby, Gratton, Mini Denton, Musgrave. I talk about nothing in particular and I think they all think I need a holiday.

I don't call Stefan and I don't call Athena.

I ring the bell once, then wait, then again, then wait. The sky is darkening, the winter afternoon giving way to early dark. There are clouds over the lake and the first whisper of something that could be rain, or hail. I turn up my collar and finally Elaine answers.

"Who is it?"

"It's Cal Sounder, Elaine."

There's a pause, long and thoughtful.

"How lovely, Cal. Bring the car right up."

"I already let him go."

"Oh. Then I'll come down."

She does, too, in a little golf cart with off-road wheels. The electric motor sounds like the biggest mosquito in the world. She's wearing what looks like a flight suit and an aviator scarf for the five-minute trip: Amelia Earhart by way of Jane Fonda. In the golf cart, she looks happier than I've ever seen her.

"I love this thing," she says. "It's pointless and stupid but it does no harm and I love it."

"How do the bears feel about it?"

"Ambivalent, Cal. They're bears."

She takes the corner fast enough that we lean into one another, and laughs. It's the first time she's touched me since Athena's accident.

"Welcome home," she says as we climb the steps, and I don't know what she means.

Elaine fixes two of her Molotov martinis and takes a bite out of the first. We sit in the living room because it's just too cold for the deck.

"What can I do for you, Cal?"

"I have questions I need to ask."

"Don't you always?"

"Yes. But also, before I do—"

She raises her hand.

"You and Athena had a moment. No one knows what it means yet. It's all terribly new and special again. You're nervous. You're both different people now. But you're hopeful too. You don't want me to lean too hard on it. You don't want this conversation to make trouble for it."

"Yes."

I must look surprised, because she sighs. "Athena and Stefan both think I'm losing it a little, and I am. I know that. It's past time I went and got bigger again, cured again. But I don't want to just yet. There's a place in my head, between when I'm just me and when I'm a little bit crazy that's . . . special. Free."

"Okay."

"I'm a Titan, Cal. I'm rich and I'm strange. I'm already not like everyone else. I just don't want to travel too far from who I was. Become something too different. I know you understand that. You're almost the only one who does."

"I do. I didn't think you did."

"I don't, when I'm well, do I?"

"It would probably make life easier with the bears. You could play with them a bit more, without worrying."

"Yes, I suppose. But maybe I wouldn't want to, any more. It's not important. They're just bears. And you want to know something. Let's get it done."

"I figure he came to the event a month ago to see you. Roddy Tebbit. And he was Roddy, wasn't he? Not Peter."

Elaine sighs and takes another drink.

"It was so odd. He looked like Peter, all bulked up and a bit worn about the edges. He sounded like him, when he was young and idealistic. I thought perhaps a relative, or just a fluke of genetics and identity. They say everyone has a doppelgänger. He was genuinely nice. A good boy. Then he said he wanted to ask me something difficult and of course I thought it would be sex. It so often is. I got ready to make a polite withdrawal."

She stretches, unself-conscious, and it's weird because for almost the first time ever I can see Athena in her, in the way she moves.

Down under the house, something thumps and thuds and argues with something else: Elaine's bears, doing bear things.

"It wasn't about sex, of course. He wanted my help. He'd gotten it in his head that I'd separated from Stefan because Stefan was cruel, and he thought that made me an ally. He told me that sad, strange story, about his perfect wife and their perfect love, and how Stefan had stolen her away, had killed her and made her disappear. He'd made Stefan into Peter Antonin, I realised, and he was hunting him with all the fire he had. This weird, new little man, peering out of a monster's face, and saying he'd never rest until it was done. He'd never stop coming, and would I help? Could I? Did I have an idea where Lillian was buried? And I realised: not a relative or a coincidence. He was Peter—or whatever was left of him. It was . . . the worst thing I've ever seen, I think."

"That's a high bar."

"It is. Well, you know. You've seen things too. I was so grateful when Athena told me you'd come through the door, at last. Even if only tentatively. I thought: there's someone who will understand."

That wide-eyed, clear smile; not mad at all, but completely terrifying.

"And I thought: how dare you come back? Not about you, dear. About him. How dare you be this new person you don't deserve? This little pathetic broken-winged thing, on a righteous mission. How dare you take on that role, and come to me—of all the women in the world—come to me for help? How dare you?"

"So you said no."

She shakes her head vigorously. "I told him: 'Yes! Yes! Of course! I'll go undercover, Dr. Tebbit. I do so completely understand, better than you might know!' He was awfully excited. Thrilled to be believed at last by someone close to the monster. He urged me to be cautious, not to give myself away. He went home, and I laughed and laughed and laughed. I thought I'd won—again. Oh, I was angry with Stefan. I saw immediately what he'd done, of course, but he would. He would. And here I was, still standing, and I had nothing to be afraid of. But when I stopped laughing, I found I had tears all down my face, and it was hurting so much. My whole body, as if it was still bruised. I tried to sleep through it. Drink through it. I even thought of fucking my way through it, but . . . I knew it wouldn't work. So I called him and said I'd found out what happened to his wife. Then I went around to his apartment and told him everything, from beginning to end."

"How did he take it?"

"I thought he'd deny it at first. I had all this proof in my head, ways to make him believe. But it was like dropping a glass. I saw him hit the floor and break all at once, and he screamed. It was awful. He screamed and screamed and screamed and he said he wanted to die. He deserved it. I said: 'Yes, Peter, you do.' And just for a moment, I thought I saw him there, in Roddy's eyes. All his fire and anger. I saw him come to the surface, and I thought he was going to fight me. Survival instinct, you see, deep down in everything that lives. But he didn't. I held his hand, the way I did when I first knew him. I stood behind him and wrapped my arms around him. I said . . . something . . . as I put the gun to his head. For just that one moment I was perfect. I was myself across all the long years: all the women I've been. I saw everything, and what it meant.

"And I shot him in the head."

She crosses her arms. A bear circles away under the house towards the dustbins. We sit there, listening. Elaine shrugs.

"So. Take me in, copper."

I open my mouth to say I'm not a cop, but someone else gets there first.

"No," Maurice Tonfamecasca says. "In fact, he won't."

Figure Doublewide hedged his bets a little, waiting for delivery of Roddy Tebbit's organs. Figure he got tired of waiting.

Maurice doesn't make the same mistake twice. He looks at me and he smiles, and hits me with a Taser. He aims low, gets my thigh, and I spasm and drop. My back hits the floor hard and the gunshot wound turns molten in my side. I say something, but it's not a word, and he hits me with another jolt.

"Hi, Cal," Maurice says. "Fuck you, Cal."

"Maurice," Elaine murmurs reproachfully, "we were talking."

"It's all right," Maurice tells her. "You don't have to talk to him any more. No one does. It's over."

He tugs on the Taser and I feel the needles wrench out of my leg, which doesn't hurt because the discharge site is still tingling. I twist, sympathetic spasm, and the gunshot wound makes a noise like bubble wrap and starts to leak. I pull myself up on the arm of a chair.

"I'm not a cop," I say, because it was ready in my mouth and I have to say something.

"I know," Maurice says, and punches me in the face. His fist is like a solid block of stone. Of course it is. There's only one way he's mobile right now. He's been in a T7 suite: bone surgery, muscle graft, and a few microdoses to join it all together. He's probably only about seventy-five percent healed, but he's also an extra twenty kilos of bone and muscle already, maybe the new carbon tube bone struts. And he got the first shot in.

Sam would say this is what happens when you're not professional about everything.

I wish he was here.

I can't fight a two-dose Titan bare-handed from a standing start. I need an edge. I've always known that. I fight fast, smart and hard, because the longer it goes on and the fairer it is, the more likely I am to lose.

This isn't even fair; it's tilted the other way already.

I let Maurice's next punch throw me across the room. I lose track for a moment in mid-air, fight to stay conscious, then come back to a big-style tumble with lots of furniture. A table smashes under me, thank god not made of glass, just old dry wood, local work.

I could die here. Hell, maybe I already have and I'm just catching up.

I go into my pocket and hope like hell what I'm looking for

hasn't fallen out in all the commotion: the folding corkscrew Athena gave me on our first anniversary. In my pocket, with my left hand, I flip it open, then grip it as if I'm going to uncork something two and a half metres tall and north of two hundred kilos. I don't want Maurice to see it before I'm ready.

He's having a fine old time stalking me through the mess in Elaine's living room. She's saying something, but he's ignoring her, because he has a plan. I'm pretty sure it goes: kill Cal in front of Elaine, receive her eternal gratitude and admiration. I'm pretty sure his whole thing this last while has been covering for Elaine. He knew she killed Roddy and everything he did was to keep that from everyone else. I'm pretty sure she never asked him to. As if she'd need him to cover for her: Elaine Tonfamecasca, killing the man who almost murdered her, who came back into her life under another name. I doubt it would even go to trial.

"Get up," he tells me, "I want you to see this one coming."

I get to my feet slowly, as if I'm worse off than I am. It's not hard, because I'm worse off than I want to believe. There's a lot of blood coming down out of the bullet wound. I already know it's going to get worse. I need him to overcommit. Trouble is, he doesn't have to do that to kill me.

"You're pathetic," I tell him. "You know it took hardly any time at all to get your blood out of my carpet, it was so fucking thin."

He throws a punch, and I slip it, just. Shake my head as if that was what I had in mind.

"Pathetic."

I try to make my voice sound like Stefan's. Pretty sure he says the same thing to Maurice every day at the office.

It must be working because the next punch is much bigger. It'd take my head clean off if I let it land. I sag under it, feeling the oblique muscles on the gunshot side tear a little more.

I dodge again, and again, try not to vomit, and finally I see him wind up, and then at last he lets it go. I don't slip this one. I stand straight, twist at the hip, and use my right hand to guide his directly into the path of my left.

With the corkscrew sticking out between my fingers so it drives hard in between the bones and sticks.

Maurice screams.

I drag the corkscrew back and he tries to follow. I'm pulling him around with his agony, with the feeling of violation, the metal lodged in him. Part of him wants it out, part of him knows that would be fine, he can get it fixed, but deep inside the animal that lives in all of us can't let a hand just get torn apart like a chicken bone. It takes training and practice to make sacrifices like that, or you have to believe in your own death, and Maurice has none of those things.

I fire off a couple of knees and an elbow while we're dancing, weak as hell because I can't rely on the muscles in my trunk, then wrench back the other way and feel the corkscrew come loose, bringing a chunk of something he probably needs. I slap him, open his hands like a window, and bring in my left with the blood still all over it. I'm going to tracheotomise the fucker as amateur as I know how. And that is how I'm going to win. Like Sam says, you go hard early.

Except I don't.

I don't win.

I'm just a little too slow. I can't twist right now, so I have to stretch my arm, and the point stops short. A couple of centimetres, not more.

Maurice catches my hand and makes a sound like pure joy.

He puts a couple into my ribs and I feel them crack. Then he throws me through the glass doors onto the deck. He's laughing, but it's not like Stefan. It's just a big, dangerous asshole laughing while he takes me down.

He follows me out onto the balcony, into the wind and the dark, and stalks me across the pine floor. It's slippery with hail, half melted and half set into ice. I'm not sure I can still stand, but I have to try. In between footsteps I can hear him singing to himself: gonna kill Sounder, gonna kill Sounder. His arms are spread wide. I wonder if he's hopped up on something, but I think it's just hate. He'll feel that bloody hand tomorrow. He'll know he was in a fight.

I'm not sure I will.

Fight smart, fight dirty, fight on.

He comes and I step to meet him as if I'm going to try to skewer his hand again, as if I'm mad enough to take the invitation to grapple, as if I think I can skip around and under on the ice, as if I could do that even without everything that's wrong with me. He hits me again and something goes pop inside that isn't bone. Kidney, maybe, or one of those little things you need that no one who isn't a doctor can name. I make a little noise I've never made before. He tries for the same result on the other side, like there's extra points for style. He's loving this: all the drama, all the power. This is his moment.

I drop and pull him forwards onto me as if I'm going to kiss him at a picnic, push him onwards with my legs towards the balcony rail. There is no part of me that thinks this is a good idea. He weighs too much and I'm too broken, but it's all I have. If I get it right I won't be carrying him, just helping him along.

I get it right. It's still impossible. The weight of him slams me down, every vertebra pressing into the ice and wood, every muscle in my legs giving up, my bullet-wound side white fire as we skid together. He's supposed to go over, not on, but it isn't happening that way. It isn't. I don't have any more tricks.

Everything screams, and so do I, but he flies at last, and he flies high, towards the drop to the canyon.

Falling any distance is bad for Titans: they're like spiders, too dense, too brittle. His face changes in mid-air to alarm and fear. I hear him clip the balcony rail and then a complex sequence of thuds and slithers. I can't turn my head to look. It's cold and comfortable down here on the ground. Then, after a moment, I hear him breathing, and I realise he hasn't gone over. He's hugging the flat-topped beam Elaine serves drinks on, both legs dangling, but good hand and right arm gripping the wood. In a minute he'll be safe, and then I'm done.

I try to get to my feet, but there's something wrong. Everything's hard.

Maurice laughs again, and gets one foot up on the rail.

Elaine Tonfamecasca walks past me and hits him twice in the face with a cast iron skillet. He stares at her.

"I liked that table," she says, and then: "And Athena loves Cal, and I didn't ask you to do any of this."

She hits him again.

"You remind me of Peter, ever so much. You always did. So now . . . go away and leave me alone."

Maurice's forehead looks soft and strange as he stares at her, as she draws back with the skillet and hits one more time in the same place, with everything she has.

And then he tumbles backwards and down to the bears.

Elaine looks after him for a moment, and then goes back inside the house.

7

Somewhere there are lights, and someone is shouting. She seems very angry. Someone hits me hard in the chest and tries to smother me with a mask, but the joke's on them because the mask makes it easier to breathe.

"St. Helen's," I say, before remembering that was last time.

Marcus is going to be so pissed.

Am I still on the deck at Elaine's, in the comfortable ice?

I think so.

I hope the bears are okay.

No one wants Maurice dropping in on them. Not even bears.

"Cal? Can you hear me?"

"No."

"You can't hear me?"

"No."

"You realise there's a certain cussedness in that statement?"

I don't want to talk right now. I don't have to, if I don't want to, while I'm dying.

"Doctor, do you mind if I try?"

The doctor does not mind.

"Cal?"

"Athena."

"Cal, don't hate me."

"Not possible."

"It is."

"Nope. I'm scared. Will you hold my hand?"

"I am."

"That's all right, then."

I wake, and it's summertime.

I sit up, with the feeling I have done all this before. I'm cold and yet not. The hospital room is pale and warm. The machines are very expensive, very discreet. The one that's telling them I'm upright is barely audible in here.

I put my feet down on the floor. They seem farther away than they should be, the way they do sometimes when you've been asleep for a good long night.

I stand up. I'm naked but who cares? Hospital room. They've seen it all before. I must have been here a while. My limbs feel heavy and a little clumsy, probably from lack of use. Maybe blood loss. They've fixed the bullet wound, and I don't even have an ass-hole pattern there.

Athena comes in and throws her arms around me. She's small against my chest, and that's when I understand.

It takes another month before they're willing to let me out on the street. When they do, I realise nothing will be the same. People look at me differently now. They see power in what I am. They make assumptions that are not entirely wrong.

Athena takes me to see Stefan, because I owe it to him. He's with a date, a professor of neuroscience from Mumbai. They are swimming together, looking out over Othrys, with the smell of honeysuckle from the garden all around. Bees drift over the pool to settle in the flowers in her hair. She waves a greeting to me as he hauls himself out, and you can see the water level change. I realise that sex, in so far as it is possible for them at all, must be much easier in the pool. Athena wanders over and sits on a lounger by the professor, and they chat. I wonder which of them is learning more, and about what.

"It's good to see you up and about," Stefan says.

"Yeah. Thank you."

"Oh, you're welcome, of course. As I said, you turned out to be more interesting than I'd imagined. A seasoning process, no doubt. Suffering and age. I might have done it anyway, even without Athena's urging. If I'd heard in time."

"Maybe Elaine would have called you."

"Maybe. Thank you for that, by the way. Not just for taking care of her, but she was so moved by your situation that she's in treatment now herself. Out in a few more months—the brain takes longer, you know. All's well that ends well. What will you do now?"

"I think we can say the cops aren't interested in retaining my services any more."

"No, I fear not. Rather too messy and ambiguous an outcome."

"Are you asking me if I want a job?"

"Genuine curiosity."

"The same, maybe. But from the other side of the line."

"Ah, yes. Perhaps. I think that would be . . . helpful."

He shrugs, water running down his back, then looks over at Athena.

"It's so nice for her. Finally, she has everything she wanted. You, of course. But also Elaine getting better, and Maurice out of the picture. The man who tormented her mother is dead. And she even has a little something to hold over me, if I ever get too patriarchal with her. Quite the fortunate outcome, and she never had to lift a finger. I'm very proud."

He flashes me a grin, and I see all his teeth.

"Excuse me, Cal. I must get back in. I find the water infinitely more convivial than dry land, these days."

"Sure. See you round."

"Count on it, Cal."

He splashes into the pool like a child.

Athena waves at me from the lounger.

I think about what happened in the spaces between what I've already found out: how did Roddy Tebbit hear that Elaine might be an ally in Stefan's camp? How did Maurice come to know who Roddy really was? The smallest intersections of lives; coincidences that add up to one particular ending.

I remember Elaine's face as she hit him, and the years of pain drained out of her into the dark.

I realise I'm proud of Athena too.

ACKNOWLEDGEMENTS

It's been a tough few years in our house, just as it probably has been in yours. Thank you, Clare, as ever, but moreso. Thank you, kids, for surviving and even thriving. Thank you to Ireland, and to Inchinattin in particular, for welcoming my father home. Thank you, everyone who's reading this book, and thank you doubly for reading these acknowledgements. Thank you Patrick, Edward, Olivia and your amazing teams. Thank you to the anonymous security guard at the Royal Cornwall Hospital on the morning of December 13th, 2020, who understood, and was kind.

Thank you public health professionals, vaccine researchers, doctors, nurses, paramedics and volunteers. Thank you, teachers. Thank you delivery drivers and grocers.

Thank you, everyone.

Together, we go forward.

A NOTE ON THE TYPE

The book was set in Utopia, a typeface designed in 1989 by
Robert Slimbach (born 1956). The stroke and proportions of
the letterforms stem from eighteenth-century transitional
typefaces like Baskerville and Walbaum but are redrawn
with a contemporary aesthetic. The typeface was designed
in a range of weights and incorporates both a titling case
and an expert case, which makes it flexible for a variety of
applications.

Typeset by Scribe, Philadelphia, Pennsylvania

Printed and bound by Berryville Graphics,
Berryville, Virginia

Designed by Betty Lew